The Shepherd

Society Lost – Volume One

By Steven C. Bird

The Shepherd: Society Lost

Steven C. Bird

The Shepherd
Society Lost – Volume One

Published by Steven C. Bird at Homefront Books

Illustrated by Hristo Kovatliev

Edited by Carol Madding at hopespringsedits@yahoo.com

Final Review by Sabrina Jean at fasttrackediting.com

Print Edition 7.23.18

ISBN-13: 978-1519474551
ISBN-10: 1519474555

www.homefrontbooks.com

www.stevencbird.com

facebook.com/homefrontbooks

scbird@homefrontbooks.com

Table of Contents

Disclaimer

The characters and events in this book are fictitious. Any similarities to real events or persons, past or present, living or dead, are purely coincidental and are not intended by the author. Although this book is based on real places and some real events and trends, it is a work of fiction for entertainment purposes only. None of the activities in this book are intended to replace legal activities and your own good judgment.

Dedication

With each book I write, my list of people to whom I owe a great debt gets longer and longer. There are many people in the indie-author community that help to make the dream of writing a reality for myself and many others. That list is, of course, too long to detail here, but for each and every one who has given me guidance or encouragement along the way, I owe you all an eternal debt of gratitude.

To my beautiful wife and loving children: may this book be only one of many more that I write that helps to secure our future together; living the life that we dream of.

Introduction

One year ago today, most of the fighting ended. The fighting, brought about by the *great collapse* as some referred to it, concluded with no clear victory, no fanfare, no resolution to the turmoil the world had faced. For quite some time, it had seemed that modern society was headed down a self-destructive path. Corrupt politicians, regardless of party affiliation or claimed ideology, sold their influence to special interests while pandering to a growing voter class who would cast their lot with whoever paid them the proper lip service or offered them the most in exchange for their vote, always paid for at the detriment of others.

As nations all over the world began to go bankrupt, their economies began to fail from the crushing debt of the promises made to voters in exchange for power. The world's financial systems started to collapse, piece by piece, starting slowly at first, with most governments hiding their eyes from the fact that their economies were based on fiat currency, backed by nothing but the word of collapsing governments. When this financial house of cards began to fall, those who had been waiting in the shadows began to come into the light and take advantage of the situation spreading all across the globe.

The politicians, most of whom were merely well-paid pawns in the game, were blamed, and either jailed or lynched by mobs of angry and desperate citizens as the hopelessness began to set in. Meanwhile, those who actually pulled the marionette strings from behind the dark curtain of financial manipulation began to take control.

What many referred to as the New World Order, a vast web of international conspirators hell-bent on dominating the world with a totalitarian global government, ascended to power, masquerading as those who would save the common citizen from the chaos caused by their very own puppets, who now took the blame.

Utilizing unholy alliances with terrorist organizations and organized crime—who also had their sights set on carving out a piece of this new world for themselves—the New World Order accelerated their goals under the guise of a violent, total societal breakdown, the chaos of which masked the true perpetrators.

As each of these groups advanced their end goals, their courses diverged, creating struggles within what had started out as a symbiotic relationship seeking the mutually beneficial destruction of society. The world's elite, the powerful financial, governmental, and corporate leaders of the New World Order would come to regret their alliances with religious extremists, which looked to the total annihilation of all non-believers in their cause as the ultimate culmination of their work. To that end, they unleashed the widespread use of weapons of mass destruction against all major population centers, killing off as much as seventy percent of the world's developed societies.

Those attacks did not spare the NWO elite—a betrayal that would have gone the other way if they had simply acted first. Neither side had ever intended on truly coexisting with one another, dividing up the new world in an equitable fashion as they had agreed. Many of the NWO elite and their families fell prey to the horrors of the large-scale, indiscriminate use of chemical, radiological, and biological weapons utilized by the Jihadi extremist factions.

In retaliation, the NWO elite employed their remaining governmental controls in counter-attacks against the jihadists, although in the end, it made little difference, as the lack of adequate controls in employing their own weapons of mass destruction took a significant toll on their own populations as well.

The Shepherd: Society Lost

As the fighting subsided from the attrition of leadership and the near-eradication of organized forces on both sides, the world was left a crumbled, decaying shell of its former self. For those who had survived, every day would be a challenge. Not only would it be a struggle for the basic necessities of life, it would be a fight for those who hoped to retain their humanity in this new and violent world, while they faced those who saw the road to survival as being paved with violence, intimidation, and aggression.

Chapter One

Taking a sip of warm, homemade herbal tea from his thermos, he felt the heat from the liquid radiating upward, warming his face against the cold morning air. Sitting on top of the ridge, looking down at his flock below, he gripped his Winchester Model 70, chambered in .30-06, with his right hand, while he scratched his Karakachan sheep dog behind the ears with his left.

"Duke, old boy," he said as he gazed at his flock down below. "You can almost feel winter's chill starting to set in. It won't be long and all of this green will be white again. I guess we'd better get to the task of reducing our flock and stocking our stores with meat before it comes to that."

Duke turned his head, looking at him as if he understood what the man was saying. For the next few minutes, the two enjoyed the peace and silence of the still morning air and the tranquility the Rocky Mountains provided them.

Jessie Townsend was the man's name. Before the great collapse, Jessie, or "J.T." as many called him, was the sheriff of Montezuma County, Colorado, nestled high in the Rocky Mountains. At forty-four years old, he was the husband of Stephanie Townsend, and the father of daughter Sasha and son Jeremy, ages ten and eight, respectively.

Before the collapse, Jessie had the foresight to cash out his retirement and buy a remote cabin deep in the Rockies. Over the years, as he watched the world spiral out of control, he prepared the cabin with provisions, supplies, tools, and everything they would need in order to survive for an extended time on their own, in the event that his fears eventually came true.

Jessie lost his bid for reelection in what many in Montezuma County considered to be a travesty, an act of voter fraud so great that it appeared that his challenger won in a landslide, though virtually no one would admit to having voted for him. Jessie could see the writing on the wall, though, and did not contest the vote.

His successor was politically well connected and had the financial backers to bankrupt Jessie with lengthy court battles if he had challenged the outcome. Add to that a legal system that had become heavily controlled by those who were connected to the right circles, and Jessie knew it would have been futile to even try. Instead, he decided it was time to quietly relocate his family to their simple mountain hideaway to ride out whatever might come to pass.

A day didn't go by when he wasn't thankful for his fortuitous decision to follow his gut instinct. Acting early had given his family time to adapt to their new lifestyle, as well as giving them time to grow their flock of sheep to a size that provided them with both meat and wool. Jessie now saw himself as a simple, humble shepherd and spent many of his days watching faithfully over his flock as a means of protecting his family's future.

This morning, as he reflected on the past, which was ever-present on his mind, he turned to thoughts of the future and the upcoming winter. Winter often came with little warning in the mountains, and he knew that once you started to feel it, it would be upon you before you knew it.

Jessie's thoughts were interrupted by Duke springing up on all fours while letting out a restrained *woof,* followed almost immediately by a loud and aggressive bark and a lunge forward. Quickly picking up his binoculars, Jessie scanned the area below to see his flock running rapidly up the side of the hill toward his position.

Catching a glimpse of one of his sheep going down in his peripheral vision, Jessie quickly focused on the abrupt movement, to see a wolf ravaging the defenseless animal. Cycling a round into the chamber with the bolt and slipping off the safety, Jessie held his rifle steady and took aim as he estimated the yardage, adjusted his hold, and gradually applied pressure on the trigger until he felt the shock of the powerful .30-06 cartridge as it discharged and sent the one-hundred-and-sixty-five grain projectile toward the offending animal.

He immediately grabbed Duke by the collar and said, "Steady boy. Not yet. Where there's one, there's more. Don't go gettin' yourself killed on me."

He then continued scanning the area below through his rifle scope, catching only a fleeting glimpse of a second wolf as it ducked quickly back into the woods.

"Mongrels," he mumbled. "We're gonna have to do something about your cousins down there," he said. "They're getting too brave, attacking in broad daylight."

Climbing to his feet, Jessie slung his rifle over his shoulder, let go of Duke's collar and said, "Come on, boy. Let's go put that poor sheep out of its misery."

~~~~

Looking out the front window of the small three-room cabin, Stephanie shouted, "Kids, there's your dad. It's time for breakfast," as she saw Jessie approach on horseback with his packhorse in tow.

Pulling his horses up to the front of the house, Jessie dismounted and greeted Stephanie with a hug and a kiss as he met her at the door.

"Breakfast is ready," she said. "Lamb and eggs. Your favorite."

Stepping inside, he closed the door behind him to keep the crisp morning air out of the cozy little cabin and replied, "It smells great. You three go ahead and eat without me. Just save me some. I've got to deal with something before I settle in."

"You've been out there almost all night. You need to get some rest. Eat breakfast and take yourself a nap. Whatever chores you think you have to do right now can wait."

"This can't," he said, pulling the curtain to the side and pointing to the load draped over the back of his old gray pack-horse, Jack.

"What's that?" she asked.

"A sheep and a wolf."

"Again? Damn it! Uh... I mean, dang it," she said, correcting herself as she realized the kids were in the room. "Is Duke okay?"

"Yeah, Duke's fine. He's out there with the flock dutifully standing guard like a sheepdog should. It seems there are more and more wolves every day," he said as he hung his old weathered, wide-brimmed hat on the coat hook. "It's gonna be a rough winter once their food sources start to thin out. We're gonna have to be on our toes. We may even need to reduce the flock more than usual, so that we can bring them in close to the cabin."

With a disappointed look on her face, Stephanie said, "I suppose you need your knives and bone saw?"

"Yeah. I'll butcher the sheep up for us and make dog food out of the wolf."

Stephanie scrunched her face and replied, "Yuck! Dog food out of a wolf? That's cannibalism. Wolves are dogs, too."

"It's a dog-eat-dog world out there," he said with a chuckle.

"Very funny, mister," Stephanie said, crossing her arms while giving him 'the look.'

"Relax. Meat is meat," he replied. "Besides, like I said, it's gonna be a rough winter. We can't afford to waste anything. I'll keep the pelt, too. You never know what it will come in handy for. Maybe you can make me some wolf-pelt house shoes," he said with a crooked smile.

Pushing him toward the door, Stephanie said, "Just go get done what you have to get done, so you can get back in here and relax for a while."

"Yes, ma'am," Jessie said, tipping his hat to her as he placed it on his head and started on his way to pull Jack, the pack horse, to the meat-processing shed.

Chapter Two

Stephanie, who now homeschooled both Sasha and Jeremy, was a middle school English teacher before society began its final death throes. Unlike Jessie, who seemed to prefer their new way of life over the way things used to be, even when times in the past were good, she often missed her old life. Even though their little mountain homestead grew on her more each day, she couldn't help but catch herself getting lost in her own reflections of the past. Often times, she would watch the children doing their homework and flashback to all of the smiles of the children she used to teach. She wondered what had become of them, although she knew the sad reality was that more than likely, most of them would not have made it through the collapse and the subsequent attacks.

Denver's population had been decimated by a bioterrorism attack with a weaponized strain of Marburg hemorrhagic fever and the entire city and surrounding areas were now considered to be dead zones by most. Although, with the fractured state of the nation, there was no way to get a reliable report of the city's true status, especially considering the secluded nature of the Townsend's self-sufficient, mountain hideaway.

As she gazed out the window, Stephanie heard young Sasha ask, "Mommy, are you okay?"

Snapping back to her present reality, Stephanie realized that a tear was rolling down her cheek, as she was lost in her nightmares of the recent past. Wiping the tear from her cheek with her hand, she said, "Yes, dear. I just had something in my eye." Pausing for a moment, she continued, "You two have been working very hard. Why don't you take a break? Run outside and see if your father needs a hand. You could use some fresh air."

The children's eyes lit up with their mother's suggestion and they both ran straight for the door. "Don't stay out there all day!

We've got to go over your work while it's still fresh in your minds," she shouted as they quickly disappeared outside, the front door slamming shut behind them.

Stephanie walked into the kitchen and poured herself a cup of piping hot herbal tea that she had been keeping warm on the old-fashioned wood stove. She then walked over to the old antique upholstered chair that Jessie had placed in the corner of the room by her favorite window. As she sat down on the chair, she gazed out the window and lost herself to her emotions, breaking down into tears. "Oh, God, why? Why did you leave our children this world to grow up in? Why couldn't things have just stayed the same?"

Putting her hands over her face, she heard the door open softly, followed by Jessie's voice. "Steph, are you okay?"

Attempting to regain her composure, she replied, "Yes. Yes, I'll be fine," as she wiped the tears from her eyes and turned to continue her gaze out the window at the beautiful and serene mountains.

"When the kids came out and said you sent them... well, I figured you might have been having a moment. I just wanted to make sure you were okay and see if there was anything I could do."

"You can turn back time," she replied tersely, intensifying her stare through the old pane of glass that separated her from the outside world.

Jessie walked softly over to her, knelt down, reached up and gently nudged her chin toward him. As he looked into her deep blue eyes and brushed her long brunette hair aside, he smiled at her and said, "I know. I know how bad things seem. We've all lost a lot. Humanity and the entire world has lost a lot. But we... our whole family, you, me and the kids, made it through it all. Most people weren't that lucky. We've got a lot to be thankful for, and I for one am grateful that God has blessed me with you.

The Shepherd: Society Lost

Things will get better. The world will move on. If history has taught us anything, the entire story of human history has been filled with struggle, wars, sickness, suffering, and tragedy, but even with all of that we've always managed to persevere. Think of how bleak things must have looked to the Europeans during the plague of the Middle Ages. To them, it truly was the apocalypse. And just look at how humanity persevered through the horrors of it all. We will make it through this as well, and someday our kids, our grandkids, and our great-grandkids will be rebuilding this world into a much better place than we left it for them."

Taking his hand and holding it against her cheek, Stephanie looked into Jessie's dark brown eyes and said, "You always know what to say. You always have. You are my world, Mr. Townsend. And I thank God every day that you are in my life."

As he rose to his feet, he kissed her on the forehead and said, "I'd better get back out to the kids. I think Jeremy was about to try his hand as a butcher before I stepped away. I'd better go try and rescue the meat."

With a laugh and a smile, she said, "Yes. You'd better go and supervise that boy. He and his fascination with knives are going to give me gray hair. That boy is attracted to sharp things."

"He's a smart kid. He knows a good blade is man's second-best friend on a homestead."

"And what's the first? Duke?" she asked.

"A rifle," he replied with a smile. "But then again, Duke is in a category all his own. That dog really earns his keep."

"Speaking of Duke, I get worried about him being out there with the flock by himself, with all of the wolves that are starting to come around. He's no match for a pack of hungry wolves."

Putting his hands on his hips as he searched for words, Jessie said, "Yeah. Me, too. The flock has to stay out on that grass just a little longer, though. We can't bring them in and start them on our winter hay supply too soon. We'll never make it through the winter. No, I'll get our flock size down and our meat stores up, and then when the weather turns, I'll pull the sheep in closer to the cabin so I can watch them myself. But for now, Duke is gonna have to hold his own out there."

"I wish we would have gotten Duke a mate while we still could, back before all of this," she said as she walked over to the front door of the cabin. "I worry about what we're going to do when he is gone. I mean, he is a dog. He's only got so much time."

"Yeah," Jessie replied. "I think about that all the time. Right now I just couldn't get by without him. Maybe when the time comes, if we are lucky enough for Duke to make it to a ripe old age, the kids will be old enough to help guard the flock and he can enjoy his well-earned retirement."

"Our little shepherds," she replied with a smile. She turned and opened the door, shouting with her hands cupped around her mouth, "Sasha! Jeremy! Break time is over! Come on back!"

Kissing her on the cheek as he walked by, Jessie said, "I'll send them if they don't come running. I love you."

"I love you, too," she said with a smile as he walked back toward the cellar where he processed his animal harvests.

Before the door could even close behind him, Sasha and Jeremy came bounding in from the outside, full of energy. "Okay, you two hellions," Stephanie said, getting their attention. "Let's put all that energy to good use and go over what you've learned today."

Chapter Three

Later that evening, just before the sun retreated over the mountains to the west, Jessie walked over the ridge to see his sheep grazing on the grassy hillside down below. From a distance, Duke spotted him with his keen eyesight and snapped to attention, his tail wagging anxiously.

Jessie lowered his binoculars and whistled through his fingers, bringing Duke running in his direction eagerly answering his master's call. "Hey, there, boy," Jessie said as he aggressively scratched Duke's black and white splotchy fur behind his ears. "You won't be alone tonight, boy. I'm gonna stay with you and help you keep an eye out for your fellow canines. Let's head back down the hill and set up camp with the sheep."

As Jessie walked down the hill, his rifle on his pack and Duke by his side, he scanned the area and tried to commit it to memory as best he could. He knew that once the sun went down, the lay of the land would be hidden until the next morning, and knowing he was probably in for some excitement that night, he wanted to be as mentally prepared as possible.

Reaching the flock, Jessie found a dry, level spot, leaned his rifle against a rock, and tossed his pack on the ground. "This looks like it'll do fine, boy." Kneeling down to his camouflaged hunting pack, Jessie detached the small tent he had secured to the bottom of the pack with bungee cords. After just a few moments, the tent was erect with the opening facing a majority of the flock.

Next, he gathered some kindling and some old dead tree limbs to use for firewood and ignited a fire with his magnesium fire-starter and some homemade char-cloth he kept in a small tin container. After tending to the fire for a few moments to ensure that it would continue to build on its own, Jessie looked at Duke and said, "Stay, boy. I'll be right back," as he gave him the hand signal to stay put.

Walking off into the trees in search of more firewood for the night, before the evening's failing light was completely gone, Jessie searched through the dead tree branches scattered across the forest floor. He looked for just the right mixture of age and lack of moisture, in order to ensure an efficient burn. It hadn't rained for what seemed like a few weeks, so there was plenty of adequately seasoned dry wood to be found. As he reached down to pick up a fallen branch that fit nicely into his desired criteria, he paused, taking notice of a large paw print. Immediately recognizing it as a wolf print, and a fresh one at that, Jessie's senses perked up as he began to scan the nearby woods for a potential threat.

"I know you mongrels are watching me," he said calmly. "You're lying back waiting for nightfall to make your move. You think you're in for an easy meal. Well, bring it on," he said as he placed his hand on the revolver he nearly always had on his side in an old brown leather holster.

Handed down to him from his now-deceased father, his cherished handgun was a six-shot, first-generation Colt Single Action Army revolver, chambered in .357 Magnum.

Though the pistol was originally chambered in the old .38-40 cowboy-era cartridge, his father, having put considerable wear on the old gun that had been manufactured way back in 1908, opted to have it rechambered by a local gunsmith for the more modern and available .357 Magnum cartridge, fitting it with a new barrel and cylinder. Although his father mostly carried the pistol with the lower powered .38 Special during his own tenure as a sheriff's deputy, the more powerful .357 Magnum cartridge was available with a simple reload if it were ever needed.

The Shepherd: Society Lost

With a well-worn blue finish and wood grips that also showed their age, his father's pistol was more than just a tool to him. It was a link to his own past and was an heirloom that he refused to simply allow to collect dust in a closet or safe. By carrying it daily, Jessie was always reminded of his connection with his father, who had raised him to be the man he was today.

With his thumb resting on the old spur hammer and three of his fingers around the grip, Jessie listened as the woods seemed eerily silent. Not even the birds were chirping. Jessie could hear his own heartbeat pounding in his chest as if it were a drum beating in preparation for war. Being one-half Native American, descended from the Ute tribe of central and western Colorado, Jessie had always felt as if his ancestors were with him, watching over him when he was in the mountains alone. Although he hadn't had the blessing of growing up in an environment where he could learn and be immersed in the Ute culture, Jessie had kept his heritage close to his heart all his life, reading, and visiting the ancient sites of the Ute people whenever he had the chance. With nightfall rapidly approaching and a hungry pack of wolves stalking his flock, he hoped the instincts of his native side would be with him tonight.

Despite the trouble they caused, Jessie found himself conflicted as to his outlook on the wolves. As a shepherd, he saw them in the view of his flock—as a predator. As a descendent of the Ute tribe, however, he was torn. The Ute saw the wolf as a cultural hero of the Ute people, in the form of a man, only taking the literal form of a wolf when necessary.

In Jessie's previous life as a sheriff, he remembered ranchers complaining about the government's reintroduction of wolves into the Rockies and how with them being on the endangered list, they weren't legally allowed to defend their herds and flocks from them. As a homesteading shepherd, he understood their plight completely. Only now, he faced a much greater threat than the ranchers had. The reduction of the human population all throughout the American West due to the collapse had left the wolf population to grow exponentially, making them a clear and present threat to his family's livelihood.

Taking a deep breath and looking up into the trees, Jessie could once again hear the chirp of the birds, as well as the other sounds of nature, return to the forest. Nodding as if he was communicating with the wolves, he turned and walked back into the grassy clearing, rejoining his flock with an armload of firewood.

As Duke dutifully watched over the flock, Jessie finished setting up camp by stacking the wood neatly near the fire for easy tending throughout the night. "Come here, boy," Jessie said, calling out to Duke.

Running over to Jessie, Duke licked him on the face and curled up on the ground beside him while keeping his head pointed in the direction of his flock, always on guard.

"Good boy," Jessie said, handing Duke a piece of venison jerky, then patting him on the back. "We may be in for a long night, boy. I have a feeling we aren't gonna get a lot of sleep."

~~~~

Running through the woods, Jessie could hear the pack of wolves gaining on him. Facing exhaustion, he knew he needed to stand his ground and fight, or die like a deer isolated from the herd. Turning to face the threat, Jessie reached down to his holster to draw his Colt, as he could see the light in the eyes of the wolves rapidly approaching. To his horror, his holster was empty. His gun must have fallen out of the loose fitting, cowboy-style brown leather holster during the pursuit.

Jessie looked back up just in time to see a large Canadian gray wolf leap into the air, its fangs exposed as it came at him for the kill. Just before the hungry wolf's teeth clamped onto his neck, he felt the paws of another tear down his back as one attacked simultaneously from behind.

Jessie twisted to avert the attack when Duke yelped and jumped up on all fours, nearly knocking the tent over from the inside and waking Jessie from his terrible nightmare.

"Holy crap, Duke! Oh, my God!" Jessie exclaimed as he realized Duke had awakened him by pawing him on the back. "Whew. That seemed way too real." With a smile, now that he realized none of it was really happening and that it was only a dream, he rubbed Duke on the head and said, "I'm sorry, boy. I guess I scared you half to death." Looking at his watch, he then said, "Two in the morning, already? I had no idea I would fall asleep so quickly, all things considered. Well, I'm up now," he said with a yawn. "I might as well make my rounds and check on the sheep."

Pushing the tent flap to the side, Jessie climbed out of the tent, stood up, stretched, and picked up his rifle. As he always did, he double-checked the condition of the action and made sure the safety was engaged with a round in the chamber. Reaching down to his side, ensuring that his Colt was really there this time, he smiled and began to walk into the darkness, away from the relative safety and security of his campfire.

Several of the sheep jumped to their feet, startled by Jessie as he approached. They initially scattered, but quickly rejoined the flock once they realized it was only him and Duke. Although sheep generally don't take to humans for companionship, they do learn over time to see their shepherd as a protector and food source, making somewhat of an uneasy alliance between man and animal. One thing that's embedded in a sheep's mind is that nearly everything on earth that doesn't eat plants—eats sheep. They'd gladly seek protection from wherever it may come, even from their shepherd, whose own intentions might be suspect.

As Jessie reached the outer edges of his flock, just one hundred feet shy of the treeline, he looked up at the bright, nearly full moon. Once again, the eerie feeling he had felt early in the day came over him, sending chills throughout his body. Thankful for the moonlight helping to illuminate his surroundings, Jessie stared into the woods intently, hoping to catch a glimpse of movement if a threat lingered in the shadows. Jessie could sense a nervousness among the flock. Over the years, he had learned to trust the instincts of animals above his own, which on this occasion, served to reassure him that his own feelings of unease were well warranted.

Feeling a cool breeze blow across the back of his neck, goosebumps came over him as he saw movement in the trees ahead. A dark figure moved silently from right to left in front of him as if it merely floated through the trees without touching the ground. Thinking he saw the silhouette of a man, Jessie's heart skipped a beat as he heard a howl in the distance behind him. Turning around instantly, he heard rustling in the woods in the direction that was now directly behind him. Swinging his rifle around wildly in the direction of the noise, he became disoriented as he once again heard rustling off in another direction, this time to his immediate right. His heart pounded in his chest as he realized he and his entire flock were surrounded by an ominous threat that loomed in the darkness.

He clicked his rifle's safety off as he heard a ferocious bark and growl in the darkness toward his tent. Unable to focus his eyes in the darkness due to the flickering campfire in the distance, Jessie began jogging toward the growl. Having made only a few steps in that direction, he heard a vicious fight break out in the darkness between what he assumed was Duke and one of the invading wolves. Initially on the offensive, Duke's aggressive voice quickly turned to yelps of pain as he suddenly appeared to be outnumbered.

"Get the hell away from him, you filthy beasts!" yelled Jessie as he fired a shot from his rifle into the air, quickly chambering another round while running to Duke's aid. As he approached the vicious struggle, he pulled a flare from his jacket pocket, ignited it, and threw it high into the air while letting out a fearsome scream. "Get out of here! Get the hell out of here, you filthy beasts! I'll kill every last one of you!"

As the flare fell back to earth, it illuminated the nightmarish scene, revealing four wolves on top of Duke. As the flare bounced once and then came to rest on the ground, it provided Jessie with the necessary light he needed to fight off the invading animals. Knowing that follow-up shots with his bolt-action rifle would be too slow given the desperate, close-range situation, he took a quick aim, fired a shot at one of the wolves, and dropped his rifle to the ground. Still running in the direction of the struggle, he blinked several times in an attempt to regain his night vision from the bright muzzle flash of his rifle as he drew his revolver and fired three more shots at the wolves. The repeated shots caused the wolves to release Duke as they scattered in all directions.

"Duke! Duke! Are you okay, boy?" he said in a panic as he ran up to his dear friend.

Duke quickly bounded to his feet and winced in pain with a yelp.

"It's okay, buddy. It's okay. Sit, boy. Sit," he said as he nudged Duke back to the ground. "Let me check you out."

Pulling a small flashlight from his pocket, Jessie began looking Duke over in an attempt to determine the extent of his injuries. With the light beginning to fade after only a moment's use, Jessie said, "Well, hell. Looks like my rechargeable batteries are on their last leg. It looks like I might be back to a caveman torch before long. It's not like I can run to the store and get more," he said, trying to calm his own nerves with humor.

"I think you're gonna be just fine, boy. You're cut up a bit, but those mongrels didn't hurt you too bad. That thick ol' fur of yours sure seems to come in handy."

Duke panted and looked at Jessie as if he intended to reply and then laid his head on the ground, exhaling as he gave in to his own exhaustion.

Patting him on the side, Jessie said, "It's okay, boy. Get some rest. I'll take over the watch from here."

Chapter Four

The next morning as the sun's rays shone through the cabin's windows, Stephanie said to Sasha and Jeremy, "You two stay put. I'm gonna go let the chickens out and check the coop for eggs."

"Am I in charge, mommy?" asked young Sasha.

"Yes, dear. You can be in charge, but I'll only be gone a minute."

Looking at her little brother with a crooked smile, Sasha said, "Now you have to do what I tell you. I'm in charge, now."

Before Jeremy could rebut her statement, Stephanie interjected, saying, "Hey, now. Don't get carried away. You're in charge as in you're responsible for anything that happens while I'm outside, but you're not his boss."

Jeremy smiled, sticking his tongue out at his sister.

"Hey. You knock it off, too, young man."

With the smirk instantly leaving his face, Jeremy replied, "Yes, mommy."

"Good, now you two behave. I'll be right back."

"Let me come, too, mommy. I don't want to stay in here with him," said Sasha, as she shot Jeremy the stink eye.

"No," Stephanie quickly replied. "By the time you got your jacket and shoes on I'd back already. Just sit tight. I'll only be a few minutes."

As Stephanie left the cabin and began walking toward the chicken coop, which was only about fifty yards away, she saw Jessie's horse, Brave, off in the distance. Immediately noticing that something wasn't right, she saw that Jessie was walking alongside the horse instead of riding him. As he got closer, she saw Duke stretched across Brave's bare back while Jessie carried his saddle.

Turning to look at the cabin, Stephanie saw the kids watching her through the window. She pointed at them sternly and mouthed the words, *stay there.*

With a hurried pace, she walked out to meet Jessie to see what was wrong and to find out what had happened. As she got closer, seeing the blood stains on the white of Duke's fur, she shouted, "Oh, my, God! Is he dead?"

Hearing her voice, Duke raised his head and looked in her direction, indicating to her that he was still alive.

"He's gonna be fine. Just a little roughed up."

"Wolves?" she asked with a concerned look.

"Yep. About four of them from what I saw. They were all over the place. It seemed every time I turned around I heard another one behind me. They didn't like the flare one bit. I'm gonna need to start carrying several of those things with me every time I'm out there."

"I'm not too crazy about you spending your nights out there with the sheep anymore. I don't want anything happening to you. We've made it this far, through all of the hell of the collapse. I can't bear the thought of losing you now."

"I know, babe," he replied as he reached up and helped Duke down from the horse. "There you go, buddy," he said, scratching Duke behind the ears as Stephanie knelt down and began loving and petting on him.

Standing up to give her a moment with Duke, he said, "The sheep are our livelihood. If we lose the sheep, we lose everything. They are our meat, our fabric, our leather, our everything. If the wolves pressure them too much, the flock will be on the run and we'll lose them. No, I've got to nip this in the bud. I'll be careful. I'm also gonna go out a little better prepared tonight."

With a look of understanding, Stephanie nodded and said, "Well, you had a long night. I'll clean Duke up. You go and get your nap in. I'll wake you for lunch."

"Thanks, babe," he said with a smile and a quick kiss on her lips.

~~~~

Walking through the woods in the darkness of the night, Jessie felt as if he was not alone. It was though he could feel the stare of eyes with ill intent all around him. The cold night's breeze slowed to a stop, the air now silent and still. Even the sound of insects chirping in the distance faded into silence.

Hearing a twig snap in the woods to his right, he fought the urge to focus on it. He knew the real threat would come from the front once his attentions were turned. Hearing the slow and deliberate breath of a large animal just ahead, cloaked by the darkness, he reached down to his side to slowly bring his revolver to bear. As his hand reached the holster, to his surprise, he found an ancient Native American bone handled stone knife. He then realized he was dressed in the traditional Ute clothing of the past. He wore a buckskin shirt, a breechcloth, and leather leggings. Looking up, in an almost trance-like state, he saw a large gray wolf slowly emerge into the moonlight directly in front of him.

He drew the knife, looking down at it in a moment of bewilderment and confusion. When he looked back up, a Native American man stood in front of him where the wolf had been, wearing a wolf headdress with grey fur extending down over his shoulders

"What... who?" Jessie stammered, at a loss for words. He simply could not believe his own eyes.

The man held his hand up as if to silence him and said, "You must leave this place. Take your family and go."

Hearing movement in the brush behind him, Jessie looked back, but saw nothing. He then turned back to face the man, but the man was gone. Glancing down at his hand, he saw that he now gripped the Colt pistol tightly. "What the…?" he began to say as he looked around quickly, only to realize that the sounds of the forest had now returned and the breeze blew gently once again.

He holstered the pistol and started to turn and walk back to his home, when he heard, "Daddy. Daddy. Wake up. Mommy said to come and eat."

Finding himself in his bed, Jessie flinched, startling his son. "I'm sorry, son," he said apologetically. "I was having the strangest dream."

"Mommy says come and eat," Jeremy repeated.

"Okay, I'll be there in a minute. Let me get dressed," Jessie said as Jeremy ran back into the main room of the cabin.

I'm losing it, he thought. *Must be all the isolation.*

~~~~

After a filling bowl of Stephanie's lamb stew with vegetables and natural herbs, Jessie went outside to the barn to gather a few items in preparation for tonight's watch. Climbing the ladder into the barn's loft, he moved several bales of old, stale hay, to uncover a wooden chest. Brushing the loose hay aside, he dialed in the combination on the padlock, popped it off, and opened the chest to reveal his sheriff's uniform and his law enforcement gear from his previous life.

Carefully removing his old uniform and laying it off to the side, he then removed a disassembled Bushmaster AR-15 carbine with a lightweight profile barrel, a rail-mounted tactical flashlight, and a 1-4X Nikon scope that had once served as his patrol rifle. After a quick inspection for contamination, he rejoined the upper and lower receivers by pushing the takedown pins into place, test cycled the action, and then placed it off to the side.

Next, he removed his old duty belt from the chest. His Smith & Wesson M&P 40 was still in his Kydex button retention holster along with two extra magazine pouches on the belt. Holding the holster and belt with his left hand, he drew the pistol from the holster and cycled the action several times to ensure it was still clear. He then reholstered it, snapping it firmly into the holster's retention mechanism.

After a few moments of thought, he took the pistol and duty belt and wrapped it in an old towel. *Some things just feel right,* he thought, opting to continue to carry the old six-shot Colt revolver instead of the modern hi-capacity semi-auto. *At least this will come in handy for Stephanie if she ever needs it.*

Climbing back down the ladder with the AR-15 slung over his back, he was greeted at the bottom by his children.

"Whatcha doing, Daddy?" asked young Sasha.

"Oh, just getting some things together to watch over the sheep tonight."

"Is everything okay?" she asked.

"Oh, yes. It's fine. My other rifle is just a little heavy compared to this one. This one will be easier to carry while on horseback," he said, trying not to worry them. "Here you go, Honeybear," he said, fishing a picture out of his pocket, handing it to Sasha.

Sasha took the picture and began looking it over, with Jeremy tip-toeing, trying to see over her shoulder. "It's you, Daddy," she said with a smile on her face.

"Yeah, that's me. That's the day I was sworn in as sheriff."

Beaming with pride, Sasha asked, "Can I keep it?"

"It's for both of you," he answered. "Run and give it to your mother. Ask her to put it in a safe place where you can both look at it anytime you want."

Answering with only a smile, the two children turned and ran back toward the cabin. Jessie stood there for a moment, watching them run with such excitement. He was glad they were young enough to be able to adjust to their new world easily. He couldn't imagine how a modern, urban teenager would adjust to such a rough and basic life after having been raised with all of the conveniences of the modern world.

Once the children were inside the house, he turned and walked toward the chicken coop and the woods that stood just beyond it. Entering the woods, he walked over to an old steel barrel, which to most, would simply look like a rusted old relic from the past, refuse that had simply been left behind. He picked up a nearby rock and banged underneath the lip of the lid, knocking it loose. Setting the lid off to the side, he looked down into the barrel to find a small cache of ammunition. There was several thousand rounds of 5.56 NATO for his AR-15, as well as .40 S&W and .357 Magnum. Additionally, there were 12-gauge shotgun shells for the shotgun that Stephanie kept within reach at all times, as well as several hundred rounds of .30-06 hunting-grade ammunition, and fresh, rechargeable batteries suitable for the flashlight mounted to his rifle, as well as several others in his possession. Picking up the batteries, Jessie looked at them and said, "Well, heck. I forgot all about having these. They'll sure come in handy."

Jessie knew that what he had at this point, was more than likely all he was ever going to get. With that in mind, he kept it all disbursed in hidden locations throughout the property to prevent a total loss if someone happened upon their cabin and attempted to rob and loot their home. Polite society was a thing of the past, and Jessie knew thinking in defensive and preparedness terms was what had kept them alive this long. It was a practice he planned on continuing.

Chapter Five

As Jessie gathered his things for the night's watch over the sheep, he turned to Stephanie and said, "Keep Duke with you and the kids tonight. That poor dog needs a break."

"What if the wolves come back? Can you handle them alone without Duke to keep them at bay?" she asked in a concerned tone.

"I hope you're right."

"What? You hope I'm right about what?" she asked, bewildered by his seemingly misplaced statement.

"If," he replied as he pulled his belt tight and secured his holster.

Glaring at him with a perturbed look, she asked, "What the heck are you talking about?"

"*If* the wolves come back. I hope you're right that it's an '*if*,' and not a '*when*.' Although, I have a feeling the latter is true. They know where a food source is. A contained group of domesticated sheep is easier to chase down than the wild game in the area that are adept in predator avoidance. No, they'll be back for sure. This is just the beginning, I'm afraid," he said in a serious tone. "It's gonna be a long winter if I don't rid us of this threat soon. Once the snow falls and game animals are even more scarce, our sheep will be impossible for them to resist."

As she wrapped her arms around him from behind, Stephanie kissed Jessie on the cheek and said softly, "Be careful out there. Do whatever you need to do. Just be careful."

Turning to her with a serious look, he replied, "You, too. I don't want you leaving the house unarmed anymore."

Interrupting before he could finish, Stephanie insisted, "I can't carry that shotgun around with me everywhere I go. I won't even be able to carry the eggs without breaking them."

"I didn't mean the shotgun," he replied. Reaching into their top dresser drawer, he removed the towel he had retrieved from the loft in the barn and unwrapped it, revealing to her his former service pistol. "I want you to keep this by the door and put it on every time you go outside. I also don't want the kids going outside alone or getting out of our sight."

"What? Do you really think that's necessary?"

"Absolutely. If we still had the internet, I'd tell you to look it up. Wolves have been known to attack children all throughout history. They're easy prey. Just before the collapse, the wolf population had rebounded so successfully from the government's reintroduction programs—well, successfully for the wolves at least—that some places in southern Colorado actually had to build shacks for children's school bus stops to protect them from hungry wolves in the area. We're not taking any chances. We have a clear and present threat, and we're going to treat it that way."

"Yes, Sheriff Townsend," she said with a salute.

"Hey, don't act that way," he protested. "We can't take any chances in this world. It's not like we can rush one of the kids off to the hospital or something if they were to become injured. We need to be as safe as we can as much as we can."

"I know. I'm sorry," she replied, giving him a hug and a kiss. "I guess I just don't want to have to think about such things. I just want some semblance of normalcy."

"This is normal, now. We'll be okay. We're survivors. Look what we've already overcome. We had the foresight to move up here to the mountains and get off the grid while everyone else just kept living the same lives, hoping it would all get better. Then when it all started going down, it was too late for most. The ones not killed became refugees or worse. We've been a step ahead of the game. We just need to stay that way."

"I love you," she said with a smile, feeling a sense of security in what Jessie had said. "You're right. I'll carry it. Show me again how it works."

"I love you, too, babe," he said with another kiss. He then picked up the gun belt, wrapping it around her waist and adjusting the fit. "There we go. The last notch on the belt, but it'll work. Now, do you remember the rules of firearm safety from back when I took you to the range all the time?"

"Yes, I think. Don't put your finger on the trigger. Don't point it at anyone. And... um, oh, treat it as if it is always loaded."

"Pretty much," he replied. "Never put your finger on the trigger, or inside the trigger guard until you are ready to take a shot. Pay special attention to that when you're drawing it from the holster in a hurry. Clasp the grip like this with your index finger straight and on the outside of the holster," he explained as he simulated the position on his side.

Grasping the grip of the pistol as instructed, she said, "Like this?"

"Exactly. Now, when you draw the weapon, keep that finger straight. There have been a lot of accidental discharges during the draw when people grab the trigger in a hurry. Once you clear the weapon from the holster, rotate it forward, and join your hands together with the supporting grip. Next, push it out to the target, your finger only reaching the trigger once you're on target."

"Like this?" she said, simulating a draw.

"Yep. You've still got it," he replied with a flirtatious smile. "The next rule is to be sure of your target and what is beyond it. Just remember, when you take a shot, you can't call the bullet off. If you miss your intended target, what's the next thing in its path? In a panic, your aim will likely be rushed and less than perfect. There have been many instances over the years where even trained police officers have accidentally shot innocent people during the heat of the moment. You need to react quickly, but don't have an automatic instinct to just start pulling the trigger. Every shot needs to be well thought out. When you're handling the gun outside of the holster and not in a position to shoot, just imagine a laser beam projecting out of the end of the barrel. Never let that imaginary beam touch anything you love."

She replied with a nod and a serious expression.

"And the third important safety rule is just like you said; treat every gun as if it is loaded," he continued. "Even when we break them down for cleaning and maintenance, we always treat them as if they are loaded, just in case."

"Thank you," she said with a smile.

"You know, you look kind of sexy with that gun on your hip. You look like a woman who means business," he said with a devious grin.

"I do mean business, Sheriff," she said, pulling him in close for a kiss. "Unfortunately, you've got business to attend to as well. It's getting late."

With a deflated look, he replied, "You're right. I've got to get out there. I don't like the thought of the sheep being out there without Duke."

Chapter Six

Riding his horse, Brave, along the trail to get to the grassy hillside where his flock was grazing, Jessie kept a keen eye out for any sign of trouble. Paying close attention to the birds, as they always seemed to have a way of alerting him to potential danger, Jessie was pleased to find them chirping away as if everything was right in the world.

As he approached his flock, he paused and scanned the area from a distance and did not see anything particularly out of place. Riding up to the ridge that overlooked his flock, Jessie dismounted and tied Brave's reins to a tree branch in the shade. "We'll just sit here and observe for a while before we set up camp. We've got plenty of time," he said, patting Brave on the back. "I have a feeling you're not going to be as talkative as Duke tonight, are you?" he said with a chuckle as Brave seemed to pay him no mind.

Using his binoculars to glass the area below, Jessie panned from right to left, pausing on each cluster of sheep, with everything seeming to be secure. Then, once his scan reached the left-most edge of the grazing area, he caught a glimpse of a lone ewe separated from the rest of the flock. "That's not right," he said aloud, as if Brave could understand. "Let's go check it out."

Mounting Brave and spurring him into action, he carefully traversed the steep hillside to the area where he had seen the ewe from a distance. As he neared, he could hear the distress in her *bahh* as she called out for something. Knowing that sheep are generally quiet animals unless there is a problem, he sped Brave up to a trot, startling the ewe as he rode up in such a hurry.

When he reached her, he saw her standing over the remains of a young lamb that had been torn to pieces by a predator. "Well, heck," he said as he climbed down from his horse. The young mother ewe refused to leave her tiny lamb's side, even though it was a gruesome scene to behold. She called out to her lamb as if it would somehow hear her and respond, not fully understanding the situation.

"Oh, momma. I'm sorry, girl," he said as he approached slowly. The skittish ewe backed away as her distress-filled calls only intensified. "Go on now," he said, trying to urge the ewe to leave and rejoin the flock. "There's nothing we can do for him now. I'm sorry, but you'll forget all about this soon," he said, referring to her relatively simple cognitive abilities. "Go," he repeated again, pushing her away.

Finally giving in to his urging, the young mother turned and slowly walked towards the flock, leaving him to deal with the remains of the young lamb.

"Those thieving mongrels," he said under his breath. Standing up and walking back over to where Brave was standing, he took his collapsible shovel out of the pack that he had secured to the horse's saddle. "We've got to bury the remains. We don't want the smell of blood to linger."

Once he had dealt with the remains of the slain lamb, Jessie looked up at the evening's sky and said, "Well, Brave, no tent tonight. It looks like it's gonna remain dry and I need to keep my head on a swivel. A tent would be the equivalent of wearing blinders. Besides, I can't fit you in the tent like I could Duke, and you're my only company," he said jokingly to the unimpressed horse.

~~~~

As Jessie set up his open-air camp and prepared his kindling and firewood for the night, a feeling came over him that he was being watched. Turning around quickly, he was startled to see a large ram standing behind him. The ram was also frightened by Jessie's sudden movement, taking several steps back.

"Oh, hey, boy. Thank God, it's only you." The ram studied Jessie for a moment and then walked toward him, lowering his head and rubbing his horns on Jessie's leg.

Seeing the number on the ram's ear tag, Jessie looked to his horse, Brave, and said, "This is Lobo. Lobo was a bottle lamb who was rejected by his mother at birth because he was too small. Now look at him. He's magnificent," he said with admiration, scratching behind Lobo's horns. "You've always been a little different, Lobo. I guess having Stephanie and the kids bottle-feed you took away some of your instinct to distrust us mean ol' humans. Here, I've got something for you," Jessie said as he walked over to his horse.

Reaching into the pack on the saddle, Jessie retrieved one of the horse treats that he had brought along for Brave. "Here ya go, Lobo. You'll love these. Stephanie makes them out of oats and dehydrated apples."

Sniffing the treat in Jessie's hand, Lobo happily took it into his mouth and vigorously consumed it.

Turning to look at Lobo, Jessie said, "I guess you saw what happened over there, huh, boy?" pointing to where the young lamb was killed. "I don't envy you sheep these days. Those wolves have gotten a taste for you and it's gonna to be hard to break them of it now. Short of killing each and every one of them, that is. Grazing domesticated sheep are just too dang easy compared to hunting and catching wild game." Scratching him on top of the head, Jessie added, "I'll do my best, but no promises."

~~~~

As the evening slipped off into the night, the world seemed at peace to Jessie; the sounds of nature all around him, a faint breeze blowing just hard enough to keep the mosquitos away, and his flock grazing on the rich grasses of the hillside, seeming to not have a care in the world. Tending to his fire, Jessie looked off to his left to see Lobo lying in the grass on the edge of the light provided by the flames.

"Not too keen on fire, are you, boy?" Jessie asked. "I guess no animal is, though. Fire in the natural world means a forest fire, which is bad. As far as animals are concerned, fire outside of the natural world means humans, which is also bad. Yeah, I guess it's just about right for you to all be leery of fire."

Turning his head quickly, Lobo looked into the darkness as he and Jessie heard a howl off in the distance.

"There they are, boy," he said, staring off into the blackness of the night. Poking at the fire with a stick, he added, "Having a campfire is a double-edged sword. On the one hand, it does a good job of keeping the critters away—no offense intended to you, of course. On the other hand, it destroys my night vision. When those fleabags make their move and I have to engage them in the dark, I feel as blind as a bat in a soundproof room."

Brave, shifted his hooves restlessly at the sounds of the distant menacing howl. Walking over to him, Jessie stroked his neck and said, "Easy, boy. They sound like they're pretty far away right now. Don't worry. I'll cut you loose if it comes down to it."

~~~~

Awakened by the sounds of wolves in the distance, Stephanie sat up in bed and reached over for her shotgun, which she still kept handy for its firepower, despite having the pistol. *That sounded close,* she thought. Duke, who had been sleeping by her side, perked to attention, having heard the howl as well.

Just then, Sasha and Jeremy came running into her and Jessie's bedroom, frightened by the ominous sounds.

"Mommy, Mommy!" Sasha cried. "The wolves. They're outside."

"It's okay," Stephanie said reassuringly. "They're off in the woods somewhere far from us."

"No! I saw one out the window," Sasha insisted.

"What?" Stephanie shouted as she pulled the covers aside and climbed out of bed.

"I woke up when I heard them howling. I looked out our bedroom window and saw a dog go by in the moonlight out near the treeline."

Duke sprang to his feet with a whimper, haunted by his previous injuries and began to growl under his breath.

"Shhhh, it's okay, boy," Stephanie said as she scratched him on top of the head. "We're safe in here."

Just then, she heard a disturbance near the chicken coop as the sounds of frantic clucking shattered the silence of the night. Springing out of bed with her shotgun in hand, Stephanie ran to the front of the cabin, opened the front door, and yelled, "Get the hell out of here!" Followed by the loud crack of the shotgun as she fired into the sky with hopes of scaring them away.

To her horror, the flash of light from the muzzle illuminated the night, exposing the silhouette of a large wolf standing just ten yards in front of her. Redirecting the shotgun, she racked the pump action, chambering another round, and fired into the darkness where the wolf had stood. With the muzzle flash once again lighting up the darkness for a fraction of a second, she saw that the wolf was now gone.

As she began to pull the door shut, Stephanie felt Duke push by her, knocking the door open as he ran out into the darkness. "Duke! No!" she screamed in an attempt to call him back to the cabin.

~~~~

Hearing the sounds of distant gunshots toward his home, Jessie sprang to his feet as his heart pounded with the thoughts of what might be happening there. Quickly mounting his horse, he rode as fast as he could through the darkness with the faint moonlight guiding his way as he raced toward the cabin.

Nearing the cabin, he heard the ferocious sounds of a struggle in the direction of the coop. Dismounting Brave before he even came to a stop, Jessie hit the ground running, bringing his AR-15 to bear, switching on the barrel-mounted tactical light. To his horror, he saw three large wolves ravaging Duke.

Flipping off the safety with his thumb, Jessie began firing at the wolves, striking two of them while the third dashed off into the darkness. He then quickly scanned the yard, seeing feathers and blood scattered throughout the area.

"Jessie!" he heard from the cabin.

"Stay in the house with the kids!" he yelled in reply, as he continued to scan the area for threats.

Unable to see any other predators in the immediate vicinity, he quickly ran over to Duke and was horrified to see him take his last breath, as he bled to death from a gaping neck wound. Placing his hand on Duke's side, he muttered, "I'm sorry, boy. I'm so sorry."

Reluctantly turning his attention to the chicken coop, Jessie shined his light on the chain-link fence that had been torn loose, allowing the wolves access. The coop was a horrific scene, with at least seven dead chickens that he could see. The others had either fled and escaped or were killed off in the darkness away from the coop. The answer to that he knew he would not know until the morning's sun gave them the safety of daylight to investigate further.

Chapter Seven

The sun's first rays of morning light shining over the horizon illuminated the fog of Jessie's breath as he sat silently in an old rocking chair on the front porch of their cabin. As he began to doze off, relieved that the long night was finally coming to an end, Stephanie opened the front door and came out bundled up in her robe, carrying a fresh hot cup of coffee.

"Coffee?" he said with excitement in his voice. "What's the special occasion that we're dipping into our reserves? Aren't we down to the last of it?"

"Yes," she replied. "We only have about two pounds left. You've had a rough night, though. You look like you need it."

"Thanks, Steph. Are the kids still asleep?"

"Finally. They couldn't go back to sleep after all of the commotion last night. They kept asking where Duke was—and I just didn't know what to tell them. They saw him run out when the wolves came, but they never saw him come back," she said with a deflated tone. "They fell asleep about an hour before the sun started coming up. Hopefully, they'll sleep for a while. You can have Duke taken care of by then, can't you?"

Taking the cup of coffee, Jessie stood up, took her by the hand, and said, "Here, sit. I've been sitting in that chair for hours. I need to stand anyway." As she took a seat on the rocking chair, he said, "Of course. I'll deal with Duke first thing. We can't lie to them about what happened. They need to know the truth. They need to know that there are real dangers out here. If it can happen to Duke, it can happen to them. Or even you or me for that matter. We can't sugar-coat this world for them anymore."

Taking a sip of his coffee and then placing it on the small table next to the rocking chair, Jessie sat down on the front porch directly in front of Stephanie, leaning back against her legs to feel her warmth. Leaning forward and draping her long, brunette hair over his shoulder, she kissed him on the cheek and said, "Let me run in and change clothes. I'll deal with the chickens while you deal with Duke. The kids should sleep long enough for us to get it all cleaned up."

"Thanks, babe," he replied, turning his head toward her and kissing her.

~~~~

A little while later, after Stephanie had changed out of her robe and into a pair of jeans, a flannel shirt, a jacket, and a pair of old muck boots. Jessie led Stephanie to Duke's grave which he had just finished covering with large rocks to deter scavenging. After a few moments of silence honoring their fallen friend and four-legged family member, they surveyed the rest of the night's carnage together. They were horrified to find that only three chickens remained alive, all three of them hens. The rest were scattered around the coop like bloody confetti, their bodies torn to shreds by the vicious attackers as they had begun consuming them on site before turning their attention to Duke.

"They're all hens," she said softly.

"What?" he asked.

"They're all hens. The roosters were killed trying to protect the flock, no doubt."

"Knowing Rex, he would have gone down swinging for sure," Jessie said, referring to Stephanie's favorite rooster, a mix between a Barred Rock and a Golden Red.

Picking up one of his feathers, Stephanie began to shed a tear, only to quickly wipe it from her cheek, saying, "Well, what's done is done. We'll get an egg or two per day for a while, and then they will eventually dry up. With no rooster, there will be no more fertilized eggs to keep our flock going."

"What about the ones you have in the incubator?" he asked, referring to the electric incubator they had been keeping warm using a small solar panel for power.

"There are only four eggs in there right now," she said. "Odds are only one or two will hatch. Who's to say one of those will even be a rooster? Remember, don't count your chickens before they hatch. Do you remember when we first started incubating? I had twenty eggs and thought I was going to have twenty new chicks, to end up with only six."

"In hindsight, I should have built a second coop away from this one to mitigate our risks of such a thing. Having all of the chickens in one place was just plain stupid," he said as he kicked a rock on the ground out of frustration.

"You can't prepare for everything that comes along," she said.

"Maybe not, but I can try," he said with determination. "I need to take a good look at this place and see where our other weaknesses may lie and deal with them before something like this happens again."

"You just focus on the sheep. They need to be your priority. We can't afford to lose them, too. If we do—"

"Yeah, I know," he said, interrupting her before she got a chance to say what was on both their minds.

Hearing the bell-chime on the front door of the cabin jingle, their attention was diverted toward the sound as they heard Sasha yelling, "Mommy! Daddy! Where are you?"

"We're right here," Stephanie shouted in reply. "Stay in the cabin. Your daddy will be right there." Turning her attention to Jessie, she then said, "You've been up all night. I'll finish up out here. Go spend some time with the kids. They need you. You've been spending so much time out there with the sheep."

"I have to. If I didn't—"

"I know," she said as she pulled him toward her and gave him a kiss. "Now, don't argue and just go be Daddy for a while.

You can be the shepherd again tonight, but for now, you're just Daddy."

Answering with only a smile, Jessie turned and shouted, "I'm coming, kids. Who wants to help me brew some chicory?"

Chapter Eight

Over the few weeks following the wolf attack on the Townsend's chickens, Jessie continued his ever-vigilant watch over his sheep, knowing that they were now his family's only reliable source of protein. Encounters with wolves had dropped off sharply since that fateful night. Perhaps having killed several of them, he had made it clear to them that his homestead was not a place where they could expect an easy meal, or perhaps they were just biding their time. Only time would tell for sure. Until then, though, Jessie would remain on guard, keeping an eye out for any sign of potential wolf presence.

Being high in the Rocky Mountains, the winter was creeping up on them much earlier than in the lower regions. Morning frost was now a daily occurrence, and the occasional light dusting of snow seemed to be warning shots fired across their bow by Old Man Winter. This morning was no exception. Jessie peeked out of his tent to find that four inches of fresh snow had fallen during the night.

"Well, hell," he mumbled to himself. "It'll be feet deep before we know it. Then I'll be back on snowshoes instead of horseback."

Wishing his flock of sheep a good day as he always did, Jessie mounted his horse and headed for home. As he pulled his collar close to his neck and his hat down tight, he thought, *I sure hope Steph has something piping hot ready to eat.*

Approaching his cabin, he saw that some of the night's snowfall had been freshly disturbed off in the distance. Urging Brave toward his discovery, he immediately dismounted at the realization that they were the boot prints of what appeared to be a fully grown man. Instinctively putting his right hand on his Colt revolver, Jessie looked back to see that his rifle was still in the scabbard attached to his saddle. He began to visually scan the area looking for any signs that someone might still be in the vicinity.

Looking back down at the footprints, Jessie thought, *Snow has fallen on these tracks for at least a few hours. I'd better get to the cabin.*

Quickly mounting his horse, he spurred him into action and raced toward the cabin. As he approached, he was relieved to see smoke billowing out of the chimney and no sign of tracks anywhere in the immediate vicinity. As he pulled back on the reins, bringing Brave to a stop directly in front of the cabin, Stephanie greeted him on the porch, saying, "Put Brave in the barn and get your butt in here. It's freezing outside."

Taking another look around, Jessie nodded in reply. Dismounting his horse, he asked, "Did you see or hear anything unusual last night?"

"Unusual? What do you mean?"

Hesitating for a moment, not wanting to face the fact that they now had a potentially much more dangerous predator in their midst, he answered, "I saw footprints just back that way, on the other side of the trees," pointing back in the direction from which he had come.

"Wolf prints?"

"I wish," he replied with reservation in his voice.

"Well, then what?"

"Man prints."

"Man prints?" she queried, hoping she had misheard him. "You mean someone has been prowling around here?"

"I'm afraid so. On my way back from the flock, I saw a disturbed area in the fresh snow. They were definitely large boot prints with a rather long stride. I'm guessing an adult male over six feet tall, from the depth of the impression and the stride."

"Did you see any other tracks?" she asked.

"No. We have to assume there are others, though. Perhaps he was just an advanced scout, with the rest of the group lying back until he reports back to them."

"So what now?" she asked.

Just then, Jeremy opened the cabin door, saying, "Mom, Sasha and I are done with our math work." Noticing that Jessie had returned from another night with the flock, he turned and shouted to Sasha, "Daddy's home!"

"Close the door, you're letting the snow inside," Stephanie insisted. "Your father will be inside as soon as he puts Brave away."

"Okay," Jeremy sheepishly replied, closing the door and disappearing back into the warmth of the home.

"Now, you were saying?" she said, prompting him to continue.

Pausing to look around the cabin while forming his words, Jessie said, "I think it's safe to say I can't leave you and the kids here alone at night anymore. With the snow coming early, I may as well bring the sheep into the corral and start them on the hay. If we butcher enough of them and can get the meat safely stored, we should have just enough hay in the barn to make it through until spring. It's a little early, but... without Duke out there with the flock, we can't keep spreading ourselves so thin with others in the area. We don't know who they are or what they're up to, but I don't have a good feeling about it."

"How will you drive the sheep back without Duke?"

"Yeah, that'll be tough. I suppose I can bait them with corn and grain. Moving them from one feed spot to another until we get them back to the homestead. There's just no way I can handle them on horseback alone. Those ewes are too skittish for that. I would just end up pushing them off into the woods or something, scattering the flock. Duke—he was priceless. That dog could drive those sheep to me all day long, never letting even one get away."

"You do what you have to do," she replied. "Now put Brave in the barn and get in here. Breakfast is ready. We can talk about it more after you eat and take a good nap."

~~~~

Removing his napkin from where he had tucked it into his shirt, Jessie patted himself on the belly and said with great satisfaction in his voice, "Oh, how I love those potato pancakes. You're the best, babe. And that syrup you make out of honey— it's the perfect touch."

"Thanks, hon. And yes, I'm thankful for our friendly little bees every day."

"Daddy," Sasha said, batting her eyes with a smile from ear to ear, "May I be excused? I'm working on a birthday present for you. Mommy made it part of our art lessons."

"That's right, it's almost my birthday. With all that's been going on I guess I've just totally lost track of everything. Of course, sweetheart. Go right ahead."

"Me, too! Me, too!" said Jeremy with excitement as the two of them ran off into the other room.

Walking over to Jessie, Stephanie threw her leg over him and sat in his lap, giving him a hug and a kiss on the forehead. "They're so excited about the birthday presents they're making. Putting some meaning behind their art projects sure has gotten them motivated. I can't wait for you to get those sheep back over here so you're around at night again. Our bed has been getting cold at night without you," she said with a flirtatious smile.

"Me, too. Trust me," he replied. "Sleeping out there in the cold every night isn't my idea of a perfect situation, either. I'll get everything I need together today before I head back out. That way, in the morning, I can just get the things I need at first light and start to move them back this way, corn pile by corn pile."

"Why not get it done today? It's early still. I don't like the thought of being alone here with the kids with someone prowling around out there. I mean—what could they be up to? How did they find us here? It can't be someone we knew from before. If they simply needed a helping hand, they would have come to the cabin like others have before, instead of lying low in the woods. Wouldn't they?"

Looking out the window at the treeline in the distance, Jessie paused and said, "No, I imagine if not for the snowfall showing their path so clearly, we still wouldn't even know they were in the area. They probably had or have more recon to do. Then again, who knows how long they've been out there. In hindsight, we should've had more dogs. We should have had more than one sheepdog, and we definitely needed a dog or two around here for security at the cabin. A good Rottweiler would've taken care of someone sneaking around in the area already, or at a minimum, we would have known they were here immediately. That is, of course, assuming this wasn't the first visit."

"You can't think like that."

"Like what?" he responded defensively.

"You can't rehash every move we've made in getting ourselves up here on the homestead and getting ourselves prepared. Before the attacks, when things were only slowly getting worse, most people thought you were crazy for wanting to sell our home that was the symbol of the American dream to many, to move your family off-grid into the mountains. You couldn't have possibly covered every scenario, but you have done a damn fine job with the time and resources we had, getting us to a safe place away from most of the horrors in the cities. We wouldn't be alive if not for you, Jessie. I'm sure of that. So stop looking to the past and look at our present. What can we do with what we have today and the threats we face? Focus on that."

"I'm glad I married up," he responded with a smile. "You're the brains of this outfit. I'm just the mule that carries the load," he said, putting his arms around her.

As Jessie leaned in to give Stephanie a kiss, the moment was interrupted by the sound of a gunshot off in the distance. Jessie's heart sank as the sound he heard shattered the perceived safety of the isolation of his family's homestead. They had managed to live off-grid in their mountain hideaway virtually undetected by what remained of the population down below, avoiding the horrors of the rest of the world until now. The uncertainty of what might be their future sent chills through his body, a nervousness and uncertainty that he hadn't felt since his first officer-involved shooting as a young rookie sheriff's deputy so many years ago.

Those thoughts and fears swept through his body like a wildfire as he turned to her and said, "Get the kids in the bedroom under the bed. Keep the pistol and the shotgun with you at all times. Throw the board in the hangers across the door to barricade it shut."

"Where are you going?" she asked in a distressed voice.

"That shot sounded like it came from the direction of the flock—"

Before he could finish, the crack of another gunshot could be heard echoing through the mountains.

"Those sheep are our livelihood. If we let someone just start walking in there and picking them off, causing them to scatter— well, we could starve this winter. I've got to deal with this and deal with it now!"

With a quick hug and a kiss, Stephanie nodded in agreement and simply said, "Hurry back. Be safe. I love you."

"I love you, too," he replied, staring deeply into her beautiful blue eyes before turning to run out the door. As he began to pull the door shut behind him, he shouted, "Remember, throw the board into the hangers and stay put."

As the door closed with a solid thud, Stephanie flinched with fear of what her husband might be running off to find. Quickly snapping herself back into dealing with the tasks at hand, she did as he asked and barricaded the door. As she turned to grab Jessie's old duty pistol, Sasha and Jeremy ran into the room, with Jeremy asking, "Mommy, what's Daddy shooting at?"

With a warm and reassuring smile, Stephanie quickly replied, "Oh, it's nothing. Let's go play hide-and-seek."

Chapter Nine

Riding Brave through the trees at a breakneck pace to avoid being seen out in the open on the trail leading from the cabin to the sheep's grazing area, Jessie dodged limbs and branches, occasionally taking a swat to his face, unable to miss them all. As he approached the treeline of the grassy hillside, he slowed the horse to a stop, dismounted quickly, and tied his reins to a small tree branch. Patting him on the neck, he said, "There you go, boy, this won't really hold you, but maybe it will fool you for a while. If you end up being left out here alone, hopefully, you'll eventually figure out you can break it off and get away."

He then quietly pulled his Bushmaster AR-15 from the saddle mounted scabbard, pulled back slightly on the charging handle to verify that a round was in the chamber, ensured that the bolt went back into battery with the forward assist, and tapped the bottom of the fully loaded magazine to confirm that it was properly seated. *Here we go,* he thought as he crept up to the treeline, still hidden from plain view.

Zooming his 1-4X Nikon scope out to its maximum zoom, Jessie glassed the area looking for any signs of movement. His panicking sheep seemed confused, scattering in various directions, and then returning to the flock, unsure of the source of the threat. His sheep had been exposed to gunfire in the past, but it was always from Jessie's own gun, and never directly presented them with harm. They clearly knew something was different on this occasion, however.

As Jessie patiently searched the area, he spotted movement on the far side of the clearing, against the trees. His relatively weak 4X zoom didn't present him with an overly detailed picture. However, he could tell that there was an armed individual carrying what appeared from a distance to be either a

CETME or FAL rifle. Looking down at his AR-15, Jessie thought to himself, *Dammit, I sure would trade this thing for my good ol' .30-06 right now. That guy has the range advantage with a .308 over my .223. On the bright side, he doesn't seem to have an optic on that rifle. He may have the advantage of firepower, but I've got the advantage in the battlespace intel department.*

As another shot rang out, the muzzle flash from the man's rifle evident even from Jessie's distance, he knew he had to approach or engage his potential adversary. In order to close the gap to increase the effectiveness of his shots with his smaller-caliber rifle, Jessie began working his way slowly and quietly around the treeline, while remaining hidden in the woods. He knew his AR-15 was better suited for close-quarters battle and quick follow-up shots than for long-range sniping with its sixteen-inch carbine-length barrel and anemic .223/5.56mm cartridge. Closing the gap before visibly approaching or engaging the man would increase the effectiveness of his shots— should they become necessary. The last thing he wanted was to get bogged down in a drawn-out firefight. The resolution to this problem needed to come quickly.

Silently working his way around the grassy hillside, through the wooded area below, Jessie paused on occasion, looking around to try to determine if the individual in question had others lying in wait, either providing cover or setting a trap. He hoped it would turn out to simply be a man wanting to steal a few sheep carcasses, but deep down inside, the situation felt like it could be something more.

Upon reaching a range where he felt his first shot, if necessary, could be well placed and carry adequate energy to neutralize the threat, he took one last look around, covered the man with his rifle, and stepped out onto the grassy hillside to confront the intruder.

"Halt!" he shouted in a firm and commanding voice.

As the man began to turn to face him, Jessie shouted, "You're on private property. Those animals are my private property, as well. You are trespassing and stealing. Lower your weapon to the ground and don't do anything that will make me act further."

"Property?" the man questioned. "The world has changed, my friend."

"I'm not your friend. I'm a man holding his sights on you."

"Either way, the world has changed. Property is a loose term. If you can't defend it, it's not yours. It doesn't matter what some piece of paper says."

"Exactly, and I'm defending it right now!" Jessie shouted in an increasingly aggressive tone, the seriousness in his voice becoming evident.

"Are you?" the man asked.

"I've got a rifle on you, don't I?"

"What about the rest of your property? Are you defending that? It doesn't look like it. So I guess it's not yours—is it?"

His body tensed, flinching with rage, coming close to unintentionally discharging his rifle. Regaining his composure, Jessie said, "You had better tell me what you're doing and who else is with you or—"

Before he could finish, Jessie heard several gunshots in the distance, appearing to come from the direction of the homestead. His heart felt as if it had skipped a beat from the hellish realization of what might be occurring.

Taking advantage of the distraction, the trespasser began to bring his rifle to bear. Snapping back into the moment, Jessie quickly let two rounds fly, striking the man in the chest, dropping him to the ground almost instantly.

Jessie turned and sprinted into the woods in the direction of where he had left his horse. Running as hard as he could, he found the tree where he had loosely tied his reins, but Brave was nowhere to be found. This realization nearly brought him to his knees, knowing it would take him far too long to get back to the cabin on foot.

Hearing several more gunshots off in the distance, Jessie frantically looked for Brave, desperately trying to spot the animal through the trees in the distance. Placing two fingers in his mouth, Jessie whistled loudly and shouted, "Brave! Come on, boy!"

Trotting through the woods came Brave, dragging the branch he had been tied to along behind.

"Oh, thank God, boy," Jessie said as he ran up to him, placing one foot in a stirrup, throwing his other leg over the saddle, and spurring Brave into action.

No longer worried about traveling with cover, Jessie rode Brave as hard as he could down the main trail between the grassy hillside and the homestead. Attempting to keep the horrible possibilities out of his mind while he raced home to save his family, he contemplated his options and decided to ride straight for the chicken coop instead of the cabin. This would give himself a position of cover while he assessed the threats that were more than likely making a move on the home.

As the homestead came into view, his heart raced and his hearing seemed to fade into silence as he saw a man step out of the cabin and onto the front porch with what appeared to be Jessie's shotgun and Smith & Wesson M&P .40 in his hands. Leaping off of his horse before he even came to a stop, Jessie abandoned his plans to take cover behind the coop, knowing that the intruder had been inside the cabin.

Focused with more rage than he had ever felt and having left his AR-15 in his saddle scabbard in his haste to dismount, Jessie drew his Colt revolver and fired two rounds in rapid succession. One of the rounds went whizzing by the man's head, while the other struck him in the right shoulder, spinning him to the side and causing him to drop the pistol.

Still occupying a world of deafening silence, Jessie felt as if a swarm of bees was stinging his left leg. In what seemed like slow-motion, he turned his attention to the source of the pain. There he saw a disheveled, filthy man with long, greasy hair, cycling the pump action of a shotgun with smoke still emanating from the barrel, chambering another round, preparing once again to fire. Still running toward the cabin, Jessie took several hasty shots at the man, striking him in the side of the head, causing him to scream out in pain, dropping the shotgun to the ground while his hands covered his gaping wound.

Ignoring the pain in his leg, Jessie ran directly at the man in front of him, who was desperately trying to cycle Jessie's pump shotgun with one arm. With blood pouring profusely from the man's right arm, which was devastated by the close range shot of the one hundred and fifty-eight grain .357 Magnum hollow-point bullet, Jessie was able to fire two more rounds at the man before he could bring the shotgun to bear, striking him in the center of the chest and directly in the throat, knocking the man back onto the ground, dead on impact.

Running past the man, Jessie ran into the cabin. Shoving the door aside, he yelled "Stephanie! Sasha! Jeremy! Where are you?" as he ran toward the bedroom, not seeing them in the kitchen or living room.

As Jessie entered the bedroom, his entire world seemed to simply stop spinning. His peripheral vision faded to darkness, his ears still registering only silence, and his heart seeming to cease its frantic beats. In front of him lay the culmination of all of his nightmares, his Hell on Earth, the end of his humanity.

On the blood-drenched bed lay his beautiful wife and two children, their throats slit from ear to ear, their eyes staring blankly at the ceiling above.

On the floor before the bed was a dead assailant, killed by Stephanie in her final struggles to save and protect her children. For the next few moments, Jessie Townsend ceased to be. He was a madman. No logical thoughts were present in his mind—

only rage and violence. Turning around toward the front of the cabin, Jessie went from a slow and steady pace to a full-speed run out the door, clearing the front porch with a single stride.

Reaching the man who shot him in the leg, who was now writhing in pain on the ground as he held his brains inside of his own head with blood-covered hands, Jessie raised his revolver, slowly cocked the hammer, and pulled the trigger, only to feel no recoil. The gun reacted with a simple click of the hammer as it struck the primer of a spent shell casing. Unable to understand the situation due to his trance-like state, Jessie continued to cycle the revolver, click after click, yet nothing happened.

Holding the gun up in front of his own face, momentarily confused, Jessie realized the futility of his actions and dropped it to the ground. Slowly advancing toward the injured man, Jessie slid his belt-knife out of its sheath, knelt down next to him, and pushed the knife through the man's hand, into the fractures in his skull, piercing his brain, killing him instantly.

Pulling the knife out slowly, while staring into the man's now empty eyes, Jessie sheathed the knife as his world went completely dark, and he, too, fell to the ground.

Chapter Ten

As the wolves circled in the darkness, Jessie drew his knife and closed his eyes so the shadows could not play tricks on his mind. He listened intently to each step they took and each breath the wolves drew as they seemed to be spiraling in closer to him. Just as it seemed they were nearly upon him, Jessie opened his eyes slowly, now adjusted to the darkness of the night, to see a large, young male wolf square off in front of him, its head held low, its front legs crouched down as if spring-loaded for an attack, its fangs exposed, and a look of pure evil in its eyes, which glowed brightly in the darkness.

With little warning, the wolf leaped at Jessie's throat, its jaws wide open and its ferocious fangs exposed. With every ounce of strength he could muster, Jessie thrust his knife forward, striking the mighty beast in the chest, just before it was able to clamp its teeth into him.

The force of the animal's powerful leap knocked Jessie backward, the animal, now dead, falling on top of him. As the back of Jessie's head hit the ground with a mighty thud from the momentum of the fall, he awoke to find himself lying next to the man he had killed. Surrounded by darkness, the sun having escaped over the horizon, Jessie's painful memories came flooding back into his heart.

"God, if you're there...why didn't you let them kill me? Why did you let me live to see my family," pausing to choke back the tears, he continued, "why did you let me see my family in such a way? If I couldn't save them, why didn't you let those men kill me, too, so that I could be with them? Why did you leave me in this place that you have so clearly forsaken, to suffer without them? What kind of a God could do this? First you let the world die, now you let my family die. Why? Why have you turned your back on us?"

Lacking the will to survive, Jessie lay there on the ground, staring up at the night's sky as if in a trance. Occasionally slipping off to a fond memory of how the world used to be, of how safe and well-cared-for his family used to be, Jessie wavered between sorrow and rage.

As the morning's sun began to shine over the eastern horizon, Jessie sat up, a shell of his former self, and looked around at the dead bodies of the intruders. His hearing had returned, as well as the pain in his leg, but his soul was still absent. Jessie was not the man he had been the previous day, before his life was shattered forever, and the lives of his wife and children stolen from them.

Jessie looked at his leg, riddled with birdshot from a number 7 ½ shot shell and said aloud for God to hear, "Let it kill me slowly. Let it become septic. It's what I deserve. Just let me suffer and die. After all this, you owe me that."

Struggling to his feet, Jessie looked at the two dead men and said, "I wish I could kill you again." Fighting back his tears, he said, "You've stolen my entire world, you filthy sons of bitches." He took the first man by the feet and dragged him to the family's outhouse. Once he opened the door, he picked the man up under the arms and tossed him headfirst down into the wretched, fly-infested pit of human waste. Repeating this action with the second man, once the body was properly interred, Jessie said a few words as if there was anyone around to hear them. He said, "God, if you're there—if anyone is there—have Satan reserve his most horrendous demon for these sons of bitches. If he doesn't have a demon vicious enough to do the job, take me, I'll gladly go and see to the eternal deed myself. I would gladly trade you my own soul, just for the satisfaction of knowing that I contributed to their hell."

Standing there with his gaze fixed upon the sky, the gentle, cold morning breeze blowing against his face, Jessie's eyes lowered to what he had once considered his home. The cabin he and his wife worked so hard to build—the cabin they worked so hard to make a home for their children—was now his family's tomb. He wanted no further part of it. He could never erase those horrible memories from his mind.

He looked to his left, where the blood of the man who came from within his home still remained as a fresh dark red stain in the dirt, and saw his shotgun and pistol. Making his way over to them with a limp, he paused, staring at them, wondering what Stephanie's final moments must have been like, using those very weapons to try to protect herself and their children. Leaning forward with a grimace of pain, he picked them up and began to walk to the barn. Realizing that his AR-15 had been left in the scabbard attached to Brave's saddle, he looked around and saw no sign of the horse.

Reaching the barn, he looked inside, and there stood Brave, waiting alongside Jack, the packhorse, hiding from the horrors that had occurred in front of his own eyes. Jessie walked over to Brave, who seemed to understand Jessie's pain, lowering his head as if offering his condolences. Jessie patted him on the neck, removed the rifle from the scabbard and leaned it against the wall. Staring at the rifle, self-destructive thoughts swirled around in Jessie's mind. He wanted to put the barrel in his own mouth and end his suffering. Perhaps, he thought, he would be fortunate enough to have God grant him his request to meet the killers in hell, where he could himself seek eternal vengeance.

No, I've got to take care of them first. I can't just leave them there.

Jessie walked to the back of the barn and entered a livestock stall that he had converted into a storage room. Picking up a gasoline can and a barbecue grill lighter, he turned and walked back through the barn, heading for the cabin. Reaching the cabin, he stood there, the gas can in one hand and the lighter in the other, reflecting on the wonderful memories they had all shared. He could almost see Stephanie and the children coming out the front door to meet him. In his mind, he could hear the children's voices saying, "Daddy's home!" as they ran out to greet him with a smile.

Tears streamed down his face as he approached the front porch. *At least they're together,* he thought.

Placing the gas can on the porch, Jessie hesitated, and then entered the cabin. Reaching the bedroom and the horrific scene, his legs felt weak as a feeling of sickness came over his body, his emotions rushing back into the forefront of his mind. Leaning down and taking the assailant that Stephanie had killed by the feet, Jessie dragged the man outside, disposing of his body in the pit of filth, piled atop his cohorts underneath the outhouse.

Walking back over the the cabin, having removed the foul man from his former home, Jessie stepped back onto the porch and contemplated his next move. Looking down at the gas can, he unscrewed the cap, instantly smelling the varnished smell of stale gasoline. He walked across the porch, opened the front door to the cabin, and with a flood of tears, he poured the contents of the can throughout the living room. He could not bring himself to enter the bedroom again. His heart couldn't bear the grizzly scene once more.

Turning to walk back outside, he paused for a moment, nearly opting to remain in the inferno with his family. Reluctantly, he continued outside where he lit a dry washcloth and tossed it back into the home. Jessie was barely at a safe distance by the time the all-wood cabin was engulfed in flames.

Jessie watched the fire until the structure that was once his home was completely consumed and became nothing more than a smoldering heap of burnt wood and ashes. There was nothing in there for him now. He needed nothing else from the world and merely waited, hoping for his own demise.

Chapter Eleven

With the doors and shutters shaking violently, the winter winds pounded against the barn as snow rapidly accumulated outside. If not for being a shelter for his horses, Brave and Jack, Jessie would have simply wished the barn to collapse on him, ending his suffering and anguish. It had been over a month since tragedy befell the Townsend homestead. Jessie, still a shell of the man he once was, just could not bear to go on. His only motivation to keep himself alive had become the care of Brave and Jack, whom he planned to release when spring arrived, hoping they could somehow find a way to care for themselves lower down in the mountains.

Having used the barn for a winter workshop in the past, Jessie had outfitted it with an old wood-fired stove for warmth during the coldest of the winter months. The old iron stove was small, but did the job and even had a flat cooking surface on top that he used for the preparation of his simple meals. Oftentimes, when he was shivering and cold, he would melt snow and heat water in an old pot just to have something warm to drink. He felt that was often just enough to stave off the creeping death of the below-freezing temperatures of the Rockies in winter.

His sleeping quarters were a corner of the hay loft with several bales of hay arranged as a bed to keep him off the floor. He covered the straw with several old wool horse blankets that he felt were simply too worn and filthy even for Brave and Jack. It was basic and crude, but in his emotional state, almost entirely devoid of the will to carry on, it was more than adequate. Perhaps the misery of his surroundings somehow eased his tortured soul.

Despite a lack of hygiene and medical attention, his wounds had healed up nicely. Additionally, Jessie had experienced noticeable weight loss induced by his simple diet, but he was still of sound physical condition, although he was uncertain if he would ever be mentally healthy again after the losses he had endured.

Gazing out a partially opened window from the hay loft, Jessie watched as the heavy snow came down, covering the entire area in a deep blanket of powdery white fluff.

Jessie had been subsisting on his emergency food stores kept in plastic buckets in several caches spread throughout the property. It was simple food, consisting of MRE's, rice, and beans, but it did its job and kept him going. For what, other than the horse's care, he did not know. Hearing a deep *baah* outside, Jessie looked down to the ground level to see a large ram with a full curl of horns wandering in the storm. "Lobo?" he said aloud.

Snapping out of his near trance-like state, Jessie climbed down the ladder to the barn floor and retrieved a cup of whole oats from a grain bin he kept sealed with a large rock on top of the lid. He then proceeded outside where he began to call for Lobo while shaking the cup of oats in an attempt to lure him into the barn with a promise of food. "Lobo, old boy, come and get some oats, buddy. You look starved."

Lobo had lost substantial weight since Jessie had seen him last, which had been the day of the attack on his homestead. Once his family was gone, Jessie had lost all interest in maintaining the flock. He felt that since they were free-ranging and could go where they pleased, other than the occasional predator attack, they should be fine. In his state of depression, he failed to remember that in the winter months the available food sources for the sheep would be covered in heavy snow. Without his supplement of hay, they would all perish.

Seeing Jessie shaking the cup of oats, Lobo lethargically walked to him, desperate for a meal. "Come on in, boy," Jessie said, leading Lobo inside with the grain. Jessie poured the grain on the floor in a small pile and retrieved several more cups from the grain bin. "Sorry, buddy, I can't give you more than that.

You'll die from bloat if I'm too generous. You've not had oats in a while and your rumen isn't ready for a large amount of it."

As Lobo finished his meal, Jessie scratched him behind the horns and said, "How's the rest of the flock? Not good I suppose... if you came all this way by yourself looking for food. I imagine you've all had a rough go of things out there on your own."

After nearly a month of being confined to the emptiness of his own mind while merely surviving in the cold, drafty barn, Jessie found himself beginning to feel sorry for the sheep he had abandoned. With snow covering the ground and the growing season over until spring, those not picked off by wolves would surely die of starvation.

Looking at Lobo during this moment of clarity, Jessie said, "Those sons of bitches may have taken my family, but that's no reason for me to let you lose yours as well. I'm sorry I've abandoned you, old boy. Rest up. Tomorrow, we'll go get your flock."

~~~~

Up with the rising sun, Jessie began his preparations to lead any of the remaining sheep back to the homestead where he would be able to care for them until spring. At that time, he intended to lead them down the mountain and set them free, along with his horses, as he simply did not have the desire to go on.

Saddling Brave for the first time since that dreadful day, Jessie added saddle-bags to his load and filled them with a mixture of corn kernels and oats. In addition, he slid his .30-06 rifle into his scabbard and holstered his rugged old Colt revolver, topped off with six fresh .357 Magnum cartridges.

To stumble across Jessie in the mountains in his current state would be a formidable sight. His long, unkempt hair, graying beard covered in soot from his wood stove, and the dead, crazed look in his eyes, would give even the boldest villain pause. Combined with his load of formidable weapons and a large-horned Navajo-Churro ram for a sidekick, he seemed like a character straight out of an old western dime-store novel.

As Jessie mounted Brave to begin his search for the flock, he looked down at Lobo, who was watching with curiosity, and said, "Well, boy, are you coming? Or are you staying here?" With a nudge of his boots, Brave began trekking into the snow, with Lobo immediately following along behind. Leaning down as if he was sharing a secret with Brave, Jessie said, "Looks like he's going with us. Heck, I wonder if he has any clue what's going on?" Realizing the one-sided conversation he was having with Brave, he quipped, "Heck, like you even know."

As he rode toward the area where he had last seen the sheep, Jessie studied the snow and his surroundings, looking for any signs of potential threats. Unfortunately, the heavy snow of the previous night would have undoubtedly covered any recent sign of animal or human activity. As the morning sun reflected off the snow, Jessie couldn't help but feel pleased to be out of the confines of the barn. As recently as the day before, he had resolved to live out his final days there, caring for the horses until spring, but now, he felt as if he had a real purpose, even if it was only short term in nature.

Spooking a small brown mountain cottontail rabbit as they approached, Jessie flinched at the sight of movement in his peripheral vision. Reaching instinctively for his Colt, he chuckled when he realized what it was. Though not in a position to be hunting, he thought to himself half-jokingly, *I'll have to remember where that little fella is. Some fresh meat would be a nice change of pace.*

Looking back in the direction of Lobo, Jessie could see that he was having a little more trouble traipsing through the foot-deep snow than Brave. With that in mind, he eased back on the reins to slow the horse to better match Lobo's pace. "You want that corn in the saddle bags, don't you, boy? Don't worry. You'll get it eventually," Jessie said with a smirk.

Upon reaching the hilltop overlooking what was once the grassy hillside where his sheep grazed, Jessie pulled his rifle from the scabbard and began scanning the area with the rifle's scope. "I don't see a thing, Lobo. Not even a single trail in the fresh snow."

With a deep, loud *baah,* Lobo seemed to be calling for his flock. Patiently waiting and listening, Jessie said aloud to himself, "I don't see or hear a darn thing. Then again, I can't see Lobo's trail from yesterday because of this new snow, so I guess that doesn't mean anything at all."

"Come on, boys," Jessie said, nudging Brave forward.

Riding several hundred yards beyond the hillside, Jessie stopped once again to scan the lower terrain with his scope. Alternating between the lowest magnification setting of 3X to gain the widest field of view, and the highest magnification setting of 9X to scan for detail off in the distance, Jessie searched tirelessly for any signs of his sheep.

Just as he was about to give up while scanning from left to right, he saw a brown spot lost in a sea of white snow. His breath fogging his scope, he quickly wiped it bare with his glove and tried desperately to reacquire his target. "There's one!" he said aloud. Luckily for Jessie, Navajo-Churro sheep often have colors other than white, making this one easy to spot in the distance against the all-white background of the freshly fallen snow.

"Let's go, boys," Jessie said as he nudged Brave forward, down over the snow-covered hill.

As they began to draw near, Jessie whistled to the young lamb that was trudging its way through the deep snow. Every time he used to supplement their grazing with grains as a treat,

Jessie would always use the same recognizable whistle, hoping to entrench the Pavlov's dog effect within his flock, making them easy to call in. Luckily, that training technique appeared to be working in his favor today as the young lamb, probably no more than eight months old, began working its way toward him.

As Jessie dismounted, the young lamb hesitated, showing caution in regards to Jessie's movements. "It's okay, buddy," Jessie said, reaching into the saddlebag, pulling out a handful of the mixture of oats and corn. "Here you go. You must be starved," he said, tossing a small handful of grain into the snow. As the lamb devoured the bits of grain, Jessie noticed that the animal's ribs and hips were clearly visible, indicating that food had been scarce for quite some time.

~~~~

As the day progressed, Jessie was able to find only eight remaining sheep in all. With the sun approaching the horizon and the temperatures beginning to fall, he decided he had probably found as many as he was going to find. With a whistle and a handful of grain, he rallied the sheep together where they enthusiastically ate the grain and aggressively begged for more with stress-filled *baah's*.

"C'mon!" he said, urging Brave forward through the snow. As they progressed toward the homestead, Jessie occasionally tossed out another handful of grain, not enough to slow their progress while the sheep searched for every last morsel, but sufficient to keep them interested in following him. Nearing the homestead, Jessie began to have a dark feeling wash over his body. His day out searching for his lost flock had been the first day since his family was stolen from him that he had allowed his mind wander out of the agony and sorrow that he still held deep down inside.

Feelings of fear, pain, sorrow, and rage swept through his body. His heart rate increased and he began to sweat despite the cold. Once he rounded the corner and saw the snow-covered remains of what was his family home, Jessie's anxiety became overwhelming. He reached for his Colt, feeling an urgent need to defend himself—but from what?

As they reached the barn, Jessie rode Brave inside, quickly dismounted, and dumped the remaining contents of the saddle bags on the barn's dirt floor, the sheep enthusiastically following. While they were preoccupied with the nutritious morsels of grain, Jessie pulled the barn doors shut, put the board in place to barricade it closed, and immediately climbed up the ladder, resuming his position by the window, gazing lost and confused at the sky above. *What's wrong with me?* he wondered, fearing that he was losing control.

Chapter Twelve

It had been several weeks since Jessie ventured out to find the remainder of his abandoned flock. Since then, he had made steady progress with his anger and depression. The return of a few of his sheep had given him something to focus on besides the tragedy that had occurred. Taking care of the sheep, his horses, and the three remaining hens had given him a daily routine with a purpose that seemed to keep his mind out of the deep, dark abyss he had been lost in for so long.

The last few weeks had been relatively uneventful, with the exception of the occasional howl of a hungry wolf off in the distance during the night. This gave him little concern, however, as the barn provided ample protection from the threats he had faced with a much larger flock out in the open grazing area.

Looking up at the sky, Jessie realized it was time to begin rounding up his sheep and leading them into the barn for the night. The sheep had become accustomed to this routine and had started to expect their nightly allotment of grain right on schedule. Stepping out into the barnyard, placing two fingers in his mouth, Jessie prepared to whistle for his sheep when he saw a glint of light down the gravel road leading up to the homestead. Fearing he was being glassed from a distance, Jessie went about his routine, pretending not to have spotted the potential threat. As he shook the old metal coffee can full of corn to lead the sheep into the barn, Jessie maintained constant movement in the event a rifle scope was trained on him at that very moment.

Once inside, he quickly barricaded the door and retrieved his Bushmaster AR-15, along with several fully loaded thirty-round magazines. Slinging the rifle over his back and placing the magazines in his coat pockets, Jessie climbed out a side window on the far side of the barn and slipped off into the treeline, disappearing into the cover of the wintery woods.

As he worked his way down the hill, parallelling the now snow-covered gravel road while remaining hidden in the trees, Jessie's heart began to pound as the painful memories began to flow back into his mind. *Not again, you filthy maggots,* he thought to himself as he felt the rage build in what was left of his blackened heart. *You'll regret ever stepping foot on this mountain.*

Once he was in a position abeam his estimated location of the threat, Jessie shouldered his rifle and began to scan the area with his scope. Working his field of view in a grid pattern, he came across a man in his late thirties to early forties, wearing hunting-style camouflage clothing. The man appeared to be observing Jessie's homestead with a large pair of binoculars. Next to the man was an SKS rifle leaning against the tree that he was using for cover.

"Not the most well-equipped looter, are you?" Jessie whispered to himself. "Now, where are your friends? You scumbags always travel in a pack—just like the wolves."

Jessie continued to scan the area, not seeing any signs of other intruders in the immediate vicinity. Continuing his way downhill, Jessie began to slip through the woods, working his way around and behind the intruder. Jessie assumed any potential cohorts would be focused on the homestead, rather than on their own six.

Once directly downhill from the intruder, Jessie handrailed the gravel road, remaining hidden in the trees until he was within thirty yards of the man. Reducing the magnification on his rifle scope to 1X for the widest field of view and rapid-fire, both-eyes-open shooting, Jessie shouted, "Tell your friends to drop their weapons and step out onto the road or you're a dead man! We've got you surrounded."

Freezing in position, the man replied, "Don't shoot! I'm alone!"

"Bull!" Jessie replied with ferocity. "Now call them out or you're a dead man."

A rustling in the brush behind the man drew Jessie's attention momentarily, followed by the man turning his head while continuing to hold his hands in the air, saying, "No! No! Stay put!"

Having discovered the man's ruse, Jessie was enraged. "If you lie, you die!" he shouted. "And you lied, you son of bitch!"

Before he could finish his sentence, a young girl wearing a purple bubble-style jacket, ski pants, and winter boots came running into the road waving her arms, screaming, "No! Don't hurt my daddy! Please don't hurt my daddy!"

"Cindy, no!" the man shouted.

Lowering his rifle, confused by what he was seeing, Jessie yelled, "Kick the rifle over to the ground and walk out onto the road with the girl."

Complying with Jessie's instructions, the man kicked the rifle over with his foot and stepped into the road with his hands clearly empty and in the air. The young girl, who appeared from a distance to be around ten or eleven years old, rushed to the man's side, embracing him with tears rolling down her face.

"Please don't hurt her, mister," the man pleaded.

Stepping out into the road, exposing himself to the man and the young girl, Jessie said, "What are you doing here? What good could you be up to, creeping around people's homes? In this world, that can and will get you killed."

"We're just looking for a place to hunker down for the winter before moving on. It's not safe out there. And with the weather, well, we were running out of options."

"Why were you spying on me?"

"We didn't know anyone lived here. We could see the burned down cabin from a distance and thought maybe the barn was abandoned. I didn't see you until you began to round up your goats a little while ago."

"Sheep," Jessie replied tersely.

"Huh?" the man asked, momentarily confused.

"They're sheep. Not goats," Jessie replied.

Jessie could sense real fear in the young girl. She had clearly seen things that no ten-year-old girl should have seen and she was willing to risk her own life to protect her father. She clearly knew the outcome of such scenes in the new world.

"What's your name, young lady?" he asked

Looking to her father for guidance, he motioned for her to reply. After a brief pause, she said, "Cindy. My name is Cindy Walker."

"What's his name?" Jessie asked, expecting a pause from the young girl if she was lying.

"Mark Walker. He's my dad."

Jessie slung his rifle over his back to show that he meant them no harm and said, "You look hungry. Walk up the hill toward the barn. I'll follow you out of sight to make sure you don't have any others hiding around here like she was. If you do, I will kill them, so you had better call them out now," Jessie said with a cold and serious voice.

"No. There's nobody else," Mr. Walker replied.

"Okay, then. Walk on up the hill toward the barn. Stop when you reach the doors. Wait for my instructions from there."

"Yes, sir," the man replied.

Covering them as they proceeded up the hill, Jessie watched the man and the young girl closely until they were approximately thirty yards ahead. He then slipped out of the trees and onto the road to retrieve the man's weapon. Slinging the SKS over his back, Jessie ducked back into the treeline and followed the man and the girl at a safe distance the rest of the way to the barn.

Reaching the barn, Jessie stepped out into the open with his rifle at the low ready, and said, "Open your jackets wide and turn all the way around so that I can see you clearly."

They did as he asked, and seeing no other weapons, Jessie said, "Okay, wait right here," as he ducked around the side of the barn and out of sight.

In just a few moments, the barn opened from within, catching the Walkers off guard. "Come on in," Jessie said while gesturing for them to follow.

Once inside, he closed the door and barricaded it shut. With a nervous expression on his face, the father said, "Why are you locking us in?"

"I'm not locking you in. You're free to go, but remember, I just found you snooping around on my property. What if you've got someone else lying low, waiting for the opportune moment to attack? You see that burned down cabin out there?" Jessie said, pointing out the window. "My wife and children's ashes are in that pile of rubble. Forgive me if I am less than trusting of outsiders."

"I'm sorry," the man replied. "Where are my manners? Like Cindy here said, my name is Mark Walker. I'm pleased to meet you," he said, extending his hand to Jessie.

Refusing the handshake, Jessie coldly answered, "You can call me J.T."

"Pleased to meet you, J.T.," Mark replied, awkwardly pulling his hand back. "We're sorry about all of this. We've also lost a major part of our lives in all this mess. My wife, her mother," he said, pausing to look at his daughter, "well, we assume she didn't make it out of Denver."

"Denver, huh?" Jessie responded, curious about the situation in Denver. "What happened?"

"I lost my job early on when things all started to unravel and the economy started to fall apart. We had recently sold our home in Dallas and moved back to Colorado to be closer to my wife's family. We were renting while we got settled in, and since we were renters, well, we found ourselves on the street shortly after the paychecks stopped flowing.

"Luckily, we had a family motorhome that we could fall back on as a place to call home until it all got sorted out. I always used to joke with my wife that no matter what happened, as long as we had that RV we'd never be homeless. Anyway, we were staying at an RV park in Cortez when the worst of it began to hit. My wife's aunt was still living in Denver when we heard about the fever that was sweeping through the area. I think they said it was Marburg hemorrhagic fever or something. Anyway, my wife wanted to get her aunt out of there and bring her to Cortez with us, where she would be safe. We figured if people in the RV park started getting sick, we could just fire the motorhome up and drive off into the middle of nowhere."

Cindy began to become emotional at the sound of her father's words, prompting Jessie to say, "You don't have to go on. I get it."

"So anyway," Mark continued, "when things really started to get ugly, Cindy and I drove out to Pleasant View where we were basically hijacked by another family who faked a roadside emergency just to get us to pull over."

"A family?" Jessie inquired.

"Yes, sir. Kids, a dog, the whole thing. I guess they needed our motorhome more than they thought we did. Anyway, we basically gave it up without a fight. With just Cindy and me, well, if something happened to me, she would be all alone. I just can't take any chances like that."

"You were taking a pretty big chance snooping around my property. If you had come a few weeks ago, I'd have probably dropped you where you stood without asking a question. I've not been in my right mind lately."

"I completely understand," Mark replied apologetically.

Turning to walk over to the wood stove that was still smoldering, Jessie leaned his AR-15 against the wall and put a few more pieces of wood on the fire. "Let me get you something warm to drink. It's freezing out there. After that, I'll work on dinner."

Looking out of the corner of his eye, Jessie could see Cindy's facial expression go from one of sorrow to one of relief. He couldn't be sure, but at least for now, he believed their story. "It's not five-star accommodations, but you're more than welcome to stay the night here. I'll fix you up a place to sleep near the stove to keep her warm."

Looking at his daughter and then back at Jessie, Mark said, "Thank you, sir. And again, I'm sorry I caused you the hassle of chasing us down."

"Just be thankful she's with you." Jessie replied.

"What?" the man asked nervously.

"Just be thankful you had a young girl with you. If not for her, you would probably be bleeding out down on the road right now. If what you say is true, I can't blame you for being cautious, and I'd sure be heading for the mountains with my little girl," pausing to wipe his watery eyes and to search for his words, "If I were in your shoes, that is. So what's your plan—you know—for the long term?"

After a respectful pause allowing Jessie to regain his composure, Mark replied, "We've been camping along the way to get this far. We would hike at night and sleep in a discreet camp during the day. Unfortunately, this early winter weather has put a damper on our plans. I wanted to get us far enough into the mountains that we could safely have campfires at night, build a shelter, and go from there. I didn't want to be too close to a major road or town and light a fire. I was afraid it would attract the wrong people. People are desperate out there. After the run-in with the people who stole our motorhome, well, let's just say I have some trust issues, too."

"Build a shelter?" Jessie asked, looking at Mark and Cindy's lack of supplies.

"I've got a pack with some basic woodworking tools, what's left of our food supplies, and a Ruger .22 pistol for small game.

We left it behind down the mountain. It was with Cindy in the woods while I scoped things out up ahead. With you pointing a rifle at us before, and looking like you meant business, I didn't feel it was the right time to explain everything."

"Right," Jessie replied. "It looks like the water is almost boiling. Have you ever had chicory coffee?"

"You have coffee?" Mark asked in an inquisitive tone.

"Chicory coffee, so not actual coffee. It's made from the chicory root. It doesn't have caffeine, but it tastes pretty good and it brings back a semblance of civility to sip a hot drink on a beautiful mountain evening, or in the morning as you watch the sun rise above the ridge and watch as its rays dance through the trees. It's those little moments of life that help me keep it together now."

"We'd both love some," Mark replied. "Thank you very much. Thank you for the hospitality. It's been a long time."

Handing them each a camping-style stainless steel coffee mug full of piping hot chicory coffee, Jessie said. "You two just relax and enjoy that while I get you a place to sleep situated by the stove where you can keep her nice and warm. It's a clear night, so it will be a cold one. I'll lock the sheep in the stalls so they don't bother you tonight. There's some beans in the pot on the stove. Help yourselves. I know you've got to be hungry. I'll be sleeping in the loft up above like I always do. If you need anything tonight, let me know. If you need to go outside to take care of business, don't open the door without waking me first. I don't need any surprises right now and if I hear the door opening, I'll assume the worst and will react accordingly. Tomorrow, when you're good and rested, we can talk more. I'd greatly appreciate some updates from you, if you don't mind."

"No. Of course, that will be fine, and thank you again. The last few nights we felt as if we were going to freeze to death in our sleep. This will be a very welcome change."

And with that, Jessie retrieved his rifle and climbed up into the hayloft. Reaching the top rung of the wooden plank ladder, Jessie turned and said, "Don't think I won't be watching."

Seating himself up on several bales of hay that he had previously arranged into the form of a chair, Jessie laid his rifle across his lap, keeping an eye on the barn floor below. *What's wrong with me?* he thought. *Letting strangers into the barn to kill me in my sleep.* Chuckling at his own thoughts, *That would actually be a gift. I could escape this world without it being by my own hand. My very own angels of death.*

Lying down on his straw bed, he stared out the window, watching the moon slowly move across the sky while he awaited the elusive luxury of sleep. As his eyelids became heavy, he whispered quietly, "Lord, if you mean for them to kill me, let it be soon."

Chapter Thirteen

As Jessie trekked through the boot-top deep snow in the darkness of the night, tracking the wolf that had killed one of his sheep, he could tell by the freshness of the tracks that he must be getting close. Hearing a twig break just up ahead, Jessie froze, attempting to focus his eyes with the failing light of the moon as it was intermittently obscured by the passing clouds.

Jessie called on all of his senses to detect the presence of a potential threat. As he focused, it seemed as if even the insects had gone silent, leaving the darkness of the woods entirely devoid of sound. The breeze that had been plaguing his dry lips now seemed calm as well.

As the clouds drifted past the moon, its light once again illuminated Jessie's way. Although he could now see, an eerie feeling came over him, as if he was being watched. Despite his misgivings, Jessie pressed on further, knowing that the safety of his sheep depended on his stopping a wolf that had gotten a taste of their blood.

Just ahead of him lay a large tree that had been blown over during a storm. Its massive roots created a wall of tentacles that had once held the mighty tree in place. As he crept around the tree, Jessie saw a large wolf staring intently at him, the moonlight reflecting in its eyes.

Mentally preparing himself for an attack, Jessie eased his Colt revolver out of its holster, cocked the hammer, and slowly began to bring it to bear. Hearing a sound just in front of him, Jessie peered down and saw a litter of wolf cubs between him and his ominous foe. The wolf, although a fierce opponent, lowered its head and calmed its breath as if to signal to Jessie that a conflict was not desired.

Looking back down at the cubs, Jessie began to back away slowly, and with distance, the wolf and her cubs faded from view into the darkness of the night.

~~~~

"Mr. J.T.," the young girl's voice called out from down below, waking Jessie from his dream.

Looking around and regaining his situational awareness, Jessie responded, "Yes, can I help you?" as he stood up and looked from the loft down to the floor.

"Yes, sir," she replied. "I just need to go use the ladies' room."

"You do realize we don't actually have a ladies' room, don't you?"

"But I saw an outhouse by the remains of the cabin," she said inquisitively.

"Oh, that's off limits. Trust me," he replied, thinking back to his gruesome deed, realizing that he needed to deal with that situation a little more completely. "If you need to go, have your father go outside with you to stand watch. I've had a wolf problem around here lately."

"He's still asleep," she said sheepishly. "He's not slept in days. I'd really rather not wake him. He's not been feeling well lately."

"Is he ill?" Jessie asked.

"I think he's just tired. Tired of it all," she said in a humble voice.

Pausing to think about the situation and if it was a ruse, Jessie could sense sincerity in the girl's voice, "Wait right there. I'll be right down."

Climbing down from the loft with his rifle slung across his back, Jessie walked over to the barn's double doors, removed the board he was using as a barricade, and partially opened it to get a view of the barnyard before proceeding outside. Flicking on his weapon-mounted flashlight, he scanned the surrounding area, and said, "It looks clear. Come on out."

"You've got batteries?" she said, seeming to be surprised.

"Rechargeables. I've got a few small solar panels that were designed to keep boat and RV batteries up when not in use. They work great for charging my rechargeable flashlight batteries. They're not holding a charge like they used to, but for now, they do the job."

Escorting Cindy into the barnyard, Jessie said, "Go right over there. I'll stand here with my back to you while you go. If you see or hear anything, let me know."

Nodding in the affirmative, Cindy slipped off into the darkness beside the barn. After a few moments, she came back into the light of the moon in the barnyard and said, "Okay. All done."

As she turned to walk back inside, they both heard the howl of a lone wolf off in the distance, causing them to momentarily pause. "See what I mean?" Jessie said. "Let's get back inside."

~~~~

Early the next morning as the sun rose over the mountains, Jessie sat at his window, watching his favorite event unfold with the awe of a true naturalist. He desperately craved a hot cup of chicory, which had become his morning ritual, but opted to let Mark and Cindy sleep as long as they could, knowing they needed the rest. Since he had made their bed by the stove, there was no way he could brew his morning treat without disturbing them, so he just deferred his craving until later.

Shortly after the sun was fully over the horizon, he heard rustling down below. Looking over the side of the loft to the barn floor, he noticed that Mark and Cindy were both up. Mark sat on the floor leaning against the wall with Cindy sitting sideways in his lap, her arms around his neck. Jessie found himself lost in the moment. He could see the true comfort Cindy felt being in her father's arms and the peace Mark seemed to have just having her to hold. Jessie ached for a chance to once again hold his children in such a loving embrace.

As a tear began to roll down his cheek, Jessie snapped out of his sorrows, and said, "Good morning, down there."

"Good morning, up there," Mark replied, looking up at Jessie. Cindy also turned and gazed up with a smile. "I think that's the first full night's sleep I've gotten in as long as I can remember."

"Give me a moment or two and I'll be right down," Jessie replied. Once he got himself together, Jessie climbed down the ladder and said, "Breakfast won't be bacon and eggs, but I do have some instant oatmeal."

"You must have had a fairly well-stocked pantry before it all began to fall apart if you still have instant oatmeal," Mark replied.

"Being way up here in the mountains we tended to buy in bulk," Jessie answered. "Besides, in the mid-winter months, our roads aren't very passable. My old F-150 out behind the barn could barely make it to town even with four-wheel drive when the winter was at its worst. With that and the apparent fragility the state of things were at the time, we tended to overbuy, which I am now very thankful for. In the quantities we bought, we knew shelf life would be an issue, so we used mylar bags and oxygen absorbers in construction-style buckets, along with vacuum sealers to help our bulk items stay fresh longer. Again, something for which I am now very thankful."

"It's almost like you knew this was all going to happen," Mark said.

"The funny thing is, I did," Jessie replied. Seeing the confused look on Mark's face, he explained, "Well, I didn't exactly know things were going to happen, but the way things were going, I just had a bad feeling. We used to live down in

Cortez, but moved up here to get away from it all. It was more than just a bad feeling of the state of the world."

"I wish I had your foresight," Mark said regrettably. "I kept telling myself it would all blow over and get better. The things that happened in the rest of the world always just seemed like something for the evening news, and weren't things we could see happening in our own reality. Boy, was I wrong."

"You didn't do too bad," Jessie replied. "You had that motorhome, and you had the brains to make it this long."

"Yeah, but I shouldn't have let my wife—"

"Don't blame yourself for that," Jessie interrupted. "There was no way you could have known, or could have foreseen the extent of what was about to happen. Besides, you were smart to keep your daughter with you at the motorhome while your wife went into Denver. I mean, you obviously didn't know the extent of what was about to happen, but if you'd all gone into the city together, well, you know."

"I see your point, but there's not a day goes by when I don't rethink every decision I've made," added Mark.

Kicking a rock on the ground, thinking about how he and Mark had a lot in common on a basic human level, Jessie said, "Me, too. Trust me. Me, too. But here we are."

"Yep, here we are. So, what can I do to repay you for last night?"

"What do you mean?"

"For room and board. We owe you for taking us in. Especially considering the situation in which we met."

With a chuckle under his breath, Jessie replied, "Yeah, that could have been a close one. I'll make you a deal."

"A deal?" Mark inquired.

"If you tell me everything you know about the state of the world out there, you can stay here on a night-by-night basis. If you just help me keep an eye out for other trespassers and put in a hard day's work to earn your supper while Cindy helps me tend to the sheep, we'll call it even. If you give me any reason not to trust you, though, well, I simply won't put up with being double-crossed. You'll find yourself back in the cold—or worse. Understood?

Caught by surprise by Jessie's overly generous offer, Mark said, "Are you sure? We'd hate to wear out our welcome. I already feel like an intruder here."

Looking off to the side as if to gather his thoughts, Jessie said, "Yeah. I'm sure. After what happened, I've not been myself. Some days I've barely been clinging to sanity. Having you two around, if it works out, would be a big help. But like I said, we'll take things on a night-by-night basis."

Reaching out to shake Jessie's hand, Mark said, "Anything we can do, just let us know."

"Great!" Jessie replied, taking Mark's hand. "I'll get breakfast going and we can talk more afterward."

~~~~

After a generous helping of instant peaches and cream oatmeal, Jessie asked Cindy to keep an eye on the sheep in the barn while he showed Mark the lay of the land. Once clear of the barn, Jessie asked, "So what's going on down there?"

"I don't know how much I can tell you," replied Mark. "I'm assuming you know about all of the attacks on our infrastructure and the accusations from every direction about who was complicit and who was simply asleep at the wheel? The biowarfare? The bombings? The poisoning of municipal water supplies? The crash of numerous major computer systems due to hacking? And the physical conflict between the UN troops sent as peacekeepers and the local militia types?"

"Yeah. I got that much. I used to listen to the radio reports every day. I'm more interested in the security situation on the ground in the local area. What's the day-to-day for the average Joe just trying to get somewhere?"

"Well, there are still plenty of good people out there, but there are just as many who aren't so good anymore. Hunger and desperation can get the best of people. Heck, the family that stole our motorhome might have made fine neighbors before it all went down, as far as I know. Anyway, fuel is hard to come by since the refineries were all hit. The only vehicles you see out and about on a regular basis are government types. Mostly military, DHS, or UN. People steer clear of them, generally speaking, as they have some pretty broad authority given the declaration of a state of emergency and the executive orders issued by the president. Most people find it prudent to avoid contact with them altogether and simply let them move about freely with little interaction. If you're in a private vehicle, however, you'll be a target for anyone with eyes on your fuel and provisions."

"And law enforcement?" Jessie asked.

"Outside of the protection of government assets, you won't see much, and the bad guys know it. It's pretty rough out there. No one can call 911 and without the threat of law enforcement coming to the rescue, well, let's just say the bad guys know they have free rein. Most of the country's communication and power infrastructure is still down. Even if you could call, what few police assets that remain wouldn't respond. They're on guard duty and don't really answer calls or patrol for crime. There are also very few veteran police officers left. When the attacks started, a good number of them were killed trying to defend their cities and towns. They were caught up in all the mess that everyone else was, only they were intentionally and selflessly on the front lines. Many more officers abandoned their posts to protect their own families. I can't say that I blame them, either. The ones who stayed had very little support, as most of the remaining government assets not directly involved in the fighting were busy protecting the government facilities, the bureaucrats, and their families. What few of them that remain on the job just can't handle it all. Many of whom are new recruits, barely trained and paid in food rations and behind-the-fence shelter for their families."

"Behind the fence?" Jessie asked.

"FEMA had set up camps in the more secure locations. They are heavily guarded and receive supplies from the remaining government stockpiles. Those won't last forever, though, as there really isn't anything being produced right now. Because of that, access to the camps is limited."

"That's funny," Jessie replied.

"What's funny?"

"People always used to joke that FEMA camps would be used to lock people in, not out," he answered.

With a half-hearted chuckle, Mark said, "Oh, those are there, too." He continued, "I have seen a few farms attempting to get up and running again, but they're raided so often by looters and refugees desperate for food that they don't stand much of a chance."

Scratching his chin, trying to take it all in, Jessie listened as Mark continued, "The organized criminal element is also becoming a huge problem. Gangs, drug cartels, and your basic thug types operate unimpeded. The collapse of civility has emboldened them to the point that the violence of pre-collapse Mexico looks tame compared to how they conduct their daily business today. Long story short—there's a reason Cindy and I were heading for the hills."

"What about airspace?" Jessie asked.

"Shut down from what I've heard. Whether they have the assets to enforce it, that is another story, of course."

"Is there any hope that the government will get things under control soon?" Jessie asked.

Steven C. Bird

"Therein lies the problem," Mark explained. "The population was so fed up with the corrupt, inept, and complicit government before everything fell apart, no one trusts anyone anymore. Especially considering the fact that those who pulled their strings also pulled the strings of those who initiated the attacks. The only sort of government or law enforcement presence that anyone has any faith in these days is the local citizen militias who've stood up to protect their own communities. But even some of them have let the power go to their heads."

"That's to be expected, I guess," Jessie replied. "If people think no one is watching, it's easy to let things get out of control. You know, *Lord of the Flies* type stuff."

"That's been the story of humanity from the beginning," Mark said in agreement. "Add to all of that the fact that there are groups who want to rebuild in the name of a one-world government on one side and those who are willing to fight a war to re-establish America to its former glory on the other, and it's just no place for children. The horrors we watched others go through around the world on television, from the safety and comfort of our air-conditioned suburban homes, is now right in our own neighborhoods."

Jessie shook his head in silence as he absorbed everything Mark was saying. "And to think we shifted our food production from local family-owned farms to mega factory-farms, leaving us unable to adequately produce what we need locally. Heck, the same could be said for our manufacturing, I guess."

"I'm sure there is a lot going on out there, especially the global big picture, that I don't have a clue about. All I know is what I have seen and heard, but the one thing I am confident about is that society is lost and I have to keep my daughter safe. She's all I have left in this world, which is why we stumbled across you."

"Speaking of that, heading into the mountains in the onset of winter might have gotten her killed. The mountains can be unforgiving if you get caught out in the weather."

"It was a chance we had to take. Something has been telling me, from deep down inside, that I needed to get her up in the mountains where we could be safe while things got straightened out."

Stopping to look around at what once was his beloved homestead, Jessie said, "That's ironic. Something has been telling me to leave."

Chapter Fourteen

Over the next several months, the Walkers stayed on with Jessie, who they still only knew as J.T., and helped him prepare for and work through the harsh winter. Jessie and Mark would rotate the duties of collecting firewood and gathering food with that of security, while Cindy tended to Jessie's remaining sheep. The deep snow and impassable road conditions had kept them safe and secure from any outside threats during the winter months, allowing each of them to begin the process of healing from the emotional scars they had all suffered.

Cindy seemed to be a natural shepherd. The animals gave a sense of structure and balance to her life, which was something she desperately needed. Against Jessie's better judgment, knowing where some of them were destined, he allowed her to name each of the sheep. Even Lobo had taken a liking to her, following Cindy around like a dog.

Over time, Jessie and Mark utilized scrap wood from around the property, making Mark and Cindy a proper living space in one of the stalls near the wood stove by adding a floor and finishing the walls of the stall all the way to the ceiling. This gave Mark and Cindy a feeling of permanence and security, which was what they had both prayed for since their journey had begun.

With signs of spring's early arrival all around them, excitement was in the air. Mark and Cindy, now completely comfortable with their simple mountain life, both felt that the oncoming spring would bring new beginnings for them.

~~~~

The Shepherd: Society Lost

Waking to the chill of a cold, clear morning, with the sunlight beginning to shine through the gaps in the old barn's plank walls, Cindy left her father sleeping while she went to add wood to the glowing embers in the old wood stove. Not only did she want to warm the space up a bit, but she also wished to get a head start on breakfast. She wanted to surprise both her father and Jessie with fresh eggs as the three remaining hens had once again started laying.

As she added a few pieces of split firewood to the old wood stove and stoked the coals, she noticed the absence of rustling in Brave's stall. Brave would normally greet whoever awoke first with a few snorts to get their attention, but this morning, she heard nothing but silence.

Walking over to the horse stall to investigate, Cindy found Jack, the pack-horse, standing alone. Brave was simply not there. In a panic, she ran to the center of the barn, looked up to the loft where Jessie slept, and shouted, "J.T! J.T! Brave is gone! He's missing!"

Hearing no reply, she began frantically climbing the ladder to the loft as her father awoke, and in a startled voice, asked, "Cindy! What's going on?"

"Brave is gone, Daddy! Brave is gone!" she yelled as she scurried up the ladder. To her dismay, she found Jessie's bed neatly made with a note and a cigar box lying on top of his old, hole-ridden blankets. She sat down on Jessie's makeshift straw bed and picked up the note as her father joined her in the loft.

"What's going on? Where is he?" Mark asked.

Fearing what it might say, she turned and handed the note to her father, who slowly took it from her hand, and opened it. As he sat down beside her on the bed, he began reading the letter aloud,

"Dear Mark and Cindy,
I thank God every day that you stumbled across my little homestead in the mountains during both your time of need and

mine. *When you arrived, I was at the lowest point in my life. I simply did not have the will to go on in this world. Your companionship helped me to make it through the winter as well as helping me to push aside the demons that still haunt me to this day, giving me hope for the future. Hope for what? That I do not know. I only know that whatever lies out there in this world for me is not on this mountain, so I must go find it.*

I have a sister that I haven't spoken to in years that I have set out to find. I do not plan to return, and even if I did, the likelihood that I would actually make it back would be low. Considering that, I would like to give you both a few things:

First, my homestead. Inside the cigar box you will find the deed to my property, as well as a detailed letter to whomever may be responsible for the administration of such things in the future, explaining how I left the property to both of you to do with as you wish as the rightful and legal owners. Who knows if any such future administrator will honor my decree in the absence of legal proceedings, but I pray they will.

Second, for Cindy's upcoming eleventh birthday, the box also contains a beautiful gold necklace that used to belong to my wife. It is the only thing I saved from the home. Cindy's smile has become the light of my world, which was previously filled only with darkness. Please wear it and keep it always.

Third, inside the box is a detailed sketch of the property with locations of caches of supplies, firearms, and ammunition. I hadn't previously told you the location of those items for myriad reasons, but now that you will be here alone, you'll need to take security very seriously, and you'll need to be equipped to handle situations as they arise.

All I ask of you in return is to do for me these few things: First, take care of Jack and the flock and help them to rebuild and thrive. If you take care of the animals, they will reward you with an abundant livelihood. Jack is an old boy, but he still has a few good years left in him. Give him a sense of purpose, and he will be a good asset and companion. Second, once the snow melts and you've got your primary needs taken care of for the spring, I ask that you clean off the spot where the ruins of my cabin now lie, and plant a flower garden there in memory of my wife and children. Fill it with the beautiful wildflowers of the mountains, and when it blooms, remember that there is beauty all around you even during the darkest days.

    Do these simple things and the homestead is yours. Do not be disheartened by my absence; rather, celebrate the fact that God brought us together during our darkest days to comfort and care for one another.

Your friend forever,
Jessie Townsend"

Mark's voice trembled with those final words. A tear rolled down his cheek as he looked into Cindy's watery eyes. They shared a moment of silence as they began to realize the incredible gift they had been given. Mark was now sure that he had been led to this mountain, if not for their sake, then for Jessie's. It was then that he realized, "Jessie Townsend. J.T.'s name was Jessie Townsend. Sheriff Jessie Townsend, from Montezuma County. He'd faded away after the election was stolen from him. No one ever really knew what happened to him. The irony is, losing that election probably saved his life. If he would have remained the sheriff, he would have more than likely gotten caught up in all the mess and killed like his replacement."

~~~~

With the sun just barely cresting the mountains, Jessie looked back in the direction of the homestead as he eased back on Brave's reins, bringing him to a stop in the middle of the snow-covered road. He felt bad for slipping off into the darkness of the pre-dawn morning without an explanation, and without saying goodbye, but the Walkers were becoming too much like family to Jessie, and after what he had gone through, he knew he had to cut things short and be on his way before his feelings compromised his plans.

Turning Brave around, he patted him on the neck and said, "Well, buddy. See that smoke? That's from the stovepipe in the barn. That's the last sign we will see of the homestead. From here on out, every day will be a new, unknown challenge. Let's go see where this world takes us, boy."

Chapter Fifteen

As Jessie and Brave worked their way down the snow-covered road from the mountains, they traveled slowly and methodically, surveying the area around them as they went, in an attempt to avoid any potential threats along their path. Jessie had taken only basic items with them, not wanting to over-burden Brave with a heavy load.

In his saddle-bags, Jessie had brought along a several-day supply of MRE's, a few pounds of uncooked beans and rice, a small container of salt, a magnesium fire-starter, and a mess kit. He had also packed ammunition for his Colt revolver, which he still wore on his side, his AR-15, carried on his back in a hunting backpack with an integrated rifle scabbard, and his bolt-action Winchester .30-06, carried in his saddle-mounted rifle scabbard.

Secured on top of his saddle-bags, he kept a bedroll and a small tent contained in a zip-up dry bag, as well as his lightweight compound hunting bow with a full quiver of carbon-fiber arrows, tipped with razor-sharp broadheads. As an avid hunter, Jessie was highly skilled in the use of a bow and felt its stealth might come in handy during the unknown journey ahead.

As the day progressed, Jessie was relieved to see only the tracks of wildlife through the snow, although he knew the further down the mountain he went, the likelihood of encountering a two-legged foe would significantly increase. Having not gotten much rest the night before due to his preparations, Jessie decided to make camp early and get a full night's sleep before going too far down the mountain and entering what he considered to be the danger zone. Having been isolated on the mountain for more than a year, Jessie felt hesitation about encountering others.

Stopping to give Brave a break from trudging through the snow with a load on his back, Jessie dismounted and said, "C'mon, boy. Let's get you a drink of water."

Leading Brave off the road and out onto a hillside clear of trees, Jessie pointed off to a pile of large rocks that had been working their way down the hillside with the help of the forces of nature for what he assumed were centuries. "Let's set up camp on the backside of those rocks, buddy. Not only will they give us a good wind break, but they'll also provide concealment of our camp in the event someone else is out and about."

Leading Brave across the hillside to the rocks, Jessie marveled at their size and shape. "These things are much larger than I thought from way over there."

Securing Brave's reins to a small tree growing next to the rocks, Jessie climbed the giant rock pile to gain a view from the vantage point they would provide, some fifteen feet above ground level. "I can see over the trees from here," he shouted down to Brave as if he could understand.

This will do, he thought to himself. *We know nothing is uphill from us and I can see in most directions for at least several miles from here.* Licking his finger and holding it into the air, he thought, *and the wind is blowing from the west, making these rocks an ideal shelter for Brave since he won't have the luxury of sharing my tent.*

Climbing down from the rocks, rejoining Brave down below, Jessie led him around behind the rocks to seek shelter from the wind. Removing Brave's saddle and saddle-bags, he started to set up camp. After laying his tarp out on top of the snow for waterproofing, Jessie began erecting the tent up on top of it, lashing the tent to the cracks in the adjacent rocks and one small tree. Tugging on the tent to test its security, he said aloud, "That'll do."

First things first, he thought. *We need water, then food, then fire.* With those priorities in mind, Jessie removed his mess kit from the saddle-bags and unfolded his portable backpacking camp stove. Removing a Sterno fuel canister from his kit, he popped the lid off, lit the contents, and placed it in the center of the stove, which shielded the small flame from the effects of the surrounding wind.

Taking his stainless steel bowl from the mess kit, Jessie used it to scoop up a heaping bowl of clean snow and placed it over the stove, melting the snow into drinking water for him and Brave. Once the snow was melted, but before it became too warm, he removed the bowl, poured himself a small cup of water, and then placed the rest in front of Brave, who quickly lapped up every drop, as he was thirsty from the day's trek down the mountain.

Not wanting to tap into his food supply early on, Jessie removed one of the arrows from his quiver and unthreaded the knife-edged broadhead, replacing it with a simple field point. *No need to damage these broadheads early in the trip,* he thought. *It would be overkill anyway.*

Rubbing Brave's muzzle, Jessie said, "Wait right here, boy, I'll be right back."

Disappearing into the woods, Jessie began to scan the surrounding snow for signs of small game. Following what seemed to be natural lines in the terrain, Jessie quickly stumbled upon what appeared to be a well-used game trail meandering through the woods. Taking a seat, leaning back against a large Ponderosa pine tree, Jessie sat still and silent, becoming one with his surroundings.

Taking a good look around, Jessie noticed that the tree was riddled with tiny holes. *Damn pine beetles,* he thought. *There's going to be nothing left of this place before long.*

Returning his focus to the task at hand, Jessie sat perfectly still and listened as every sound of nature resonated with him. He could hear the activity of a tree squirrel, and with his eyes closed, could see a picture in his mind of its every move. Jessie had always felt at home in nature, and this new world was putting that aspect of his life to good use.

After approximately a half-hour of sitting and listening to the sounds of nature all around him, a brown mountain cottontail rabbit exposed its position just twenty yards ahead. As the rabbit hopped to and fro, searching for plants to eat hidden just below the snow's surface, Jesse slowly and deliberately brought his bow to bear, nocked his arrow, clipped his mechanical release into place, and silently came to full draw. Using the upper pin of his fiber-optic sight for such a close range, Jessie held his breath and slowly applied pressure to the trigger on his release as he floated the pin on his target, sending the field point-tipped carbon-fiber arrow flying at his unsuspecting prey at nearly three hundred and twenty-five feet per second.

With a direct hit, the rabbit jolted from the impact, making a complete backflip, coming to rest just a few feet from where it had been standing. The rabbit lay still and silent, killed instantly from the impact of the arrow that had passed clean through the animal, burying itself deep in the snow.

With a smile on his face, happy for both acquiring a meal as well as making a clean, humane kill, Jessie approached the rabbit, knelt down and said with a whisper, "Thanks for the meal, little buddy." He then pulled his knife out of its sheath and quickly field-dressed the animal, tossing it into a plastic sack he had brought along and carried in his pocket. After a few moments digging through the snow, Jessie retrieved his arrow, wiped it clean, and then began his short hike back to camp to prepare his evening meal.

As Jessie walked back to the large rocks where he and Brave were camping for the evening, he collected what roughage he could to feed Brave. Being the tail-end of winter with spring just around the corner, the grasses had yet to begin their seasonal growth cycle, and in the mountains, had yet to begin to peek out through the remaining snow.

Arriving back at the camp with a large bundle of roughage under his arm, Jessie positioned it for Brave to eat while he prepared his own meal.

Quickly skinning the animal and removing the unwanted parts, Jessie skewered the critter on a green tree branch that he skinned with his knife. The green nature of the wood would prevent the skewer from catching fire too easily while he roasted his prize over an open flame.

Using his firestarter and char cloth to get a small campfire going, Jessie used two forked sticks on opposite ends of the fire to support the skewered rabbit while it cooked.

Leaning back against a large rock while he tended to his dinner, Jessie reached into his coat pocket and pulled out a small notebook and a pen. With the Walkers no longer serving as his company, Jessie felt the need to tell the story of his journey. Not that he expected anyone to ever read it, but the pain he still harbored deep inside gave him the ever-present desire to share his thoughts, as a release of sorts. Prior to the arrival of Mark and Cindy, he had felt trapped within his own mind. His thoughts had become a prison, but with their friendship, he had once again felt the need to reach outside of those prison walls and communicate his feelings. With no one else around, he felt a journal just might fill the void.

As he sat down to write, he held the pen in his right hand with the notepad on his lap and felt a total loss for words. *This is just silly,* he mused. *I feel like a teenage girl with her diary.* Laying it aside, dismissing his desire to share his feelings, he once again began to tend the fire and his meal, only to be drawn back to his journal. Picking it back up, he put his pen to paper and began to write:

When I was a young boy, I would sit down and watch the old western movies and long for the freedom they had. Living that open-range, cowboy way of life seemed like the ultimate life to me. Don't get me wrong, I knew I wanted to settle down and have a family someday. That's just who I was deep inside, but at the same time, the freedom of riding the open range always captivated me.

As a child, I lived by everyone else's schedule. My parent's work dictated most days, and if not, it was school and chores throughout the week with church on Sunday. Saturday was really my only day to be me. I would often play in the woods with nothing more than a stick for a toy. That stick could be anything I wanted. Sometimes it was a rifle, other times it was a sword, or maybe it was even something magical. Either way, my imagination, not the toy itself, led the way.

When I watched those old westerns, I would see how the cowboys on a cattle drive would face perilous journeys along the way, fighting off bandits and the Native Americans they called Indians, even though I personally took issue with that, as they traveled.

It wasn't their struggles that lured me to their way of life. It wasn't the concept of the cowboy versus the Indian as Hollywood put it; it was their freedom from the clock and the calendar. When cowboys in the old days set out on a cattle drive, it would often take them months to reach their destination. Their only deadline was the oncoming winter or other such things, but along the way, things like where they ended up that night, was all up to fate. They didn't have to be somewhere the next day, leaving their wonderful world of freedom behind. They were totally immersed in it. The day of the week didn't matter to them, and the only time that mattered was based on the position of the sun to light their way.

The Shepherd: Society Lost

To me, despite all of the hardships and horrors that came along with those glory days of riding the open range, that freedom from society, that freedom from the calendar or clock, was like a magnet drawing in my soul.

So here I sit with my horse, looking out into the wild of the Rocky Mountains and the vast expanse of America that lies before me, and for the first time in my life I am without a calendar and without a clock. If it weren't for the turmoil going on in my own heart, I would, for the first time in my life, in some twisted way, be free.

I celebrate this freedom with deep heartache and regret. I wish more than anything to be back in that small cabin with my beautiful wife and children, but alas, that is not the hand I have been dealt. I have nothing in my life left except the glimmering hope that my sister is out there, still alive, just waiting for me to find her. I will pursue that glimmer of hope to the ends of the Earth, and if God were to take me before I reach her, so be it. At least I will experience true freedom during the journey.

Jessie closed his notebook and slipped it back into his pocket, tucking the pen securely into the spiral binding. *Almost ready,* he thought as he admired the smell of his dinner as it cooked over the fire.

Once his meal was safely cooked, he held the end of the skewer while he shaved off a few slices of meat at a time onto his plate and enjoyed the simplicity and the beauty of the evening.

"We're gonna be just fine, boy," he said to Brave, who almost appeared to understand, replying with the toss of his head.

Chapter Sixteen

Awakened by the sound of distant howl, Jessie quickly sat up in his tent and listened to the sounds of his surroundings. Brave was obviously anxious, indicating that something was indeed afoot. Slipping out of his tent, Jessie walked up to Brave and stood alongside him, stroking his mane to calm his nerves. "Shhhh, it's okay, boy."

Seeing that his small campfire was now nothing more than smoldering coals, Jessie quickly began to place more wood on it in an attempt to get it going again. As he poked at the coals, amber sparks were carried up into the darkness of the night by the gentle breeze as it flowed around the large rocks. Jessie was thankful that he had put their camp in such a position to prevent a predator from easily creeping up on them from behind.

Hearing a twig snap directly ahead of Brave off in the darkness, Jessie dropped the piece of wood, stood up, and placed his hand on the grip of his trusty Colt. He quietly stepped around and in front of Brave, putting himself in between the potential threat and his beloved horse. As his eyes struggled to focus in the darkness of the night, he heard a grunt and a snort. *A bear,* he thought as his pulse quickened. *Must have been lured in by the smell of my dinner.*

Reaching into the tent, Jessie quietly slipped his AR-15 out of the integral rifle scabbard made into his backpack. Bringing the weapon up to his shoulder, he switched on the tactical rail-mounted light and shouted, "Hey, bear!" as he scanned the area in the direction from which he heard the noise.

Clicking off the safety with a round already chambered, Jessie kept his finger clear of the trigger, not wanting an accidental discharge from a nervous flinch, but was mentally prepared to engage a target if need be. "Hey bear!" he shouted again, this time eliciting a response as a fully grown black bear emerged from the darkness with a deep grunt, followed by a clacking of its teeth and a moan.

Being an avid hunter and understanding the basic vocalizations of black bears, Jessie lowered his rifle, keeping the light out of the bear's eyes, and said, "Go on, boy. Git!" with an authoritative tone, knowing that the bear meant him no harm and was simply caught up in the same situation as him.

Acquiescing to Jessie in the moment, the bear turned and bolted off into the darkness.

Stroking Brave on the neck, Jessie said, "It's okay, boy. He's gone. But that's yet another sign of spring. The bears are coming out of hibernation and are going to be hungry. I guess I need to start doing a better job of disposing of the remains of my kills."

~~~~

Early the next morning as the sun rose fully above the horizon, illuminating the valley below, Jessie enjoyed a sip of warm herbal drink he had made from wild peony root that he had discovered during an early morning stroll around his camp as he searched for forage to feed Brave. "It looks like it's gonna be a beautiful day, boy. Let's not waste it," he said as he began to break down their camp and pack up for the day's journey.

Once he had saddled Brave and had secured all of their supplies to the saddle and saddle-bags, he swung his leg over the saddle. As he took the reins, he paused and looked back over his shoulder to the mountains that just a day before he had called home, and with a nod, he nudged Brave forward as they rode off into the unknown.

As the sun traveled across the sky reaching the high noon position, Jessie and Brave reached a narrowing of the road just up ahead. As the old dirt road merged with a stream with a steepening of terrain on both sides, Jessie eased back on the reins, bringing Brave to a stop while he visually scanned ahead. "It's a funnel," he whispered to Brave.

Reaching back over his shoulder, Jessie clutched his AR-15 by the stock and pulled it out of its scabbard and over his head. He then shouldered the weapon, scanning the area ahead through the scope on its maximum zoom.

Not seeing an apparent threat in the vicinity, Jessie nudged Brave forward, murmuring, "C'mon, boy." Laying the rifle across his lap instead of putting it away, Jessie remained ready for a threatening situation, should one arise. With one of his recent encounters ending in the greatest tragedy of his life, Jessie couldn't help but be on edge about the potential of crossing paths with others.

As Jessie and Brave approached the area of concern, Jessie divided his attention between the surrounding area and signs of others who might be present on the ground. Seeing footprints along the edge of the stream, Jessie slowed Brave's cadence to take a better look. "They're going downhill, boy. They came through here... maybe yesterday. Hitting the snowline probably prompted them to head back down the mountain a bit. It gets pretty dang cold at night the higher you go. Let's just hope they either kept moving or moved off the road in another direction."

~~~~

For the next several days, Jessie and Brave traveled methodically down the mountain, stopping to camp whenever a suitable location presented itself. Jessie found himself taking his time, not being in a hurry to rejoin what was left of the world below. He continued to see signs that others had been on the mountain, but had yet to come across them. Both he and they were clearly in a mindset to avoid others, and for this, he was thankful.

As they approached the town of Dolores, the statutory town of Montezuma County, they had still yet to encounter others directly, yet Jessie had been able to see the occasional chimney or campfire smoke off in the distance. The lower levels were clearly a more hospitable place for most, being warmer at night and closer to available food supplies such as wild game and plant life. A cursory view of Dolores through his rifle scope, however, showed no such activity.

"Where the heck is everyone, boy?" Jessie said aloud. As he scanned the houses and buildings below through his rifle scope, he noticed many of the buildings had a red X painted on the front by the entrance. "Well, hell. We know what that means," he said. "I thought Dolores was far enough off the beaten path to avoid the droves of people who no doubt began abandoning Denver when the fever began to hit it hard. But then again, if people like the Walker family were going to attempt to send people back and forth to retrieve loved ones, there would be others doing so as well and it was only a matter of time. There were probably a lot of people in Denver with family in Cortez and Dolores who wanted to get away from it all and unfortunately ended up bringing the fever with them. Such a shame," he said, shaking his head as he looked at the ground.

Startled by the sound of a gunshot echoing off the surrounding mountains in the distance, Jessie scanned the area trying to determine its origin. Unable to home in on the source of the gunshot due to the echoing nature of the mountains, Jessie said, "Let's get a move on, boy."

After putting some distance between themselves and the sound of the gunshot, Jessie stopped to pull an old highway map out of his saddle-bag. With the goal of going around the mountains to the south and then paralleling Interstate 40 to head east toward his sister's last known location in Tennessee, Jessie thought, *We've got to get across the Dolores River at some point.* Following a potential route of travel on the map with his finger, he decided, *If we skirt around Dolores to the north and then cross the 145 bridge on the west side of town, we'll be able to avoid most of it. We can cut across at Joe Rowell Park and then get back off the beaten path for a while.*

Folding the map neatly and slipping it back into his saddlebag, Jessie urged Brave forward and they continued on their journey.

As the sun began to fade into evening across the mountains to the west, Jessie and Brave arrived on the northwestern edge of the town of Dolores. Jessie was heartbroken at how Dolores and the county he once served as sheriff had fared during the aftermath of the fighting and the attacks. He fought the urge to ride through town looking for survivors, as he knew the risks far outweighed the chance of doing any good.

Pulling his bandana over his face and donning his gloves, unsure of the situation in town now that those with the fever had died off, Jessie nudged Brave forward once again, proceeding toward where Highway 145 met Joe Rowell Park in order to cross the river as planned. As they slowly and cautiously rode toward the park, Jessie looked around carefully at every window, doorway, alley, and rooftop. The town of Dolores, once a bustling and happy little town, now seemed devoid of human activity and was eerily quiet.

As Jessie and Brave approached the city's water treatment plant, located on the north side of Highway 145, he noticed the pungent smell of the stagnant and foul water that was once purified by the facilities treatment tanks, now sitting idle.

Pausing with an uneasy feeling about him, Jessie started to change his plan, but hesitated due to the distance they would have to travel to find another way across the river. Nudging Brave forward, they entered the now empty Highway 145. The only cars he could see were abandoned along the streets of the town and on both sides of the bridge. One Dodge camper van that he noticed had the familiar red X painted on the side. *I guess that was someone on the run from it all,* he thought.

Riding down the center of the street, Jessie and Brave rode onto the bridge and began to cross. At the halfway point, Jessie looked down to see what appeared to be droplets of blood on the concrete. *Crap!* he thought as he heard a car horn blow. Immediately following the startling sound, armed men, who had been hiding in the trunks of the abandoned cars, began to climb out, rifles in hand, all aimed at Jessie.

Jessie slowly raised his hands and shouted for them to hear, "It's okay. I'm just passing through."

"Put your hands on top of your head!" one of the men shouted.

Complying with their request, Jessie slowly placed his hands on his head, and said, "Like I said, I'm not looking for trouble. I'm just passing through."

"I'm afraid not," the man with a long graying beard replied, seeming to be in charge.

As the men slowly and carefully approached Jessie, he studied their demeanor and attire in an attempt to assess the situation. Filthy and disheveled in appearance, with numerous visible scars and missing teeth, these individuals looked to Jessie as if they had been living life the hard way long before it all hit the fan. "What can I do for you, gentlemen?" Jessie asked.

"Shut your mouth," the man replied.

As they approached, Brave became nervous and began to shift around as if he was looking for a way to escape.

"Easy, boy," Jessie whispered in an attempt to calm him, knowing any such attempt to make a run for it would be met with a wall of bullets from which they could not escape.

One of the men took Brave's reins in hand while another put a rifle to Jessie's side.

"Don't move," the man said.

A third man then removed Jessie's Colt from its holster and began to admire it. "Nice," he said with a smile, as if he had no intention of returning it. "He must think he's some sort of old west gunslinger carrying this ol' thing around."

"Remove the pack," the man in charge then ordered.

Easing his right hand down to release the buckles on his pack, Jessie said, "Look, the others that are following along behind have a lot of food and provisions. We can work something out."

Ignoring his statement, the man that had removed his Colt also took Jessie's pack and removed his Winchester from the saddle-mounted scabbard. With a smile, the man said, "Jackpot," as he admired all three weapons.

"Now the knife," the man said.

Jessie slowly removed his knife and handed it to the man handle first.

"Off the horse," the man then ordered.

Reluctantly, Jessie swung his leg over and began to climb down from Brave's saddle. Once his leg was clear, he felt several hands clutch him and pull him violently to the ground, followed by the view of a rifle butt being shoved into his face, and then— darkness.

Chapter Seventeen

The wolves circled Jessie in the darkness. He could hear their hungry growls all around him as they almost seemed to communicate with one another through their fierce, bloodthirsty sounds. His head pounding, his pulse racing, Jessie felt paralyzed. He wanted to reach for his gun, but he simply could not move. It was as if his muscles didn't respond to his commands.

Is this how it's gonna be? Is this how it's gonna end? Jessie thought as he lay there helpless on the cold hard ground.

The alpha wolf appeared directly in front of him from the darkness. With fresh blood in its fur, it looked as if it had just returned from a kill. Still hungry, the wolf slowly worked its way closer, the sounds of its claws scratching on the rocky ground as it walked.

Reaching Jessie, the wolf stood directly over him, its menacing fangs exposed, its putrid breath smelling of rotting meat, warm saliva dripping onto Jessie's face as it stood over him.

"Wake up!" the man shouted as he smacked Jessie violently across the face.

Hurled back into reality, Jessie found himself hogtied and lying on a cold concrete floor in an old abandoned building. In a daze and with a pounding headache, Jessie looked around in an attempt to assess the situation. Several men sat around a fire in the far corner of the room while two of the men stood over Jessie, one with Jessie's own knife in his hand.

"The others—tell us about the others!" one of the men shouted.

"What?" Jessie replied in a confused voice.

"The others you mentioned on the bridge. The ones following behind you. How many of them are there and when will they arrive?"

Quickly formulating a response, Jessie replied, "They sent me as a scout. If I don't report back, they won't approach the town. They'll assume it's not safe."

"How many and where are they?"

"Ten men and six women," he replied.

One of the men patted the other on the shoulder with a devious smile and said, "Women. They've got women."

"Shut up," the other man said in a muffled voice.

"All we want is food," the man with the long graying beard said to Jessie. "We can work out a trade with them. You, for some food. It's that easy."

"Like I said," Jessie insisted, "they won't come if I don't report back."

With a crooked smile exposing his rotting teeth, the man said, "We'll see," as he turned and walked toward the fire.

One of the men by the fire handed him a plate of meat that had been cooked on a small portable campfire cooking grate they had placed over the fire, "Here you go, Wolf," the man said.

Hearing the name *Wolf,* Jessie's attention was peaked. Shaking off the coincidence, he looked around the room, trying to think of a way out of his dire situation. Having been a sheriff and knowing all too well what men like this were capable of, even when times were good, Jessie knew if he didn't make a move soon, his chances would begin to rapidly deteriorate.

Wanting to get a better look at his surroundings, Jessie shouted, "Hey, Wolf."

Pausing from his meal, with a mouthful of meat, the man turned and replied, "Are you ready to talk?" wiping his mouth with his sleeve as he continued to eat.

"I need to use the restroom," Jessie replied.

His mouth still full of food, Wolf smiled, revealing meat stuck between his rotting teeth, and said, "Then piss yourself."

Damn it, Jessie thought out of frustration.

~~~~

As the day slipped away into the night, Jessie lay awake on the cold hard floor alone, while his captors drank and partied on the other side of the room. Clearly professional looters, they had come across several bottles of hard liquor that they passed around the fire, sharing amongst themselves.

The men seemed not to have a care in the world. They were truly in their own element in a world devoid of social order and any valid law enforcement presence. The men relished the sorrow of others, laughing and joking about those whom they had found to be easy prey.

As one of the inebriated men passed the bottle off to the next, it slipped from his fingers, breaking on the floor. Outraged, one of the other men immediately pulled a knife and yelled, "You clumsy son of a bitch," as he shoved the knife into the man's stomach.

As the man fell to the ground, writhing in pain with his hands on his wound, the others joined in, cheering for the man who committed the assault. They all then began viciously kicking and stomping the injured man in a most violent manner until he struggled no more.

Once the laughter subsided, a tone of seriousness came across the group as Wolf said, "Get him out of here before he starts to stink. Toss him out back with what's left of that horse. We'll burn them both tomorrow before the flies and maggots get out of hand."

As Jessie lay there, horrified by the extreme brutality of the group, fear swept through his body as he heard the mention of a horse. "Horse, what horse?" he shouted.

With all six of the men turning to face Jessie, Wolf replied, "Why, that fine specimen you rode into our town on. Don't worry, he didn't go to waste. He was delicious." Pointing at the remaining meat by the fire, he added, "There's more if you're hungry."

A sickness came over Jessie at the revelation that he had been watching the men consume his beloved horse, Brave. Rolling over on his side, he vomited uncontrollably as the men all laughed at his pain.

Jessie's sorrow quickly turned to rage as all of the emotions and hatred he had worked so hard to suppress came flooding back into his head. The thoughts of what had been done to his family, vividly clear in his mind, drove him to struggle against the ropes, the force of which began to cut into his skin. Bleeding profusely, Jessie felt one of his hands begin to slip free from the ropes. It was then that he had a moment of clarity and eased his struggle, appearing to the men as if he had simply given up.

Not now, he thought. *Not now.*

~~~~

As morning drew near, the men had one-by-one passed out or had simply fallen asleep from their night of alcohol-fueled lunacy. Only two of them remained in the room with Jessie, both asleep by the fire. Jessie had quietly worked his left hand free from the confines of the ropes. With one hand free and no one actively watching him, Jessie patiently worked to free his other hand, and then sat up to untie his feet.

Once he was free of the ropes, Jessie took a two-foot long section of it and tied a knot in the center and one knot on each end. Holding the knots on the ends of the rope in each hand, he crept over to one of the men who was sleeping face down on the ground with his right arm under his forehead. The fire, now just smoldering red-hot coals, provided Jessie with just enough light to see, while also providing a reasonable degree of darkness, should he be discovered.

Nudging the man in the side with his foot as if trying to wake him, Jessie stood over him from behind. As the man lifted his head and turned to see who was waking him, Jessie quickly threw the rope around his neck, placed his foot on the back of the man's head, and pulled as hard as he could. The knot in the center of the rope crushed the man's windpipe, silencing any ability he had to scream. His arms shaking from the intensity of the struggle, Jessie watched as the life slipped from the man, his struggles fading into a mere shudder, and then the silence of death.

Rolling the man over and frisking him for weapons, Jessie found a five-inch-long fixed-blade knife in a sheath on the man's belt, as well as a Glock 9mm pistol tucked into his pants. Taking both of the weapons, he then walked over to the second man and knelt down beside him. After pausing for a moment, soaking in the gravity of the situation, Jessie grabbed the man by the hair, yanked his head off the ground, reached around and slit his throat from ear to ear. Nothing but the sound of gurgling blood and escaping air could be heard as the man momentarily struggled before also being consumed by the silence of death.

Feeling the man's warm blood soak into his pants as he remained kneeling on the floor, Jessie wiped the knife clean on the man's shirt and stood up. Looking around the room and thinking of his next move, he walked over to a doorway that led to a darkened hall with several doors on each side and one door at the end.

Hearing movement in one of the rooms, Jessie quietly closed the door and looked around the room in which he was being held, searching for a way to escape. Seeing only the door, and a set of stairs leading up, Jessie chose to walk over to a small rectangular metal-framed window that was mounted unusually high on the wall. The window had been opened and utilized by the men as a chimney for ventilation and exhausting the smoke generated by their small fire.

Looking up and out of the window, Jessie could see the stars of the clear and calm night as well as the ground up above, separated from the window by a two-foot-high concrete retaining wall. *I'm in a basement,* he thought.

Reaching up to the window's ledge, Jessie pulled himself up and through the opening, escaping out the window into the darkness of the night. Once outside, Jessie looked around and quickly realized that he had been held at the water treatment facility on the edge of town, adjacent to the bridge where he was taken. The pungent smell of the stagnant water made that revelation entirely clear.

Pausing to think of his next move, Jessie decided to take the prudent course of action, which would be to escape, regroup, and then deal with Wolf and the men on his own terms. He simply wasn't going to allow men like this to terrorize people passing through a town that he used to protect as sheriff, like trolls under a bridge, waiting to pounce as unsuspecting travelers attempted to use the bridge as a means of crossing the Dolores River.

Just like the wolves that had terrorized Jessie's flock of sheep, this new Wolf and his deadly pack had to be stopped.

Chapter Eighteen

Heading east into the city of Dolores on Central Avenue, Jessie slipped from house to house in an attempt to remain hidden from view on the bright, moonlit night. Turning north on 6th Street, and then back east to Hillside Avenue, Jessie felt a mixture of emotion from intense rage to sadness. He felt rage that people like the men from whom he had just escaped had somehow been spared when so many good people had lost their lives during the attacks and the resultant collapse. He also felt sadness that the town of Dolores, which he was once sworn to protect, had been decimated. Each and every red X marking the buildings of the once quaint little town was a sobering reminder of the horrible death that those who didn't flee had suffered.

Distracted by his thoughts as he rounded the corner of a white craftsman-style home, he nearly failed to see a wooden plank with nails protruding from it as it was swung violently at his head. Attempting to dive to his left toward the house to avoid being struck in the head, the makeshift weapon grazed the top of his head with a loud thud, the nails protruding from it only narrowly avoiding his scalp.

Dazed, but still conscious, Jessie slammed his shoulder against the house, and immediately took evasive action to avoid another swing, diving at the figure holding the board and tackling his assailant at the waist, rushing forward, taking both himself and his attacker to the ground.

Pulling the Glock from his waistband, he shoved the pistol into the throat of his assailant. As he began to apply pressure to the trigger to end the assault, he heard a woman's voice amidst the struggle saying, "I'll kill you, you son of a bitch! I'll kill every one of you murdering bastards!" as she pounded her fists on his back.

Encumbered by the weapon, Jessie tossed it out of reach and using both hands, subdued the woman, sitting on top of her while struggling to hold her hands still. "Stop. Stop it! I'm not one of them!" he shouted. "But if you keep screaming like that they're liable to hear us and then you *will* have to deal with them."

Easing her resistance against him, the woman, now visible by the moonlight, said, "Who... who are you?"

"I just got away from them. They may be searching for me by now. We've got to get the hell out here before they come looking."

Seeing bruises on Jessie's face and the cuts on his wrists, the woman relaxed and said, "Okay... Okay, get up and I'll take you somewhere safe."

Releasing his grip on her wrists, Jessie got off her and extended his hand, helping her to her feet. Looking around to see if they were being watched, she said, "Quick. This way," as she took off in between the two houses.

Quickly retrieving his weapon from the ground, Jessie jogged along behind the woman, following her a few blocks down the street where she climbed a chain-link fence and entered the backyard of an old two-story home.

Looking around again to see if the area was clear, she waved for Jessie to follow, where she led him to a basement cellar underneath the old house.

Once they got inside, she closed the two doors above them, locking them from the inside and bracing them by sliding a large piece of wood through both of their handles.

With the doors closed the room was pitch black inside. Jessie heard her voice say, "Just a second," followed by the sound of a match being struck against a matchbox. As the tiny flame erupted from the match, Jessie could see in the flickering light as the woman lit an old antique-style oil lamp, bringing a soft glow of light to the room.

"We're safe in here," she said as he looked around. "The house has a red X on the front. They seem to avoid those."

Looking up at the ceiling and pointing, Jessie stammered, "Is someone—"

Interrupting before he could answer, the woman said, "I don't know, I've never looked, but it doesn't matter. I've been staying here for a few weeks now and I haven't gotten sick yet."

The woman, an attractive brunette in her early to mid-thirties, had a very matter-of-fact demeanor about her. "My name is Ashley. You can call me Ash."

"I'm Jessie," he said. "What... how did—"

"How did I end up down here by myself?" she again interrupted. Looking at Jessie's wrists, she said, "Let me get you something for that. Luckily, whoever did live here, had a lot of extra supplies down here. They were either some of those prepper types or wanted to get their money's worth from one of those wholesale clubs. Either way, they've got lots of stuff down here that's been coming in handy."

Opening a large first-aid kit while she talked, she continued, "A few weeks ago, gosh, I guess it's been over a month now. I've sort of lost track of time. I was traveling with my husband and a few friends. We were coming up from Regina, New Mexico where we had been staying since the attacks. We had run out of food and were down to our last bit of fuel and decided to use it to get up to Telluride to try and hide out with my husband's brother. Being way up in the mountains, we hoped it would be a good place to ride things out."

Pouring alcohol on a cotton swab, she then touched it to Jessie's wrist, making him flinch. "Oh, come on," she said, dismissing his pain. Getting back to her explanation while she treated his injuries, she said, "Anyway, Tom's brother—Tom was my husband, by the way—is one of those hardcore survivalist types. He worked at the ski resort in Telluride and whenever he wasn't doing some sort of hardcore outdoor activity, he was shooting guns and preparing for the apocalypse. Tom used to give him a hard time and make fun of him, but look who's laughing now," she said as she wrapped a bandage around Jessie's wrists.

"Long story short," she continued, "we actually thought we were going make it until those murderous thieves at the bridge hijacked us at gunpoint. Tom resisted," she said, pausing for a moment, seeming to get lost in her own thoughts, "and started fighting back. I guess he knew we weren't going to get out of there unscathed. He could read people. He always could. Anyway, during the fight Tom yelled for me to run while they fought them off. I was hoping I would get to safety and have him catch up to me later. I heard several gunshots as I ran. I turned to see Tom's limp body falling to the ground. Two of them held him while that man with the gray beard shot him in the head at point-blank range."

Wiping a tear from her eye, she said, "So, I ran into town to try to get away. I managed to hide under the front porch of one of the houses. I could see through the lattice as they searched the streets and between the houses, but they never went inside. Not even once. It was then that I realized they must be afraid they'll catch whatever it was that everyone around here had died from."

"Marburg hemorrhagic fever," he said.

"What?"

"It was a weaponized virus used against Denver by one of the jihadist groups involved with the attacks. It spread to cities like Dolores by people evacuating Denver to get away from it all. At least that's what I've heard. Who knows what's really true."

"So, anyway," she said bluntly, "I noticed they never went inside any of the buildings with the red X painted on the front. Based on that observation, I searched for a safe place to hide and found this cellar, which is perfect because of the exterior entrance. By the way, do you think the virus could still be around? I mean... on the dead bodies and stuff? How long can it survive without a living host?"

"I'm not a medical expert, but I did have to take EMT training related to my law enforcement position. I'm not sure about this virus in particular, but it is similar to Ebola, I believe. From what I remember from the Ebola scare we had a few years back, it can live on a dead body for quite some time. Back then, the experts didn't even know. Basically as long as there are tissue and fluids, it can survive for a very long time. Again, that's all based on my limited knowledge of the subject, of course."

After a moment of awkward silence, Jessie looked around the room to speak as Ash interrupted, asking, "So, what's your story? Where are you running to?"

"I'm not running *to* anywhere," Jessie replied tersely. "Like you, I've lost everything I held dear. I lived up in the mountains north of here. Like you, I thought hiding away in the mountains was the best bet. My family and I had a small working homestead where we raised sheep."

"So you're a shepherd?" she asked.

"Uh, yeah. I'm a shepherd. Anyway, things were going pretty well. For the most part, we felt like the turmoil of the rest of the world was passing us by. We had encountered a few groups over time, but most people moved along easily enough once they learned we would not be taking them in or giving anything away. Then one day, a group of men, not unlike the trolls at the bridge here, found us, and..." pausing to look at his hand, thinking of his beloved family, Jessie's heart sank into his chest as he realized his wedding ring had been taken from him by the men at the bridge.

Fighting to maintain his composure, Jessie was unable to form his words. Ash reached out and put her hand on his and said, "It's okay. I get it."

"So as I was saying," he said after clearing his throat, "I didn't have a reason to stay on the mountain anymore. I've got a sister I haven't spoken to since this all began, and I figured I might as well spend what energy I have left trying to find her, which is basically how I stumbled across you here."

"So where are you running to now?" she asked.

Taking offense, Jessie sternly replied, "I'm not running anywhere. I was only falling back to recoup and regroup before dealing with this situation any further."

"Good," Ash replied with a smile, "maybe we can work together on that."

With a look of curiosity, Jessie asked, "What did you have in mind?"

Standing up and walking to the other side of the cellar, Ash pointed at a cot she had been sleeping on and said, "We can talk about that in the morning after you're rested up. Now that you're here, we can take turns standing watch during the nights in four-hour shifts. I'll take the first watch. You look like you need your rest. By the way, do those scumbags have a reason to want to get you back?"

"Two good reasons," he replied.

With a smile, understanding exactly what he meant, she said, "By the time your sleep shift is over the sun will be up and those scumbags will more than likely be out looking for you. We'll need to stay on our toes." Picking up an old side-by-side double-barrel twelve-gauge shotgun and throwing a bandolier filled with shotgun shells over her shoulder, she said, "Rest up for now. We'll talk more later."

Chapter Nineteen

Back at the water treatment plant, as Wolf and one of his men entered the room where Jessie had been held the previous night in hopes that he would be ready to give them more information, to their horror they discovered that two of their men had been killed and Jessie was nowhere to be found.

In a profanity-laced verbal explosion of rage, Wolf shouted for Juan, his right-hand man. "Juan! Get in here, now!"

Running into the room with his pistol in his hand and at the ready, Juan shouted, "What? What is it, Wolf?" as he scanned the room for threats.

"You've gotta get a handle on these guys," he said, pointing at the two dead men on the floor. "What the hell is this? Are you telling me not one person saw or heard anything? What is this guy? A ghost?"

"Naw, man, everybody was drunk and I guess..."

"You guess? You guess?" Wolf said, raising his hand back as if he was going to smack Juan in the face. Slowly lowering his hand, Wolf said, "This guy ain't gonna hit us like this and just get away with it. You and Jake get out there and find this guy. He can't have gone far. He has to be on foot. Search every damn house if you have to! I don't care if you're worried about getting sick. Just find him!"

Without hesitation, Juan left the room running and quickly climbed the stairs into the administration area of the water treatment plant above. "Jake!" he shouted, seeing Jake sitting in an office chair by the window with his head on a desk. "Jake, wake the hell up!" he said again, kicking the chair.

"Ah, man. My head is killing me," Jake replied, lifting his head off the desk and turning to look at Juan.

"Yeah, well, Wolf's gonna kill us himself if you don't get up. That guy that came in on horseback got away last night. He killed Paco and Hank, too. We've gotta go after him."

"Killed who?" Jake said, still confused.

"Paco and Hank, you big sack of shit! Now get up!" he again yelled, slamming his fist on the desk. "You're supposed to be on watch, anyway. How are you gonna to see anyone coming if you don't even look out the damn window?"

"Whatever, man. I'm coming," Jake said as he stood up and stretched. Jake, a six-foot-three bruiser with long black hair pulled back into a ponytail, was a formidable-looking individual. He wore desert-style camouflage clothing sourced from a looted military surplus store, smattered with various bloodstains from altercations he had initiated. Picking his machete up off the desk and sliding it into a sheath on his belt, he then reached forward, grabbing his Romanian AKM rifle, tossing it over his shoulder, and said. "All right, let's go," he said, pounding his chest with his fist.

Chapter Twenty

As he crept through the woods, knife in hand, Jessie was careful not to break a twig underfoot. Paying particular attention to the wind and how it might carry his scent, he circled around, staying downwind to avoid giving his presence away too soon.

Hearing a commotion through the dense evergreen trees up ahead, Jessie approached silently. Pushing several small branches out of his way with his left hand, Jessie was horrified to see the hungry pack of wolves devouring his horse, tearing at its flesh while it was still alive and suffering.

Fighting through the pain, Brave lifted his head and turned to look at Jessie as if he was pleading for help. Jessie could see the pain and suffering in Brave's eyes as the old gray wolf turned to see Jessie standing behind the trees. Baring its blood-soaked fangs, the wolf leaped at Jessie, crashing through the trees, knocking him to the ground.

"Wake up," Ash whispered, holding her hand over Jessie's mouth while shaking him by the shoulder. "Shhhhh, they're patrolling the streets. They look pissed. What did you do?"

Sitting up on the cot, covered in sweat, Jessie regained his composure and quietly said, "Nothing you wouldn't have done."

Replying only with a smirk, Ash turned and looked through a gap in the large wooden doors leading up and out of the basement. "We should hit them now while they expect you to be on the run and alone. I only see two of them. A big guy in some sort of desert gear. He's pretty well armed. Another guy in black cargo pants and an old army field jacket is with him. They've both got rifles, but we've got the element of surprise," she said.

"No, let's wait," he insistently replied.

"Wait for what? More people to get raped and murdered?"

"This would be acting while on the defensive. That hasn't worked so well for me in the past. If I would have been more proactive about security back on my homestead, rather than reactive, my family might still be alive today. When I was the sheriff here in Montezuma County—"

"You're the sheriff here?" she interrupted.

"I *was* the sheriff here," he replied. "Before it all started going down. I left and moved up into the mountains to the north long before the attacks. So anyway, that's one of the big differences between patrol and SWAT. Officers on patrol react to a situation that is presented to them, without any prior knowledge or planning. That's their job, though—to respond to crimes being committed or that are just being reported. SWAT on the other hand, often operates with prior knowledge of the individuals they confront and generally do it on their terms at the time and place of their choosing. If you look at the success and casualty rates of patrol officer encounters versus SWAT encounters, you'll see that SWAT generally has a better outcome."

"So, what do you propose we do?" she said.

"There's six of them left if my count is correct," he said, formulating his response.

"The others must have been out on a run," she replied. "Unless, of course, you're saying you took out ten of them."

"Actually, I only got two on my way out. They took out one of their own last night during a drunken brawl."

"Then the others are out on a run," she said.

"What do you mean?"

"I've been observing them this whole time," she explained. "They use the water treatment plant for a home base, probably because of the security of the sturdy concrete structure and its location just outside of town away from the red X's. From what I've seen, roughly half of them stay put and keep an eye on the bridge and their stash. They know that with the mountains to the northeast and the river dumping into the McPhee Reservoir to the west, the town of Dolores and the 145 bridge is the perfect setup to ambush people heading south."

Pausing to take another look through the crack in the doors, she continued, "The other half of the group seems to always head out and split up, heading south on Highway's 145 and west on 184. They're usually gone for a few days and then return. Sometimes with vehicles they didn't have before, and one time they—" she paused, looking away.

"One time what?" he asked, urging her to continue.

With an uncomfortable expression on her face, she said, "I saw them come back with two young women."

"Are they still there? What happened to them?" he asked.

"I don't know. I saw them go in, but never saw them come out. I feel like I should have done something."

"What could you have done alone?" he asked. "We all may want to go head on into something at some point in our lives, but that's not always the best course of action, even for those you want to help. If you get yourself killed in the process, you're no good to anyone. It's the same reason flight attendants on commercial airlines always mentioned in their safety briefing to put your own oxygen mask on first and then assist others. If you pass out, you're not good to anyone. The same is true in many situations in life. The two of us together stand a lot better chance doing something about these wretches of society than you could have done alone."

"That still doesn't make it feel any better... knowing that I just let something happen."

"I didn't say that to make you feel better. I said it so you would keep your head on straight. From this point on, everything we do, we need to do as a team and we need to act with purpose, not with raw emotion."

Changing the subject, she said, "So, what do you propose?"

"Let's hit them where they are at their weakest. Let's hit them on the road. If we hit them here, they'd stand far too great a chance of finding out where we're hunkered down. Just think about that, if they were to hit us right now, here in this cellar, what's our chances of getting out alive?"

"Slim to none," she responded.

"Exactly. On the road, however, we can pick them off without the safety of their own base of operations for them to fall back to. And if we're successful in our getaways, they won't even know we're their neighbors here in town. Then, we can just come back here and watch them squirm from a distance."

"That makes sense," she replied.

Standing up and walking over to the cellar doors, taking a look outside himself, he said, "Now, we just need to nail down what we have to work with. I'm afraid I didn't get out of there with much. Just this Glock and a knife. I don't have any extra ammo, though. I've got just what's in the magazine. They took my rifles, my pistol, and my bow."

"You can shoot a bow?" she asked.

"I've bow hunted nearly every year of my life since I was twelve years old," he replied.

"Good," she said. "Maybe you can put this to good use," she added, as she pulled back a curtain covering what used to be a shelf for vegetables. Picking up a recurve bow, she handed it to him and said, "Can you shoot one like this?"

Taking the bow and looking it over, Jessie said, "I've been using a compound bow for years now, so I'm probably a little spoiled, but yes, I can use this. Do you have arrows?"

"I found seven," she replied, holding up a leather quiver full of arrows. "Three of them look like hunting arrows, too," she said, referring to the blades on the broadheads.

"Oh, yes, these will do nicely," he replied. "Where did you come across this stuff?"

"The sporting goods store on the east side of town. It was one of the few buildings in town without the red X, so I scoped it out. The place was pretty much cleaned out. It must have been hit pretty hard by looters."

Admiring the bow, he asked, "Did you find anything else?"

"Just a big survival-type machete, a few boxes of shotgun shells—which, of course, come in handy—a few random boxes of pistol cartridges, and some fishing gear."

"What kind of pistol ammo is it?"

Reaching into one of the storage cabinets built into the wall, Ash removed a bag and placed it on the table in the center of the room. Opening the bag, she placed several boxes of ammunition on the table.

"Great," Jessie said sarcastically. "More .357 Magnum ammo for my pistol they took, just to pour salt in the wound." Picking up another box, he said, ".38 Special—that would also work in my Colt. It's the same thing, just an eighth of an inch shorter and less power. Oh, here we go," he said, anxiously opening a box of cartridges. "9mm Luger—this will work in the Glock.

Standing back, looking at the table and scanning the room, Jessie crossed his arms and supported his chin with his hand, saying, "So we only have a Glock 9mm pistol, a twelve-gauge shotgun, a bow, and some miscellaneous things like knives to work with?"

Putting her hands on her hips, Ash looked at Jessie, cocked her head to the side, and said, "Is that a problem?"

"No. Not at all," he replied. "We just have to be smart about it. Let's wait till nightfall so we can sneak out of town. Between now and then, let's pack up some provisions and work on a plan."

"Provisions?" she queried.

"Yes, provisions, as in food, water, etc."

In a perturbed voice, Ash said, "I know what provisions are. I'm just wondering why you want to pack up the food and carry it with us."

Looking at her with a serious expression, Jessie replied, "Just because we plan on coming back doesn't mean we will actually make it back. I didn't plan on being taken at the bridge and neither did you. We have to stop making assumptions and consider every move we make to be permanent from here on out."

With a look of understanding, Ash said, "I'll grab a bag. Let's get with it."

Chapter Twenty-One

Under the cover of darkness, after having watched for activity on the streets for several hours, Jessie slowly opened one of the large wooden overhead doors leading out of the home's basement cellar. The night was clear with a cool breeze gently swaying the overgrown shrubbery of the once well-kept neighborhood. An illusion of peace and serenity swept through the abandoned town of Dolores, as not a sound outside of nature could be heard.

As Jessie slipped out of the cellar, he stayed close to the house for cover, avoiding being illuminated by the bright moonlit night. Peeking around the corner of the house, scanning the parallel street for any signs of possible threats, he signaled Ash and stepped back over to the door, taking hold of a large duffle bag full of their provisions and supplies. Supporting it on his back by positioning the shoulder strap diagonally across his chest, Jessie then reached out and took the recurve bow and quiver from Ash, who then slipped out, carrying the shotgun and a smaller shoulder bag that she had filled with the extra ammunition and a few other supplies.

Closing the door behind her, she and Jessie crept around the corner of the house, where he whispered, "Okay, it's your plan. Lead the way."

Nodding in the affirmative, Ash began traveling through the neighborhood's fenced backyards, staying close to any shrubbery and trees that were available for visual cover. Working their way through the town, Jessie couldn't help but become distracted by his thoughts of what once was. The quaint, peaceful town of Dolores was now a ghost town filled with un-mowed lawns and the scattered remains of trash that was simply never collected as the surviving residents fled the sickness that had plagued their beloved town, claiming the lives of so many. All that remained of several of the homes were piles of ashes, reminding him of his own cabin. *Did someone burn these homes to erase the pain of what remained inside? Or was it simply to prevent the spread of the illness that claimed them?* he wondered to himself.

Recognizing the homes of several dear friends and acquaintances, Jessie's thoughts of sadness turned to ferocity as he thought of those who now preyed on the survivors who remained. Whether it was the attackers who killed his family back on the homestead, or the villainous bandits who captured him, stole his possessions, and killed his horse, Jessie resolved to never again allow such travesties of humanity to stand unanswered. If he had nothing left to live for, he could at least find peace in knowing he would someday die defending others.

Stopping to crouch behind a small tree, Ash whispered, "The sporting goods store is just down the street. There's no need for you to drag that big bag all the way over there. Just meet me down by the river by the boat launch in the park," she said, pointing toward the river with one hand while she handed him her bag with the other.

Nodding in reply, Jessie took both of their bags and slipped across the street, through the grounds of the Dolores City Park, and then hid alongside the river to await Ash's next move.

As he sat and watched the river flow gracefully by, reflecting the brilliance of the moonlight, Jessie remembered the times he had spent as a child fishing on this very river with his father. Having always wanted to take his own son fishing on the Dolores River to carry on the tradition, he couldn't help but feel the heartache and regret of never having had the chance. *I should've found the time,* he thought, pounding his fist into the ground. *I should've never let work stand in the way, putting off what now will never come.*

Hearing Ash approach, he wiped away a single tear and turned to see her slipping across the street with a canoe held high over her head, her shotgun dangling from its sling around her neck.

"Outstanding," he said, pleased with her find.

"I've had this idea in my head for a long time now," she said. "I knew with those scumbags guarding the main bridge, and with the 4th Street bridge having been destroyed for who knows what reason before I got here, this would be a good way to get across and around them. I grabbed a few other little things that might come in handy, too."

"Great," he said, helping her slip the canoe quietly into the water. As Jessie held the boat steady, he said, "Climb in. I'll hand you our gear."

Climbing onto the front seat of the two-person canoe, Ash reached out and took both of the bags from Jessie, placing them in the center of the canoe for stability. Detaching her paddle from the built-in storage rack, Ash pushed her paddle down into the water, contacting the river-bed below, and applied pressure, holding the canoe against the shore while Jessie climbed aboard.

"You ready?" she whispered.

"Yeah," he replied.

"Here we go," she said as she shoved them off with her oar against the bank. Now adrift with the slow and steady current, Ash began paddling off to the right side of the bow, pushing the front of the canoe downstream and gradually to the left, following a course to reach the riverbank on the south side of the river.

Jessie kept a vigilant watch of the shoreline from the rear, watching to make sure they weren't detected as they made their way out of Dolores.

Within minutes, as they reached the south side of the river, Ash steered the bow of the canoe onto the sandy shore, immediately climbing out and holding the canoe steady while Jessie stepped onto the shore as well.

"Let's carry the boat off the bank and out of sight," she whispered, pointing just over the hill.

Leaving their gear inside the boat, Ash picked up the front of the canoe while Jessie carried from the rear. Once they were over the hill and out of sight, they quickly gathered their things. Ash double-checked a compass she had retrieved from the sporting goods store, using the light of the moon, and they slipped off into the darkness of the night.

After hiking several miles through unfamiliar and rugged terrain, Ash and Jessie finally reached Highway 145, approximately three miles south of Dolores. Looking around, Jessie said, "Let's get some sleep. We need to set up a fairly solid ambush, being just the two of us. We'll be able to get a better lay of the land after sunup and make a wiser decision."

"Sounds good to me," Ash said, tossing her bag onto the ground. "Do you want first or second watch?"

"I'll take first," he replied. "Let's set up camp over behind that hill and get settled in."

~~~~

Driving north on Highway 145 in what had been an abandoned, faded green 1976 Ford E250 Econoline cargo van, three of Wolf's men were returning from their supply run, when Lou, the driver of the van, spotted something along the side of the road up ahead.

Reaching over and hitting the man in the passenger seat, Jorje, in the arm to get his attention, Lou said, "Hey. Wake up. What's that?" he asked, pointing up ahead.

Bringing his binoculars up to see, his passenger replied, "Well, hot damn. We're not coming back empty-handed after all."

"What? What is it?" Lou asked.

"There's a bitch on the side of the road up ahead. T, wake up man!" Jorje shouted to the sweaty, unkempt man in the back seat.

"What?" T asked, sitting up to see what was going on.

Simply pointing in reply, with a smile on his face, Jorje said, "Here. Check it out."

"Oh, hell, yes," T replied, with a hunger in his voice after getting a look through the binoculars.

Bringing the van to a stop just short of the woman, Lou put the transmission in park, leaving the engine running. "You two check it out," he said. "This seems too good to be true."

"Don't knock a gift," Jorje said as he exited the van, with T following along behind him. Jorje then proceeded around the front of the van, while T exited out of the side sliding door, walking around to the back of the van, putting one of them on each side of the seemingly defenseless young woman.

"Please. Please help me," the woman said. "My husband and I have been walking for days. He collapsed out there," she said, pointing toward the open brush to the west. "I don't know what's wrong with him. He refused to drink any of our water, giving it all to me," she said as she began to cry. "Please help him."

Looking to his cohort with a crooked smile, Jorje said, "Oh, yes, ma'am. We'll help your husband. How far out is he?

"He's right over that hill," she said. "Hurry, he wasn't responding at all. I'm really worried."

Turning to look at his friends with a smile, Jorje looked back at the woman and said, "Okay, just wait in the van with my friend over there and I'll go find your husband and bring him back so that we can get him some help."

"I'll go with you," she said.

"No, get in the van," he insisted.

"But my husband needs me," she protested.

With a scowl on his face, Jorje shouted, "Look bitch! Get in the damn van!"

Lou shouted from the van, "Just grab her, man. Stop playing games."

As Jorje began to walk over to the young woman with a devious smile on his face, he said, "Look, I tried to be nice, but I'm not very good at that. You're gonna get in the—"

Interrupted by the sound of the van's horn blaring, Jorje and T both turned suddenly to see Lou lying with his head against the steering wheel, with an arrow sticking half-way out of his skull, blood running profusely down the side of his neck.

Before either of them could say a word, a second arrow penetrated Jorje's side, piercing both his heart and lungs, instantaneously dropping him to the ground.

Drawing the Glock 9mm that had been hidden in her waistband, Ash, took aim at the remaining thug as he pulled a revolver from behind his back, bringing it to bear on Ash.

With a loud and ferocious scream, Jessie came running around the van from his hidden location on the other side of the road, knife in hand, distracting the man. As T turned to see Jessie bearing down on him, Jessie tackled him, driving him onto the ground.

As the two men impacted the ground, the revolver bounced out of T's hand. As the thug blocked Jessie's knife with his other hand, grasping his wrist, Jessie began to punch the man in the face repeatedly with his free hand, unleashing a fierce and primal aggression. As the stunned man's grip loosened, Jessie took the knife and sliced open his throat. With a large gasp of air followed by the grotesque sounds of the man choking on his own blood, the fight soon ended with the man they had called T lying on his back, eyes wide open, facing the morning sun.

As the man's blood pooled and began to soak into the dry ground around him, Jessie stood up, looked at Ash, and said, "Great job, Ash. You showed great restraint not firing on this scumbag when he drew on you. The sounds of a gunshot would have likely traveled to the treatment plant, alerting their friends. Damn fine acting, too."

Shocked by a level of aggression she had not expected from Jessie, who had seemed to her to be a very well-tempered man, Ash replied, "Uh, yeah. I'm just glad you got to him right away. One more second and I would have had to shoot."

As Jessie's adrenalin rush began to fade, he looked around and said, "Okay, let's gather what we can, drag the bodies off the road, and get out of here. We'll take a look at the map and see the best way to get over to 184 to see if we can intercept the others. It will be easier now with these weapons," he said as he knelt down to pick up the dead man's revolver.

Looking the gun over, he said, "Piece of crap import. Oh, well, it's a .38 and we've got ammo for that."

He then walked over to the one they called Jorje. Pulling his arrow from the man's side, he wiped off the blood and laid it to the side. "We can't be wasting arrows," he said. "That's our stealth weapon." He then searched the man, finding a Springfield Armory GI-style M1911A-1 .45ACP pistol hidden behind his back. "Score," he said. "Do you prefer the Glock there or are you a 1911 girl?"

"I'll stick with the Glock," she replied. "My husband had one, so I'm familiar enough with it."

With a nod, Jessie slid the pistol into his belt and stood up, stretching his back as he went. "Damn. I'm getting old," he said, feeling the after-effects of the intense struggle.

Walking over to the van, Ash opened the door and allowed Lou's body to fall out onto the ground, breaking the arrow that protruded from his head.

"Sorry about that," she said, reaching in to shut off the van.

"No big deal. We've got plenty."

Chapter Twenty-Two

After having driven the old Ford van down several small dirt backroads to intercept Highway 184, Jessie and Ash were parked behind a cluster of mature trees, in what was now an abandoned RV campground. The campground sat on a hill that overlooked the road to the north below. Jessie felt that the campground gave them an excellent tactical advantage for an ambush, as it was located on a position of elevation over their target, and since it was designed to accommodate and grant ease of access to large recreational vehicles with a road leading in and a road leading out, they were not boxed in by one entry point, should they need to escape.

From their vantage point on the hill, they could clearly see Highway 184 from a distance, keeping an eye out for signs of the other members of Wolf's gang.

Leaning back against a large shade tree, sitting on the ground in one of the campsites while admiring and inspecting the rifles found inside the van, Jessie huffed under his breath.

"What?" Ash asked.

"Wolf," Jessie said with a chuckle. "What kind of name is that anyway? Probably some sad attempt at looking tough to hide the insecurities of a battered childhood and failed adulthood or something."

"Wolf?" Ash queried.

"Oh, that's what they call the older guy with the mostly gray beard."

With a scoff, Ash replied, "I guess I haven't gotten to know them quite like you. I've been keeping my distance. My run-in with them was brief."

"Well, you didn't miss anything. Or rather, you missed a lot, I guess. I don't imagine you would have enjoyed your stay."

Glancing over at the van, Jessie said, "You know… it's funny."

"What's funny?" she asked, confused by Jessie's statement.

"In all of the post-apocalyptic movies, like Mad Max, for example, people are always running around in old vehicles they patch together, siphoning gas from other cars to keep going, but in reality, they really wouldn't last that long."

"What do you mean?"

"Well, first off," he said, standing to join her as she stared intently at the road, "the gas would go bad after a while without some sort of stabilizer being added to it. Fuel you find in a storage location may have been treated, but no one puts that in the vehicle they're driving, so if you find an abandoned car on the side of the road, it was almost certainly not treated. Also, since the government mandated the use of ethanol in pump gas, fuel that sits in a ventilated tank too long will collect moisture from the air at a much higher rate than straight gasoline. I bought an old beater truck once that had been sitting for a year. It started up and ran fine, but on my way home, the fuel-pickup screen became completely clogged with rust particles and it left me stranded on the side of the road. The tank was so rusted on the inside from all of the moisture, the fuel came out looking like milk mixed with rust."

Stopping to swat at a mosquito, he continued, "Not to mention the fact that the tires, belts, hoses, and non-lubricated and protected seals would all dry rot, leading to all sorts of mechanical failures. Yeah, for the first few years the plunder would be good, but after a while, people would find themselves back on horseback. I suppose the same future will befall us if the world doesn't somehow get straightened out."

After a brief pause to look around, Jessie gathered his thoughts and said, "And to tell you the truth. I think I'd like it that way. Without the advantages of machinery, the bad men among us would have a harder time imposing their will."

"I don't look forward to a world without medicine, though," Ash added. "Sure, the frontiersman way of life had a certain romance to it, but without things like modern medicine a lot of people simply won't make it."

"Yeah," he said, taking a deep breath. "I guess you're right." Changing the subject, Jessie said, "So anyway, come over here and I'll give you the low-down on our weapons score."

Joining Jessie, she said, "That's an AK47, right?"

"Almost right," he replied. "Well, for all practical purposes you're right. It's an AKM. Basically an early update from the original 1947 design. Most people still call anything that even remotely resembles an AK an AK47, though. Anyway, here's how it works," he said as he began to give her a run-down on the rifle's basic function and operation.

"It's no sniper rifle, but it will eat any crap ammo you feed it, as long as it's the right size, of course, and will run well even if it's dirty and abused. That's why it has been so popular around the world, especially with the groups that had less than perfect supply chains and training programs."

Checking to ensure that the weapon was unloaded and clear, Jessie handed it to Ash, saying, "Here ya go, run through the basics of what I just showed you. Get the feel of everything. Don't be easy on it, either. You can't break it with your bare hands. If you're gonna cycle it, cycle it hard. Don't half-do things when it comes to a gunfight."

Taking the rifle and holding it up to her shoulder, she said, "It fits me nice."

"Yeah, it was designed to fit a malnourished third-world conscripted soldier," he replied. "It's short and small. By the way, what's your experience with rifles?"

"My husband and I used to go shooting a lot. He had several hunting rifles. He didn't have anything like this. He was mostly just a hunter and not a recreational shooter. But I always went to the range with him. To be honest, I was a pretty damn good shot," she said with a smile. "Often times better than him."

Returning the smile, Jessie laughed and said, "That's usually the case. Women are naturals." Noticing the large man's watch dangling loosely from her wrist as she held the rifle, Jessie asked, "Where did you find that? It doesn't seem to fit. You might want to put that in your pocket or something so it doesn't clank around if you're trying to be stealthy in a sticky situation."

"It was my husband's," she replied with a somber demeanor. "It's all I have left of him."

"Oh, I'm sorry," Jessie replied softy.

Picking up the other rifle that he had found in the truck, Jessie said, "This is an FAL. It has substantially more power than the AK. They both shoot a 7.62mm projectile, but this one has nearly double the case capacity. Hence, its cartridge is called the 7.62x51 NATO or .308 Winchester."

"Case capacity?" she asked.

"Yeah. As in room for more gunpowder in the cartridge case. It basically has more power and a lot more kick. It's better at long ranges, but up close and personal, it's hard to beat that AK there," he said pointing to the weapon in her hands. "The 7.62x39 Russian that it fires has adequate knock-down power and the recoil is manageable enough to be friendly to well-placed rapid-fire shots."

"So what's the plan?" she asked.

"I've been thinking about that," he replied, leaning the FAL against the tree. "Not knowing exactly when the other group will come through, or if we've even already missed them, it's hard to put anything together. The only place we can really nail something down is back at the water treatment plant. We know where they are there. We were lucky with our first ambush, but we need to step it up a notch and we can't keep risking you as bait."

"Don't you worry about me. I can handle myself," she quickly replied.

"Oh, I know you can," he said while rubbing his head and smiling. "I can still feel the beating you gave me when we first met."

"If that's the role I need to play, I'll play it. I want to get these filthy monsters. They took everything from me," she insisted.

"Yeah, I know. But we stand a much better chance taking them all out if we don't do something reckless that will get one or both of us killed too early in the fight."

"So, again, what's the plan?" she asked impatiently.

"These guys see themselves as the predators, and everyone else is the prey. A wolf pack operates in an offensive manner. They don't really set up much of a security strategy around their own den because, well, they're at the top of the food chain. The deer, elk, and everything else don't plan many counterstrikes. These guys seem to think the same way. Just look at how those dirt-bags handled the situation where they thought you were a poor defenseless woman there for the taking. They thought they would take you easily, and they died because of that miscalculation."

Interrupted by the sounds of vehicles approaching in the distance from the west, Jessie and Ash both ducked behind the trees and quietly watched the dust trail that kicked up as the vehicles approached. Looking through the binoculars recovered from the van, Jessie said, "Looks like their friends to me. One of them found himself a Harley. What a moron," he said.

"Why does that make him a moron?" she asked.

"It's hard to defend yourself when you need both hands to ride," he replied. "I bet he feels cool, though—the wannabe outlaw biker that he is and all."

Picking up the AKM, Ash said, "So, I guess this is it," as she rocked a loaded thirty-round magazine into place, and cycled the action, chambering a round.

"No, wait," he replied.

"What? Why? We've got the element of surprise," she said.

Jessie then explained, "When I was being held by them, one of the things I noticed was a complete lack of discipline. They got drunk and partied all night. Their security was lacking, to say the least. All these guys have going for them is pure ruthlessness and a desire to commit violence on others. Unfortunately, that's all it takes to get by for many in a situation like this. He who acts first and with enough aggression often wins. Anyway, if these guys bring back supplies, they'll all no doubt live it up again, feasting on their new ill-gotten gains. Let's let them make it back. And then tonight, when the night is winding down for them and they're either drunk or tired, we'll slip into their den and show them what it's like to be the prey instead of the predator. Besides, one group not making it back on time is one thing, but if neither group makes it back, it may signal to the others at the treatment plant that something is afoot, causing them to be more on-guard than usual. If we want to get all of them, we need to keep them believing they're at the top of the food chain."

Pausing to watch the group drive by, an old Dodge pickup truck following along behind the Harley, Jessie counted five men total, two in the cab, two in the truck's bed, and one on the motorcycle.

"Looks like they've got a truckload of booty," he said, noting the boxes and bags in the back of the truck. "Ah, hell," he said in a defeated tone.

"What. What is it?"

"They've got a girl with them."

"What? A girl?"

"Yeah, looks like a young girl is hogtied between the men in the cab. Those two guys in the bed of the truck also have rifles in their hands. They could return fire pretty quickly if need be."

"We've got to do something!" Ash said in an anxious voice. "You know good and well what is gonna happen to that girl when they get her back there. There is no damn way I can allow that to happen."

"No!" Jessie replied forcefully. "We'll wait until tonight and strike them when and where they least expect it."

"But—" she said, attempting to interrupt.

"Listen, we can't fire on the men in the cab of the truck. She's sitting right next to them. There is no way we could get them separated from her while fighting off the others. We have to be smart about this. We won't leave her with them. I promise."

As the men passed them by and headed in the direction of the treatment plant, Jessie said, "Let's take only what we need. The rest we can come back for when it's all over. We need to travel quietly and light. That dust cloud they are kicking up on the road could be spotted from too far away, and if we drive there, we'll give away our position in the same way. No, let's get some rest and hike back to the treatment plant under the cover of darkness. Then, when the opportunity presents itself, we'll turn the tables on them."

Chapter Twenty-Three

Hiding in the darkness of the night, alongside one of the stagnant and foul wastewater treatment tanks, Jessie pointed and whispered, "You see that smoke?"

Squinting to see, Ash replied, "Yeah, I think I can make it out." As a cloud drifted beyond the moon, allowing its light to once again shine on the main building of the water treatment facility, she said, "Oh. Okay. I see it now."

"That's coming from a basement level. That's where they held me."

"Do you think that's where they have the girl, too?"

"That's hard to say. But the way they act, they probably wouldn't seek privacy to do what they'll no doubt all want to do."

Feeling sick to her stomach at the thought, Ash said, "So, now what?" Continuing to explain, Jessie said, "They build a fire down on the lower level where the floor is all concrete, and open that window to vent the smoke out of the building. We can use that to our advantage."

"What do you propose?" she asked.

"Well, if they stick with their routine, that fire is their heat and light source for their late night shenanigans." Looking back up at the moon, he continued, "It looks like things are clouding up. Without the moonlight to expose us, we should be able to sneak up pretty close to the window by the fire. It's guaranteed to be open because they'd smoke themselves out without it. Hopefully, they'll be half drunk, but even if they're not, their eyes will be adjusted to the fire and they won't be able to see into the darkness very well."

Ash nodded, showing her understanding as Jessie continued, "If you follow that wall toward the river, there will be two more windows, however, both were closed when I was there. The one in the very corner of the basement, the furthest one down, is in a pretty dark corner. Most of the men will be positioned around the fire. I'll create a diversion and start hitting them from the open window, causing them to disperse. I'll then enter the main basement room through one of the windows and engage them head on. While their attention is on that area, you slip in through the door facing the river. If any of them try to flee the basement they'll either do it through the hallway leading to that door or they will head upstairs and into the upper level."

"What about the girl?"

"I'm getting to that," he said. "Work your way through that hallway, which should be dark as it has no source of light that I know of, and try to find the girl. If you find her, get the hell out of there with her. Go to the river and run downstream on the riverbank. I'll join back up with you down by the reservoir if I can. Find a place to hide, and if you don't see me by sunrise, get the hell out of here and never look back. If you don't find her in any of the rooms adjacent to the hallway, just keep pressing forward and we'll eventually meet up in the main room where they have the fire. If we meet up there and haven't found her yet, we'll regroup and go with what we have in front of us."

"Sounds good," she said with a tremble in her voice.

"Are you okay?" Jessie asked.

"Yeah. I'm fine. I've just been waiting to face these monsters for so long. Hiding out in that basement all this time I've wondered what I would do when I was finally able to confront them. And now that the opportunity is here...well, it just doesn't seem real to me yet."

"It will soon enough," he remarked. "Now, remember, if we don't link back up and you don't see me by morning, get the hell out of the area and never look back. You know where the van is. Take it and get yourselves as far from here as you can."

"Be careful," she said, giving him a hug and a kiss on the cheek, before slipping off into the darkness.

Looking up at the sky, Jessie watched a mass of clouds move in front of the moon, darkening the night sky. Taking a deep breath, he said aloud to himself, "Well, here we go."

~~~~

Slipping silently down the hillside, working her way around to the side entrance of the basement, Ash made her way to the old concrete building. Being in a shadow of the moonlight, she enjoyed the benefit of the cover of darkness, even when the moonlight occasionally reached beyond the clouds.

Her heart was racing with thoughts of what she was about to do rushing through her mind. She had dreamed of the opportunity to strike back at this terrible gang ever since they stole her husband from her. Although she had helped Jessie kill the three men in the van, she had yet to inflict a deathblow on another human being herself. She knew she had it in her; she only hoped she would not hesitate when the time finally came.

With her back against the concrete exterior wall, facing the river, she could feel the familiar light breeze blow through her hair. Looking down at the river, which occasionally reflected the light of the moon, she thought to herself, *This must have been such a beautiful and peaceful place to live, before—.*

Her thoughts were interrupted by a thump immediately on the other side of the door next to her. Startled, she gripped her AKM rifle tightly, holding it against her chest. Releasing the pistol grip with her right hand, she slowly pressed the safety lever down to the fire position. As the thin, stamped, sheet metal lever clicked into the detent on the receiver, making the slightest metallic sound, she paused and listened, hoping someone on the other side of the door didn't hear the click as well.

~~~~

Using the cover of darkness while the moon was hidden behind the clouds, Jessie crept over to the open basement window. With his back to the wall to conceal his silhouette as best he could, should the moon's light return, Jessie quietly placed his bag on the ground and opened the main flap. As he listened intently to the muffled voices inside the building, he painted a picture of the scene in his head, using his memories of the night he escaped.

Okay, you filthy degenerates, here we go! he thought as he retrieved a plastic water bottle from the bag. Removing the cap, Jessie took a sniff of the contents and smiled. *You might not be getting your van back, boys, but I'll be nice enough to give you some of its fuel back,* he thought as he tossed the bottle through the window toward the fire.

Almost instantly, with a loud *whoosh,* the fire rapidly expanded, burning the volatile contents of the bottle, causing a flash of hot flames that engulfed several of the men sitting around the fire. Two of the men, consumed by the burning flames, began running away from the fire, screaming as the others began to try to figure out what had just happened, while reaching for their weapons.

Taking advantage of the chaos, Jessie tossed a second and a third bottle into the flames, expanding the fire's reach, pushing the men away from the fire. Aiming into the flames, Jessie began firing his FAL into the room in the direction of the men, although he was unable to get a good sight-picture because of the blinding light of the massive flames. At that moment, however, he knew he needed to keep the pressure on them regardless as to whether he made any direct hits, so that Ash could make her entry into the basement undetected.

With the men in the basement blindly returning fire on his position, bullets ricocheting off the concrete windowsill, Jessie tossed his final gasoline bottle into the room and then immediately ran along the outside wall to the window in the far corner of the room. He swung it open, and jumped feet first onto the basement floor below. With the men still focused on the window by the fire, Jessie took aim, firing a well-placed shot that struck one of the men firing on his previous position squarely in the back, dropping him face first into the fire.

As the man's body began to sizzle on the hot coals, Jessie quickly acquired his next target. With two men remaining in the room, Jessie fired, striking a large, longhaired man directly in the abdomen, while the other returned fire with an AR-15, narrowly missing Jessie's head. Rounds glancing off the concrete wall beside him sent concrete fragments bouncing off the side of Jessie's face.

Quickly firing another shot, Jessie took down the shooter with a shot to the throat, nearly beheading the man with the powerful one-hundred-and-sixty-eight-grain projectile, severing his spine, with a mist of blood splattering on the wall behind him.

Looking back to his left, Jessie saw the man with the abdominal wound still alive and struggling to reach his weapon. With a quick follow-up shot, Jessie ended the man's suffering and removed him as a threat.

As Jessie watched the dead man's face hit the floor, he caught movement out of the corner of his eye, on the stairs leading to the upper floor of the facility. Quickly turning to his right to face the threat, his pulse raced as he thought to himself, *Wolf!* Seeing the group's vicious leader on the stairs aiming an AK at him, Jessie dove to his left while firing several shots in the direction of the stairs in an attempt at interrupting Wolf's chance at making a good shot.

With several rapid muzzle flashes coming from Wolf's rifle, the room seemed to go silent as Jessie dove to the floor. Squeezing off several more shots of his own while in midair, Jessie saw his rounds impact the wall directly behind Wolf, forcing him to turn and flee up the stairs.

Slamming down onto the cold hard concrete floor, Jessie regrouped, checked his rifle, and said, "Oh, no, you don't, you dirty son of a bitch. You're not getting away from me that easy."

~~~~

As the silence of the night was broken by Jessie's assault on the main basement chamber, Ash heard several loud male voices inside the hallway. Quickly opening the door to see one of the men running away from her and toward Jessie's attack, Ash sent two rapid-fire shots into his back, dropping him forward, smashing his face on the floor, dead on contact.

Before she could scan the area for additional threats, a hand grabbed the barrel of her rifle as a large man slammed her into the wall, forcing the center of her rifle against her neck as he took hold of the stock as well. Unable to breathe, Ash struggled as the man lifted her off of the floor, pushing her up with her back to the wall.

Staring down at the man in the dark hallway, she could barely make out who he was. All she could tell was that the man reeked of alcohol and sweat and was missing several teeth, with the few that remained full of rot and decay. As the man pushed her harder and harder against the wall, he said, "If only you could have gotten here sooner, we could have had a real party then."

Fading quickly from being unable draw her breath under the crushing force of the rifle, Ash released her grip on the gun and desperately reached into her waistband, pulling her knife from its sheath and thrusting it into the man's stomach.

Seeing the look of fear in his eyes, the man maintained his pressure on the rifle as if frozen in place. With a side-slashing motion, Ash felt the wet warmth of the man's entrails as they spilled out onto the floor before her, forced out by the contraction of his own muscles as he struggled to strangle her.

Releasing his grip on the rifle, he dropped to his knees as Ash dropped to the floor, landing on her feet and momentarily dropping to her knees. Still alive and almost in a daze, the man held his own guts in his blood-covered hands. He slowly looked up at her, only to see the butt of her rifle come smashing down on his face, and then—darkness.

The man now lying before her on the floor in a bloody mess, Ash wiped her hands free of his blood and looked up through the open door from which he had come. With several candles lighting the room, she slowly entered with her rifle at the ready, hearing only whimpers of fear.

Rounding the corner, her rifle aimed at the sound, Ash saw a half-dressed, petite, young, blonde-haired girl shivering with fear in the corner. Thinking that the girl couldn't be more than fifteen years old and obviously the victim of terrible abuse at the hands of the gang, Ash slung her rifle over her shoulder and whispered, "Shhhhh, it's okay. We're gonna get you out of here now."

Unable to speak, the young girl's eyes filled with tears as her emotions overwhelmed her.

"Do you have any clothes?" Ash quietly asked, noticing that the girl was naked from the waist down. Looking around the room, Ash saw a pair of blood-stained pants on the floor, quickly picked them up, and took them over to the girl, saying, "Quick, put these on. We need to get out of here."

Nodding yes, the emotional and terrified young girl took Ash's hand, stood up, and slipped her legs one at a time into her jeans.

"Shoes? Do you have shoes?" Ash asked.

Shaking her head no in response, Ash said, "It's okay. We can worry about that later. Can you walk?"

Nodding yes, Ash took the girl's hand and said, "Hold on to me," as she brought her rifle back to the low ready and led the girl into the dark, blood-filled hallway.

After ensuring that the path was seemingly devoid of any new threats, Ash led the young girl into the hallway and over the dead man's body. Tired and weak, the young girl's bare feet slipped in the dead man's blood, causing her to nearly fall to the floor.

Catching her by the arm, Ash said, "Quick, this way," as she led her out the side door.

Looking up into the sky, the moon now free of the clouds and shining brightly, Ash looked around and whispered, "Screw it. We've got to make a run for the riverbank. Let's go!"

Pulling on the girl's hand, the two started to run for the river. Stepping on something sharp with her bare foot, the young girl winced in pain, slowed to a walk and began limping severely.

Wasting no time, Ash knelt down before the girl and said, "Climb on. I've got you."

Running toward the river with the girl on her back, Ash's rifle dangled awkwardly in front of her on the sling around her neck, bouncing off her knees as she ran. Once over the edge of the riverbank, taking cover out of the line of sight of the facility, Ash dropped to her knees, placed her hand on her rifle, and just watched, looking and listening for any signs of movement.

Still hearing gunfire coming from within the building, she said, "Good, he's still in the fight." Turning her head to look back at the girl still perched on her back, Ash said, "Okay, let's get going. He's going to meet up with us at the reservoir."

Speaking her first word to Ash, the young girl nervously muttered, "Who?"

"My, I mean, *our*, friend. His name is Jessie. He's fighting off the bad men that took you. He's going to catch up with us at the reservoir. From there, we'll figure out where to go next, but I promise you, it'll be far from here."

Chapter Twenty-Four

Running up the stairs in pursuit of Wolf, Jessie held his rifle at the high ready, preparing to fire at the sign of even the slightest movement. Reaching the upper floor, Jessie scanned the immediate area, seeing office chairs and furniture scattered about, as well as signs that some of the men had been using the area as their makeshift sleeping quarters. Dirty blankets and empty beer cans were strewn about, as well as a pile of discarded prescription drug bottles and hypodermic needles.

Hearing an office chair bump into a desk on the far side of the room, Jessie turned to see Wolf taking aim, followed by a click. With an enraged facial expression, Wolf rotated the gun sideways to look at the rifle's action, realizing that his weapon had suffered a failed-to-extract malfunction.

Bringing his FAL to bear, taking aim at Wolf, Jessie began to squeeze the trigger as a flash of light came into view in the corner of his eye, followed by the feeling of a thud and a deep burning sensation in his shoulder. Staggering and stumbling backward, Jessie saw Wolf running out the door on the far side of the room as another man rushed toward him, pistol in hand.

Falling backward into a desk and weakened by his injury, Jessie lost his grip on his FAL, dropping the rifle to the ground. With his attacker rapidly approaching, Jessie saw another flash of light followed by the loud muzzle report of a long-barreled revolver, as a bullet whizzed by his head.

Knowing that he must put distance between himself and the other man while he assessed his own injuries, Jessie turned to run while simultaneously drawing his M1911A1 .45 caliber pistol, firing several shots blindly in the man's direction. With his poorly aimed shots slowing the man's advances, Jessie made a break for the door.

Running out of the east-facing door of the upper level, Jessie saw the residential area of Dolores just a few hundred yards ahead. With focused determination, he ran as hard as he could up Railroad Avenue, ignoring the intense pain in his shoulder.

Hearing the pop of several more shots behind him, Jessie knew his pursuer was still in the fight. Reaching 1st Street, Jessie turned left, putting several houses between himself and the shooter. He then jogged right, cutting through an abandoned home's backyard. Hopping over the short picket fence on the other side of the yard, he then turned right onto 2nd Street, running back across Railroad Avenue and into the neighborhood on the south side of town in an attempt to throw his pursuers off of his trail.

Ducking left into an overgrown yard out of a desperate need to stop and treat his wound, Jessie knew he couldn't keep pushing all the way to the supply-filled basement where Ash had gotten by all that time. Hesitating momentarily, Jessie entered the back door of an old two-story house marked with the infamous red X painted on the front. Upon entering the home, Jessie pulled his shirt up and over his nose and mouth in an attempt to filter the potentially contaminated air. Jessie could smell an odd smell as he crept through the house. He knew it must have been a long time since anyone had died here, but was still uneasy due to his self-admitted ignorance of the sickness that had previously swept through the town.

With his pistol in his right hand and his left applying pressure to the wound on his left shoulder, Jessie carefully walked through the kitchen and into the living room of the home. With the curtains tied open, there was just enough light from the moon shining through the windows to guide his way.

Noticing the manner in which personal items and children's toys were left out-and-about around the house, it appeared to Jessie that no one had simply packed up and left. It was as if life in the home had simply frozen in its tracks. There were even several pairs of shoes on the floor and jackets on the coat hook by the front door.

Walking over to the front door, peeking outside through the small decorative glass windows going down the center of the door, Jessie didn't see any signs of activity out front or on the street. As he turned around, he couldn't help but see a pair of car keys and a woman's purse hanging from the decorative key hook. The key hook resembled an elementary school arts-and-crafts project, and appeared to spell out what he assumed were the initials of the home's occupants. *Nobody got out of here,* Jessie thought as an eerie feeling swept through his body.

Damn, this hurts, he thought to himself as he lifted his hand to look at his wound underneath. *I've got to get this properly dressed.*

Looking to the other side of the large living room, Jessie saw what appeared to be a bathroom. Entering the bathroom, Jessie went straight for the medicine cabinet above the sink in an effort to find supplies that he might use to treat his wound. Feeling around in the darkness to find his way, Jessie thought to himself, *damn it!* as he could find only aspirin and a box of small, finger-sized, peel-and-stick bandages.

Taking a deep breath, Jessie knew the best hope he had for finding medical supplies would be in the couple's main bathroom, probably co-located with their bedroom, which he assumed to be upstairs. Fearing what he might find, Jessie shrugged it off and proceeded quietly up the steps with his .45 at the low ready in his right hand.

Jessie found the upstairs to be much darker than the main floor below. The curtains on the windows had remained shut, preventing the moonlight from guiding his way. Bumping into a small decorative table at the end of the hallway at the top of the stairs, Jessie found several half-burned candles and a large box of matches.

Of course, he thought. *Surely the power had been out for some time before whatever happened to the people who lived here took place.*

Fumbling around in the dark with the box of matches, after several attempts at holding the box steady against the desk with his knee and striking the matches with his only free hand, one of the matches finally sizzled to life. The burning match illuminated the candle, which Jessie quickly lit, bringing a faint, flickering light to the hallway.

Picking up his .45 and sliding it into his waistband, Jessie took the candle with his right hand and continued to work his way slowly down the hall. Reaching the first bedroom door on the right, Jessie knelt down and placed the candle on the floor to free up his right hand. He then turned the knob slowly, with the door creaking ominously as it opened. Picking up the candle with his free hand and nudging the door open with his elbow, Jessie was horrified to see a child's bed. Lying on top of the bed, covered completely by the bed's sheets, was what appeared to be the small body of a deceased child. Jessie guessed that the child must have been no more than six or seven years old when he or she died.

Feeling his stomach twist into knots from the emotional scene, Jessie realized that the curtains for the window directly in front of him were drawn back, potentially giving away his position as the bright candle would be easily seen from the street. Ducking back into the hallway, Jessie continued down the hall, this time going to the room on the end. *This is more than likely Mom and Dad's room,* he thought.

Repeating his process of placing the candle on the floor so that he could open the door with his only free hand, Jessie nudged the door open to find yet another bed. This time, however, the bed contained an adult-sized body underneath the covers. *The entire family must have gotten sick,* he thought. Taking a step into the room after ascertaining that the curtains were closed to prevent exposure of the candlelight, Jessie began to look for an *en-suite* bathroom where the parents may have kept their medical supplies.

Several steps into the room, Jessie nudged something in the floor with his left foot. His heart skipping a beat, he held the candle lower to find the decayed corpse of a man lying face down on the floor, on top of what appeared to be old, dry blood stains on the carpet beneath him.

With a small entry hole and a large exit hole in the man's skull, Jessie looked around on the floor to find a Smith and Wesson revolver lying just out of reach of the man's hand, as if it had slid across the floor on impact.

I guess Dad just couldn't deal with it, Jessie thought. Reflecting back to his own loss, Jessie understood the pain the man had gone through and knew that he had narrowly avoided such a self-inflicted fate.

As he entered the master bathroom, Jessie opened the bathroom closet to find washcloths and towels, as well as assorted hair and skin-care items on the shelves. Seeing a box of gauze bandages in the back of the closet, Jessie reached inside to retrieve them, when all of a sudden he was slammed against the wall by a full speed tackle. Dropping the candle inside the closet during the impact, Jessie found himself lying on the floor being repeatedly punched by one of the men from Wolf's gang.

As the man beat Jessie mercilessly while shouting expletives, Jessie struggled to block the blows, with little success. Giving up on his defensive blocks, Jessie reached into his waistband and gripped his .45 pistol, clicked off the thumb safety, and brought it to bear against the man. His attacker then immediately grabbed Jessie's arm as the weapon discharged. Narrowly missing the man's side, Jessie tried to shoot a second time to no avail. *Jam!* he thought, realizing that his awkward one-handed shooting position must have led to a limp-wrist-induced failure of the weapon to properly cycle another round into the chamber.

As the man struggled with Jessie for control of the pistol, he found Jessie's wound and shoved his thumb forcefully inside, underneath Jessie's collar bone, where the bullet was lodged. With excruciating pain surging through Jessie's body, he let out a tremendous scream as he remembered his knife.

Pulling his knife from his belt, he slashed at the man, severely cutting into his arm and side, causing the man to release his grip on Jessie and fall backward, retreating from the blade, giving Jessie the opportunity to get some distance between himself and the threat.

As he struggled to his feet, Jessie turned to see that the closet was now engulfed in flames, with the fire quickly spreading. His injured attacker now standing back on his feet, illuminated by the fire that was quickly growing out of control behind Jessie, reached around his back and drew an old revolver from behind him. The man began slowly cocking the hammer as he slowly took steps toward Jessie, backing him toward the far side of the room.

"My Colt," Jessie murmured to himself, recognizing the man's weapon. "Hey, you were on the bridge that day, weren't you?"

"I guess we should have killed you right then and there," the man said as he continued his slow advance toward Jessie. "You've caused us a lot of trouble and I'm gonna make sure you burn for it," he said with a crooked smile as he glanced past Jessie's shoulder to the growing fire behind him.

The fire now covering the wall behind the man, Jessie could see that his escape options were quickly becoming limited. As the man raised the pistol up, pointing it at Jessie's head, Jessie tripped and fell backward onto the floor as the Colt discharged. The flash and muzzle report stunned Jessie with its shockwave as the bullet barely missed his head.

Landing on top of the deceased father's remains, Jessie quickly reached for the Smith & Wesson revolver, raised it to the man's stomach, and fired the remaining five shots in the cylinder.

The small .38 revolver, not having the knock-down power to take the attacker off his feet, caused the man to stumble and fall toward Jessie, continuing with the momentum of his advance. Jessie felt the weight of the man as he collapsed on top of him, pinning him to the floor.

Injured and disoriented from the struggle, Jessie strained to work his way loose from both the decomposed corpse beneath him and his now dead attacker on top of him. Finally breaking free as the room became completely engulfed in flames, Jessie retrieved his Colt revolver from the assailant and ran for the window, crashing through the glass.

As Jessie made the blind leap to escape the fire, he fell onto the roof over the front porch below and rolled off, freefalling to the cold hard ground below.

Chapter Twenty-Five

As the morning's sun came up over the eastern horizon, Ash and the young girl who she now knew to be named Lillian, waited patiently at the reservoir for Jessie's return.

Looking toward town, Ash could see smoke rising in the distance. A feeling of uncertainty and dread came over her that she hadn't felt in quite some time. After her husband was killed, Ash had felt cold and emotionless, but now that Jessie had stumbled into her life, she had once again began to feel for other people. She had been so consumed by the desire to exact revenge on those who had taken everything from her, she had forgotten what it felt like to be truly alive—until this very moment.

"Do you think he will come?" Lillian asked, sitting concealed in the trees along the bank of the reservoir.

Turning to Lillian, Ash answered confidently, "He'll be back. I know he will."

"Was he your husband?"

Caught off guard by the question, Ash quickly answered, "No. No, he wasn't," as she felt for the watch on her wrist, which to her horror, she realized was gone. "Damn it!" she shouted.

Feeling that she had touched a nerve, Lillian said, "I'm sorry. I guess that's none of my business."

"No, I'm sorry. I didn't mean to be short. My watch—it was special to me—I must have lost it last night. I just... I'm just worried about him, is all. But no, he isn't my husband. I was traveling with my husband and some others when the men at the bridge, the same ones that held you, attacked us. They killed the others, but I got away. My husband fought to the death to give me a chance to escape. It was his watch. It was all I had left of him," she said as she wiped a tear from her eye.

Regaining her composure, Ash said, "After that, I found myself living in the basement under one of the houses in

Dolores. I had almost lost track of time, thinking of nothing but how I could take my revenge against those killers, even if I had to die doing it. I didn't want to live anymore, I mean, I had nothing to live for, anyway. And then along came Jessie," she said with a smile.

"How did the two of you meet?" Lillian asked.

"His family was killed in a similar manner. They lived on a homestead way up in the mountains where they thought they would be sheltered from the world. Which they were, for a while. Eventually, evil will find you, and when it does, you've got to be ready to face it head on, with no reservations. I know that now, and so does Jessie. We both look back on things and wish we had handled them differently along the way. We both have that in common, I guess."

"Anyway," Ash continued. "He was on his way to find his sister when the very same group of men took him. They held him prisoner in an attempt to find out if others were following. He somehow managed to get away from them, which is when we met. I nearly killed him," she said with a chuckle. "I thought he was one of them at first."

Ash then turned to Lillian, and said, "You don't have to answer. I know it can be hard to talk about things, but... what happened? How did you end up with them?"

Taking a moment to gather her thoughts and compress her emotions, Lillian explained, "My father disappeared early on, when things started to get bad. One day, he went out looking for food and water for us, and just never came home. He and my mother weren't getting along very well, even when times were good, so I don't know if he saw it as an opportunity and just left, or if something happened. I try to convince myself that he left us because of my mother. That way I can keep a glimmer of hope that he is still out there somewhere and that someday, maybe I can find him again."

"My mother—well—she was a piece of work, to put it nicely," Lillian said with a rather sharp tone, "She would shack up with any man who seemed to be able to feed us for a little while or protect us. Then one day, one of them had eyes for me, and she didn't do anything to stop him," Lillian said, pausing to deal with her thoughts.

"So, anyway," she continued, "after that, I packed a few of my things and left. She didn't even try to stop me. I guess she figured it would be easier to feed herself than to have to worry about us both. It wasn't long after that that I met up with a really nice family that took me in. They were a mother, father, and son who were traveling from California to some family ranch of theirs here in Colorado. I don't know exactly where it was; they just kept telling me that we were almost there. Then one day we were jumped by a group of men in a roadside attack. They killed Frank, the father, and their son, Bradley. They raped Helen over and over again. It was horrible. I could hear her scream for hours on end until her cries were finally stopped by the sound of a single gunshot. I was afraid the same thing would happen to me next, but they told me they had to save me for the rest of their group, which is how I ended up here. They gave me to the rest of the group as a gift," she said in disgust as tears began to roll down her face.

Sitting down next to Lillian, Ash put her arm around her and said, "You've been through a lot. I'm so sorry. I don't know how the world ever got to this point. We just seemed to be spinning out of control for so long. Everywhere you looked in the world it seemed like some new bad thing was happening every day. It was truly like watching a bad reality show being filmed before your eyes. Some people seemed to have blinders on, just assuming it would all eventually get better, while others seemed motivated to help the decline continue. Others, if they were skeptical of what was going on, were labeled with whatever politically correct derogatory moniker for non-conformists was popular that day. Then all of a sudden when we were at our weakest, the attacks came and the house of cards that our world had become came crashing down. The violence, the killing, the sickness, the terror, it was awful. And then the hunger and suffering that followed," Ash said, pausing to look away for a moment.

"There have been many days that I wished I would have died early on like so many others," Ash continued. "I often told myself they were the lucky ones. But now, every time I meet someone like you or Jessie, I'm reminded that I'm actually fortunate to have made it. The fact that you and I both are still here, after all we've seen and suffered through, shows me that there is still hope for this world yet."

For the next few hours, Lillian and Ash sat silently, reflecting on the events of the recent past, while watching the birds on the bank of the reservoir in search of their next meal. Remembering what Jessie had said about moving on if he wasn't there before sunrise, Ash said, "Wait right here. I'm gonna walk up to the top of the hill to see if I can get a better look. He really should be here at any time," she said, forcing a positive outlook into her words.

Replying with only a reassuring smile, Lillian tossed a pebble into the water to watch the birds chase it as if it was something for them to eat.

Walking through the trees to the top of the hill with her rifle slung over her back, Ash took a hidden position behind a cluster of wild shrubbery and scanned the area for any signs of Jessie. "Come on, Jessie. Where are you?" she whispered to herself.

After about ten minutes and no luck, Ash resigned herself to the fact that the odds were she would have to do as Jessie had insisted and take Lillian, leaving the area, never to come back.

Walking back down the hill to where she had left Lillian, Ash pushed a tree branch out of the way and said, "We'll give him a little more time. He should be here any minute—"

Interrupted by a man's deep and raspy voice, she looked up to see Wolf, standing there with a knife to Lillian's throat. "I don't think he's gonna make it, darlin'," he said with a devilish smile.

Ash's heart sank in her chest as she realized that if Wolf had found them, then Jessie must have been killed, and now she and Lillian could face the same fate—or worse. Bringing her AKM into position, Ash aimed the rifle at Wolf and said, "Drop the knife or I'll drop you where you stand!"

Stepping behind Lillian for cover, Wolf laughed a demented laugh and said, "Go ahead... shoot me. But ask yourself if you can live with yourself if you hit this pretty little thing by accident. Besides, if you shoot me, this blade is tight against her throat. If I fall, she'll hit the ground with me. You can be rest assured of that. Just imagine the pain she'll feel. The burning sensation as this old blade slices through her pretty, little neck. You'll watch her die a slow and miserable death, and it will be by your own hand," he said, smiling to expose his rotting teeth. "Now, you nasty little bitch, put the gun down and maybe, just maybe, I'll let you both live after I'm done with you."

Fearing for the worst, Ash slowly began to lay the rifle down when Lillian shouted, "No! Shoot him! I don't care if I die. I don't want to live anymore, anyway. Just kill him and kill me, too. Save yourself!"

Seeing the madness and rage in Wolf's face as his arm tightened, preparing to pull the knife across Lillian's throat, Ash quickly took aim and pressed the trigger as the world around her seemed to move in slow motion. First there was the flash of light, followed by the thump of the rifle's recoil against her shoulder as she screamed inside at the fear of what might be happening before her eyes. Wolf's head then whipped back violently as his brains and bits of hair and skull splattered into the trees behind him.

Lillian simultaneously shoved Wolf's arm away as he fell, the knife only slightly grazing her delicate skin.

Rushing into Ash's open arms, Lillian wrapped her arms around her as they both began to cry amidst their strong embrace. Despite becoming strengthened and hardened by the events they had endured, both Ash and Lillian lost all control of their emotions, purging themselves of their pent-up agony and sorrow.

Regaining her composure, Ash knew what she must do. She could wait for Jessie no longer. Her heartbreaking revelation that Jessie must have died in the fight the night before was now a reality for her. The prudent thing for her to do now is to focus on Lillian's safety and to get her out of the area as Jessie had wished.

~~~~

Falling down onto his back with his knife out of reach, the only remaining wolf approached Jessie, hidden in the darkness. With the glowing of its eyes shining through the darkness of the forest and the sound of its heavy breath, the old gray wolf stepped out into the moonlight, revealing itself.

Jessie could see the fierceness in its eyes, the blood of its fresh kill still dripping from its fangs. With a fierce, low-pitched growl, the wolf inched closer and closer. As Jessie attempted to grasp his knife that lay just out of reach, the wolf let out a ferocious snarl as it leaped into the air directly at Jessie.

Out of nowhere, a second wolf came flying out of the darkness, latching onto the old gray wolf's throat, taking him to the ground. A fierce fight erupted between the two wolves with a ferocity and level of primal violence that Jessie could have never imagined.

Finally succumbing to the battle, the old gray wolf lay dead on the forest floor. The second wolf—a she-wolf—stood over the now dead alpha male of the pack that had terrorized Jessie's

The Shepherd: Society Lost

flock for so long. The she-wolf turned to Jessie, looked him directly in the eyes, and then slipped away into the darkness, disappearing as quickly as she came.

Chapter Twenty-Six

Lying flat on his back with the sun in his eyes, Jessie swatted a fly from his face and turned his head, looking across the street at the smoldering remains of the home, now just a pile of ashes. Jessie realized he must have managed to crawl away from the flames before it completely burned to the ground. His memory of the previous night a blur, his head pounding with pain, he tried to sit up, but his surroundings began to spin. Laying his head back on the ground and simply focusing on getting his bearings back, Jessie looked at his watch, surprised to see that it was nearly two in the afternoon.

Turning his head to look down the street, Jessie saw a stray housecat, just sitting there, staring at him.

"No free meal today, cat!" Jessie shouted. "I'm not dead. At least not yet, anyway. Besides, you don't want this to be your meal. I'm sure I'm tough and full of gristle. Probably a bit gamey, too." Struggling once again to sit up, Jessie looked at the cat, tossing a pebble in its direction, saying, "Now get out of here before I realize I'm hungry and the tables turn on you."

Watching as the cat scurried behind one of the neighboring homes, Jessie looked around and thought, *I just hope the reason Ash isn't here is because she fled to safety with the girl, like I asked.*

Struggling to his feet, Jessie dusted himself off and winced in pain. Pulling his collar away from his body so that he could get a good look at his wound, he realized the dried blood had formed a scab into the fabric of his shirt. Recognizing his urgent need for first aid, Jessie hobbled painfully through town, making his way to the basement hideaway that had kept Ash alive all that time.

Slowly working his way to the home, stopping to rest and to ensure that he wasn't being followed, Jessie made it to the basement. Waiting outside behind the neighboring overgrown shrubs, Jessie carefully watched and waited. He wanted to make sure he wasn't merely allowed to live so that he might lead the men to the other survivors. Once he was satisfied that he was not followed, Jessie slipped into the basement, closing the overhead door behind him as he descended down the short flight of concrete steps, bolting the door closed behind him.

Rushing over to the shelf containing first-aid supplies, Jessie carefully cut his shirt free from his body, using a knife to work his wound free of the cloth fibers. Once his shirt was completely removed, he washed his wound with a saline solution and then coated it with an antiseptic ointment. When he felt he had done all he could do on his own, Jessie taped several layers of gauze over the wound and searched the shelf for an antibiotic. Knowing the likely course his wound would take without surgical treatment, and considering the elapsed time from the onset of the injury until his first opportunity to treat it, he felt getting a course of antibiotics started would significantly improve his odds of survival.

Sifting through the medications on the shelf, Jessie found a container of amoxicillin that had been marketed for livestock use. With a chuckle, Jessie joked to himself, "Well, I'm just a big, dumb animal, so it should be fine."

Taking a dose of the medication, Jessie walked over to the cot Ash had slept on during her stay in the basement. *I'm sure gonna miss her,* he thought. *I hope she got the girl and made it out. God, please let that be what happened. Let them be safe out there, somewhere. There's been enough death around me. I can't take much more.*

Overcome with exhaustion, Jessie laid back on Ash's cot, closed his eyes, and returned to his thoughts of what might remain of the world he once knew. Was his sister, whom he had set out to find, even still alive? Would it even be possible to find her? Being in complete darkness about the state of the world, other than what he had managed to gather from others and over the radio back when the broadcasts were still being transmitted, these thoughts and more swirled around in his head.

Unable to sleep due to the thoughts racing around in his mind, as well as the pain his body was enduring, Jessie thought of his journal, and how it, with all of his other worldly possessions, had been taken from him by the men at the bridge. As the contempt he had for them and all those like them turned to anger, Jessie stood up and walked back over to the medical supply shelf and continued to sort through the bottles.

"Ahhh, here we go," he said aloud to himself. "T3 with Codeine. Just what Doctor Townsend ordered." Popping two of the pills into his mouth, Jessie took a drink of bottled water and once again laid down on Ash's cot.

~~~~

Flying high over the earth below, the eagle soared. Gliding on thermal updrafts, the great bird effortlessly stayed aloft, scanning the terrain below for its next opportunity for a meal. Not having eaten for days, the eagle was desperate to return home to its nest with a meal for its young offspring.

The bird's keen eyes, detecting movement below, honed in on a young hare, bounding along, stopping to eat the newly blooming spring foliage as the countryside came alive once again after the long, harsh winter the animals had endured.

Seizing on the opportunity, the eagle tucked in its wings and dove at the ground with great speed. As it approached, it spread its wings to reduce its rate of descent while opening its talons wide, going in for the kill.

Latching on to its meal, the eagle triumphantly climbed higher and higher, traveling back to its nest perched high on a rocky cliff overlooking the valley below.

As the eagle landed, bringing a much-needed meal for its offspring, it found them dead. Massacred by a predator in its absence, the eaglets' soft gray down was scattered about, covered in their own blood. Amidst the carnage lay a snake, coiled and ready to strike the eagle.

In a fit of rage, the eagle unleashed a piercing shrill and lunged forward at the snake. The eagle and the snake both struck at one another, becoming entangled in an intense struggle as the eagle carried the snake higher and higher into the air. Succumbing to the snake's entangling grasp, the eagle began to fall back to earth, carrying the snake with it, a fight to the death that would end only upon impact with the rocky ground below.

Sitting up on the cot, grunting from the pain in his shoulder caused by his sudden movements, Jessie looked around the room to see that he was still safe and sound in the basement beneath the old house. *Damn these crazy dreams. At least it wasn't wolves,* he thought.

Taking a dose of ibuprofen to address inflammation and to dull the pain without clouding his mind any further, Jessie picked up his old Colt, glad to be reunited with his father's old gun. Flipping the loading gate open and half-cocking the hammer to free the cylinder, Jessie pushed on the ejector rod, ejecting the remaining cartridges and spent cases. With three fully loaded cartridges and three empty cases, Jessie held one up and said, "That explains why my shoulder didn't disintegrate. He was using .38 Special instead of .357 Magnums. Thank God for that."

Replacing the .38 Special cartridges with fresh .357 Magnums from the basement's remaining cache, Jessie wiped the old pistol down, spun the cylinder to check its function, and placed it on the table next to the cot.

Finding an old notepad on the supply shelf, Jessie thought, *I guess I could work on my journal, even if I have to start over.* Picking up a pen, he held it over the paper, pausing for a moment to reflect on the recent events of his life, and began to write:

I'm not sure why I've been spared. For some reason, my family and I were saved from the initial onslaught of violence, hidden way safely on our mountain homestead that my wife and I felt compelled to build. Alas, it was not enough to shelter them from the violence and evil of the world, now unrestrained.

Since their tragic deaths, from which I don't think I'll ever truly recover, I've been spared multiple times. Why? Why am I still here while other good, deserving people have met horrible fates at the hands of the attackers and the sickness and mayhem they've spread?

I'm not especially deserving of this gift of life. My desire to live was extinguished the day my family was taken from me, yet here I am. Not a day goes by that I don't think of my beautiful wife. Her smile warmed me on the coldest of nights. Her laugh brought joy and peace to my heart. Her wisdom and patience brought balance to my world. My children, they gave me a reason, a reason for everything. With them, every day when I awakened, I knew my purpose for that day was to love and provide for them. To care for them. To keep them safe.

At that, however, I failed. I do not deserve this pardon from God that I have been granted. Not a day goes by that I don't wish that he had taken me in their stead, or even to have taken me with them. I would give anything to be by their sides in heaven right this minute.

I hope I find my purpose soon. I hope that soon I can see why I've been spared.

As tears began falling on the paper, Jessie laid it aside and began to weep heavily with his hands over his face and his elbows on his knees. Opening the bottle of prescription-strength pain pills, Jessie tossed several into his mouth, swallowed, and laid back on the cot once again.

Reaching down to his wound, he traced his bandage with his fingers and thought, *a few more inches. Just a few more inches and I would have been liberated from this hell.*

Looking over to the bottle of amoxicillin, Jessie thought, *Why bother? I should just let the inevitable infection take me and save the medicine for whoever comes along next.*

Chapter Twenty-Seven

Awaking from his drug-induced slumber, Jessie attempted to sit up, only to find that he was somehow unable to move. Looking down, he realized he had been tied firmly in place, with ropes wrapping completely around the cot, his hands and feet bound individually.

"What the hell?" he exclaimed as he frantically looked around the room. Seeing a well-weathered man in his mid-fifties with graying hair and a gray, unkempt beard, Jessie demanded, "Who the hell are you? What's this all about?"

"I should be asking you that same question, stranger," the man said as he took a sip of coffee, his well-worn brown leather boots propped up on a folding chair.

"What?" Jessie asked in a confused tone as he struggled to free himself.

"Calm down," the man said. "You're just gonna hurt yourself more."

Relaxing from his struggle, Jessie asked, "Who are you and what do you want?"

"I'll ask the questions," the man said calmly. "You are an intruder in my house, after all."

"Your house?" Jessie asked.

"That's what I said. Can't a man leave his house unattended without having to worry about trespassers taking all of his supplies these days?" Getting no response from Jessie, the man continued. "You see, this is my home. I've lived in this house for fifteen years. When everything started to hit the fan and the fever the jihadists spread in Denver reached us here in Dolores, I bugged out to my hunting cabin on the Front Range. Having depleted my resources there, I thought I'd better get back here and try to get the rest of my supplies before some low-life looter like you managed to find the place and clean me out."

"But what about the red X on the front of your house? Did someone die here?"

"Heck, no," the man answered. "I painted that on there myself when I left, to keep people away. It looks like it worked, for the most part. Now, back to you. Who the heck are you and what are you doing here? Are you a looter? What are you running from? I see there that you and someone had a disagreement," he said, pointing at Jessie's wound.

"I was jumped by a group of scumbags on the bridge on the west end of town. They took everything I had. They even killed my horse. That's it. I got away and ended up seeking shelter in here."

"Likely story," the man replied. "It looks to me like you've been living in here a heck of a lot longer than you've had that wound."

"Oh, there was a woman staying here. That's how I found the place."

"Woman? Where is she now? Did you kill her? Is she the one who gave you that hole in your shoulder while trying to defend herself?"

"No! No, sir," Jessie quickly replied. "That's not it at all. Let me start from the beginning."

Jessie then explained to the man his ordeal in detail. He explained what had happened to his family, and how he had set out to find his sister, but had ended up being taken by the men at the bridge, which led him to Ash and their ultimate revenge against the gang.

As he wrapped up the story, he said, "So, you see, sir. I need to get out of here soon and see if I can figure out if Ash made it out of the treatment plant with the girl. Her trail is getting colder by the day, but I've just not been physically able. I just wanted to lie low here for a while until I had the strength."

Pacing back and forth while he digested Jessie's story, the man asked, "Are you worth it?"

"Am I worth, what?" Jessie replied, confused about the man's question.

"Are you worth my effort? Are you worthy of my help?"

"I'm not asking for your assistance, sir. I'm just asking that you allow me to gather my things so that I can go and look for Ash. I'm really worried about what might have happened the other night. Those men—the last thing a woman needs in this world is to be captured by men like that."

"Good answer," the man said as he walked over to the medical supply shelf, reaching behind several bulk bottles of aspirin, producing a small, dark brown jar of liquid. Taking a hypodermic needle from the shelf, the man then drew some of the contents of the bottle into the needle, holding it up against the light to verify the dosage.

"What is that? What are you doing?" Jessie asked nervously.

"Don't worry, it'll only burn for a second," the man said as he tightened the ropes holding Jessie's arm, plunging the needle into one of his veins.

"Hey, what the—? Don't! Don't you…" Jessie argued as he kicked and struggled. Everything around him slowly became a blur, and then darkness.

~~~~

Just before the eagle and the snake impacted the ground, the great bird of prey released its grip on the snake and shook the coiled serpent's body loose. Extending its wings, pulling out of the freefall just before hitting the ground, the eagle narrowly avoided death, while the snake, hissing furiously until the moment of impact, hit the jagged rocks with great force, dying instantly.

The Shepherd: Society Lost

As the eagle circled above his dead foe, looking down at the battered body of the snake, he felt no satisfaction. Despite the outcome of the flight, his offspring had been killed.

As the eagle flew off into the setting sun, Jessie squinted as bright light shined directly into his eyes. "Wake up," he heard, still in a daze, barely conscious. "Wake up," he heard again, along with the feeling of a smack on his cheek.

Coming out of his drug induced slumber, Jessie found himself lying on a bed inside of a house. Attempting to move, he once again found himself restrained by numerous ropes.

"How do you feel?" the man from the basement asked him.

Not fully understanding the point of the man's question, Jessie responded, "What? Where am I?"

"I moved you upstairs," the man said. "That dirty old basement was no place to perform a procedure," he said as he checked Jessie's pulse. "Now just calm yourself down and relax," he said.

Reaching over the small table on wheels, he picked up a small object and said, "Here's you a souvenir," holding a distorted and mushroomed bullet in front of Jessie's face for him to see. "This was lodged just underneath your clavicle, just above your first rib and next to your costoclavicular ligament. How the bone wasn't shattered is beyond me. It was basically redirected by the bone and worked its way underneath. It must have been a low-velocity load. You'd have probably been okay for a while, but it would have hurt like hell forever and would have caused you a lot of problems later on. That would be, of course, if you didn't die from infection. You'll probably be okay now. You're all patched up and I'll have you on a course of antibiotics throughout the healing process."

"Are you a doctor?" Jessie asked, still confused about what had taken place.

"The best kind of doctor. A vet!" the man joked. "We don't need those high-dollar facilities to perform basic procedures. A barnyard is all we need to get the job done."

Just then it hit him, "Spencer Tate? You're Spencer Tate, aren't you?"

With a surprised look on his face, the man said, "Just how did you know that?"

"I guess I didn't recognize you at first with the beard and long hair. The last time I saw you, you were clean cut."

Staring intently at Jessie, the man said, "I'm sorry, but—"

"Townsend," Jessie replied. "Jessie Townsend. I was the sheriff of Montezuma County until—"

"Now I remember!" The man said, interrupting Jessie. "Sheriff Townsend. You don't quite look the same yourself, all scruffy and used up looking," the man chuckled.

"I'm not a sheriff anymore," Jessie replied, bluntly.

"Yes, that was a travesty what happened."

"I'm just a shepherd now. Well, I was," said Jessie in a defeated tone. "Once I left the sheriff's office and moved to the mountains and started raising sheep, it was the first time I felt like I had actually found my calling. It wasn't easy, but it was the most fulfilling thing I've ever done. There's nothing like taking care of something that needs you, while it takes care of you and your family in return."

"Sounds just like being a sheriff," Spencer replied. "Oh, and where are my manners? Let me get you untied." Reaching for Jessie's restraints, Spencer paused and asked, "Now before I untie you, no hard feelings, right?"

With a smile, Jessie replied, "Of course not."

"Sheriff, uh, I mean, Jessie," Spencer said, continuing. "I know I didn't know you personally before you were robbed of your reelection, but I knew who you were. I knew how the people of Montezuma County thought of you. You were held in very high regard. That's not all too common with elected officials. Well, even less so now, of course, but even back then, and that says something about you. After you left, most of us, myself included, had no idea where you and your family went, which probably kept you safe for as long as it did, but I can tell you one thing; this place just wasn't the same after you left. Under Sheriff Sanders, crime and corruption were rampant. A lot of your deputies were let go and he brought in a bunch of his own. They were less than professional, to say the least. By that point, we didn't just feel that you were robbed of your reelection, we felt we were all robbed of our local county government."

Rubbing his wrists, now free of the restraints, Jessie replied, "Thank you, Doctor Tate."

"Oh, call me Spence," he replied. "There's no reason to be formal now. Heck, we're the only two people left in town. *Hey, you* would work just fine. I'd know who you're talking to," Spence said with a smile.

"I hope we're the only two," Jessie added. "That's another reason I need to check out the treatment plant. Only one of them made it out of there to come after me. I took care of him. The gang's leader got away, though, at least that's as far as I know. I'm not sure if there were others that I don't have knowledge of. That, and I need to look for signs of Ash and the girl."

"As soon as you're able," Spence agreed. "Give yourself a few days to get the healing process started and then I'll go with you. You won't be a match for anyone in your condition, and you'll do no one any good if you get yourself killed. In the meantime, we'll lie low here."

Chapter Twenty-Eight

Over the next several days, Jessie and Spence remained in Spence's home while Jessie's healing process got off to a good start. They kept the windows closed and practiced light discipline at night to avoid drawing attention to the home in the event that any potential threats remained in the area. The spring rains had moved in, providing them with a basic level of security, as anyone who might have remained at the treatment plant would more than likely be hunkering down until the foul weather passed by.

As they sat in the main living room of the home, Spence sat by the window in his recliner, peaking through the curtains with his rifle propped up against the wall next to him. His rifle, a Springfield Armory M-1A Standard with a classic walnut stock, was simple and basic, adorned only with a brown leather sling. Spence's sidearm of choice was a Smith & Wesson 686 Plus seven-shot revolver in .357 Magnum, a handy coincidence, making Spence's ammo collection complimentary to Jessie's own Colt revolver.

As Spence held the curtain slightly open with the barrel of his revolver, watching the overflow from the heavy rain wash down the street, he said, "It's almost like Mother Nature knew this town needed to be cleansed."

Replying with a half-hearted laugh, Jessie said, "Yeah, ain't that the truth? By the way, how did you make it all the way here from the Front Range?"

"I drove part of the way and then slipped into town on a bicycle from the northeast."

"You drove? Drove what?" Jessie asked with a curious tone.

"Don't laugh," Spence said.

"Why would I laugh?"

"A 1986 Pontiac Fiero SE."

With a chuckle, Jessie said, "Really? What... uh, why, of all the choices out there?"

"It makes more sense than you think," replied Spence. "Well, it makes some sense, at least. First off, that little sucker with that old-school Iron Duke four-cylinder is super simple with no computers or the like. Parts are everywhere. They put that motor in everything back then, even the S-10 series of small pickup trucks. It can even be retrofitted with a breaker-point ignition if an EMP was the concern. Even though it's forty years old, it gets thirty-eight miles per gallon! It's so light and aerodynamic, it comes by its fuel economy the honest way, not through technology. Fuel consumption is critical when you don't have a supply chain. And on top of that, it's tiny, so it's easy to hide if need be. Besides, it was only me, so I didn't need much room. Obviously, it wouldn't be ideal for a group of people. Heck, it's hardly ideal for two unless you strap a bunch of stuff on the rear deck-lid cargo rack, since there's very little room for gear."

With a grin, Jessie conceded to Spence's argument.

Spence then asked, "So what's your plan? I mean, after this. After we check on the whereabouts of the woman and the girl, then what?"

Pausing to gather his thoughts, Jessie replied, "When I left the homestead, I set out to find my sister. She's my only living relative. At least I hope she is."

"Where was she when last you knew?"

"East Tennessee," Jessie replied.

"That's a long way these days," Spence replied. "How did you plan on getting there?"

"I had a friend near Cortez that owned a Cessna C-185 tail-dragger."

"Are those the ones that look like a Super Cub?" asked Spence.

"No, I believe you're thinking of a Husky or a Scout," Jessie replied. "A C-185 is a six-seat, high-wing, utility airplane with a tailwheel landing gear configuration, making it suitable for off-airport bush flying. They'll hold six people, or four people with a lot of gear. They're basically a flying pickup truck."

"And you can fly that thing?" Spence asked.

"I used to do banner towing and fire patrol when I was younger. I wanted to be a professional pilot before I ended up following in my father's footsteps and pursued a career in law enforcement. I did the banner tow and fire patrol gigs as a way to build flight time."

"What makes you think the plane is still there? After all that's happened?" Spence asked.

"Joe had previously lost his medical certificate, so he hadn't been flying it. He kept the airplane in his barn and not at the airport, so there may be a chance it's still there, even if Joe isn't," Jessie said in a somber tone. "He was in pretty bad shape last I heard. He had prostate cancer, I believe. So without a medical infrastructure... well, let's just say I doubt Joe fared very well after it all went down."

"So, you plan to fly a tiny little airplane across the country, having to stop for fuel along the way in today's crazy world?"

"Yeah, basically, that's it. Or at least that was the plan. I can't get ahead of myself," Jessie replied. "I have to check on Ash and then go from there."

"How would you get fuel? I would imagine the limited supply of avgas at any of the airports along the way would've been taken long ago."

"You can run autogas in those things. The government-mandated ethanol can cause a few problems with rubber components such as seals, and methanol can cause problems with getting water in your fuel, which is dangerous for aircraft fuel-system icing at higher, colder altitudes, but for the most part, it'll run. You have to watch out for conditions that may cause vapor lock, which can also be a problem, but for all intents and purposes, it's a one-way trip anyway. It doesn't need to run for long."

"So you're gonna scavenge for autogas along the way?"

"Yeah, basically," Jessie replied. "It'll be a little risky since there isn't really any fresh gasoline out there anymore. What I may find has been sitting there in some old abandoned car's fuel tank for a while, but like I said, it's a one-way trip. I'll make it work."

"I'll make you a deal," Spence said, giving Jessie a serious look.

"What kind of a deal?" Jessie asked.

With a solemn expression, Spence looked at Jessie and said, "I want to go with you. Unless, of course, that would conflict with your plans."

"Why would you want to put yourself at risk like that, trying to find my sister? What's in it for you?" Jessie asked, confused about Spence's motivations.

"Because I don't want to just sit here and wait to die alone," Spence replied. "What you described sounds like the adventure of a lifetime. I would rather go out on some incredible journey than to wait for some illness or thieves to pick me off. When we get wherever it is we end up going, if you find your sister, I'll be on my way and won't be a bother. But in the meantime, it will be one hell of a ride. Besides, I never got married. I never had kids. I'm all alone in this world. The ironic thing is that I was a closet doomsday prepper, one could say. I had weapons, food, medical supplies, everything I needed to ride out a major event like this one. People back then who knew, thought I was a crazy whack-job on the fringe—but look who is alive and eating well tonight," he said with a crooked smile.

"The one thing I didn't prepare for," Spence said, pausing to gather his words, "was to have someone to survive with. To have someone to survive for. I don't have that. Without that, I might as well be out there living the heck out of life."

"Besides, I'm your doctor and it's doctor's orders that you take a medical professional with you in the event of complications."

With a smile, Jessie said, "I'm probably not going to make it. You know that, right?"

"I know what I would be getting myself into," Spence replied.

"Well, okay then," Jessie said with a nod. "But let's not get too far ahead of ourselves. My first priority is to look for any signs of Ash and the girl. If they need me, that's where I'll be."

"I understand completely," Spence replied. "If it's not out of line for asking, was this Ash woman special to you?"

Looking him directly in the eye, Jessie quickly replied, "She's special because she took me in when she didn't have to. She's special because she's a great person, inside and out. She's special because she wanted to put herself at risk to help others, like the girl we saw them take to the treatment plant. But if you mean romantically, no. Absolutely not. My heart still aches for my wife whom I still love with all of my being. I don't imagine I'll ever move on emotionally from her. And to be honest, I don't want to. No, Ash is more like a little sister. She's good people, and in this world, good people need each other."

"I understand and completely agree," Spence said. "Whatever we find at the treatment facility, whatever direction it takes, I'm there with you. Now, let's get a good night's sleep tonight. Tomorrow, we can discuss what to take with us. After we've got that all lined out, I'll help you clear the water treatment plant and we can decide how to proceed from there."

Chapter Twenty-Nine

Peeking out of the window at first light, taking a sip of coffee, Spence turned to Jessie and said, "The rain finally stopped, but it looks like it's gonna be cloudy and overcast for a while. That's not necessarily a bad thing, though."

"I would go out there in a hurricane today," Jessie replied. "I'm obviously still sore, but I feel good enough to get the heck out of here.

Stepping away from the window, Spence said, "I couldn't sleep so I got up and put some stuff together for us." Tossing Jessie a camouflaged rain poncho, he said, "We can use these today in case it starts to rain again. It's still wet and damp out there and, if nothing else, it will keep the wind off."

Catching the poncho, Jessie said, "Thanks. What else did you pack?" he asked.

"Since you and your lady friend already took my shotgun and shotgun shells, I grabbed the remaining .38 and .357 shells, divided them up and put half in each of our bags. Luckily, you two didn't figure out that some of the shelving covered a hidden door which opened into a closet where I had a security cabinet." Pausing, distracting himself with a side thought, he continued, "Yep... I was a crazy prepper. Now, though, you can just call me a survivor. Anyway, before I derail my train of thought anymore, I've always been a subscriber to the preparedness rule that two is one and one is none. With that in mind, I just happened to have a second M-1A hidden safely away where looters like you and the girl couldn't find it. Lord knows if you did, you would have taken it with you when you assaulted the water treatment plant and it would be lost to us now."

"I can't argue with you there," Jessie said, nodding in agreement. "Just keep in mind, we thought you were dead upstairs. We didn't realize we were stealing."

"I know. I'm just giving you a hard time. So anyway, I packed us each some basic provisions and put the pain meds and antibiotics that you may need, as well as extra wound care items, in your pack."

"Sounds good," Jessie replied, nodding in the affirmative.

"Are you about ready to get on with this?" Spence asked.

"Absolutely," Jessie replied.

Picking up his rifle and pack, Spence said, "Let's get on with it, then."

~~~~

Slipping into the basement and exiting the house through the basement doors, Jessie and Spence worked their way slowly and cautiously toward the water treatment facility. Passing the burned house where he had narrowly escaped with his life, Jessie was once again reminded of how many times he had somehow managed to survive perilous situations, although not unscathed. The emotional and physical damage was beginning to take its toll on his body and mind.

Pressing on toward the treatment plant, Jessie and Spence ducked behind an old thrift store which had been looted and partially burned. Being the closest standing structure to the plant, Jessie said, "Let's observe from here for a bit. We can't get any closer without exposing ourselves."

"Roger that," replied Spence as he began to scan the area with his binoculars.

After they had spent half an hour observing the facility, seeing no movement, Jessie said, "Okay, my last known location for Ash was on the lower level. She was supposed to enter the basement door facing the river while I made an attack from the opposite side, drawing their fire. From there, it all went to hell once I got inside and I ended up escaping out of that door there," he said, pointing to the upper-level administrative office entrance facing them.

"Was it still open when you got away?" asked Spence, noting that the door was open, exposing the interior of the building to the elements.

"I was running at a full sprint, so that guy behind me probably wouldn't have taken the time to close the door. If it has been open all this time, it would indicate that there is no one inside. They would have closed it by now to keep the wind and rain out otherwise."

"That's what I was thinking," replied Spence.

"Okay, then. Let's work our way down Railroad Avenue, using the overgrown decorative shrubs as visual cover. Once we reach the upper parking lot, you peel off, hugging exterior walls for cover and work your way over to the open admin office door. I'll swing around to the lower exit where Ash was supposed to enter the building."

"Are you sure you don't want me to go to where Ash was? You know, just in case," asked Spence, concerned about what Jessie might find.

"No, I'll need confirmation one way or another. I'll go through the bottom. Anyway, if it's clear up top, work your way down the stairs and I'll meet you in the main basement space down below."

With a nod to the affirmative, the two men worked their way down Railroad Avenue as Jessie had suggested. Reaching the facility, Spence edged his way to the administrative entrance, while Jessie stuck to his plan of entering through the lower basement door.

As Jessie approached the door, he swung the M-1A over his shoulder and drew his Colt revolver. He appreciated the firepower the M-1A had to offer, but knew its weight and length made it less than ideal for close-quarters battle scenarios. Cocking his old single-action Colt with his thumb, he slowly pulled the door open, noting that it had a spring-assisted closing mechanism, which may have explained why it was still closed after the attack.

Entering the dark hallway, Jessie turned back and propped the door open with a rock, allowing light from outside to shine into the hallway, illuminating his way. Overwhelmed by the smell of death, Jessie swatted flies away from his face as he looked at the man whose guts had been spilled on the floor by Ash's blade. *Damn, girl,* he thought.

As he stepped carefully through the grizzly scene, something on the floor caught his eye. *What the heck?* he thought, as he reached over to pick it up. *Well, I'll be damned, it's Ash's watch.* Attempting to wipe off the dried blood to no avail, Jessie slipped the watch into his pocket and continued his search.

Looking into each of the side rooms, he saw no one else other than the man Ash had shot upon her initial entry into the hallway. Looking down at the blood stains on the floor, Jessie could see both Ash's footprints, as well as those of a smaller-framed person who was apparently barefoot at the time, both leading back out the door. With a smile, Jessie thought, *she got her.*

Hearing the upper door leading down to the basement creak as it slowly opened, Jessie entered the main basement area, while covering the stairs above.

Looking down at Jessie, Spence said, "All clear up top… well, no one living up top, that is." As he scanned the main basement area illuminated only by the small windows mounted high at the ground level, he said, "You did all of this?" referring to the bodies, some burned and some beginning to rot.

"It needed to be done," Jessie replied.

"I'm not arguing that. Just… Just glad you made it. That's all."

"Ash isn't here," Jessie said. "Her tracks led her and the girl back outside."

"You can see her tracks?" Spence inquired.

"Trust me, it's obvious," Jessie replied, "Now, let's get to the reservoir where we were supposed to meet up."

~~~~

Making their way to the reservoir, following along the river bank, which was Ash's most likely route of travel, Jessie was frustrated to discover that the heavy rain had washed away any sign of Ash and the girl's travel. Pressing on, he came to a secluded area where the smell of death was in the air. His heart feeling heavy in his chest, he was afraid of what he would find if he followed the source of the smell but knew he had to see for himself. As he worked his way through a small cluster of trees, Jessie came upon a dead body lying flat on his back with a devastating gunshot wound to the head that took off half of the back of the man's skull.

As Spence caught up to him, he placed his hand on Jessie's shoulder and said, "Do you know him?"

"It was Wolf," Jessie replied. "She killed him," he said as he paused to maintain his composure. With a smile, he looked at Spence and said, "She killed him. They got away. She got that poor girl away from them."

With a sense of relief, Spence asked Jessie, "Do you know where she might be now?"

"I told her if I didn't return to take the van."

"Van?"

"We took out one of the gang's scouting teams and took their van. We parked it a few miles west of town in an old pole barn at an abandoned house. They've had plenty time to get to it and get away. Ash is tough. She had been hardened by a lot since it all began. I'm sure they're fine," Jessie said with satisfaction in his voice.

Jessie wanted to be able to see Ash once again, to let her know how it had all worked out. He felt bad about the fact that more than likely, they would never again cross paths, but he took solace in the fact that he knew she would be able to make the best of her situation, and would continue to fight and survive in this shattered world they had all come to know.

Chapter Thirty

In preparation for the journey that lay ahead, Jessie set out to check for fuel in the tanks of the abandoned cars that remained in Dolores, while Spence rode his bike back to the discreet location where he had left his car before making his way to his home. No longer concerned with concealing his whereabouts in town, Spence drove right up to the front of the house so that he and Jessie could load the car with ease.

Impressed at the stealth in which the car traveled as Spence pulled to a stop, Jessie said, "Wow, that thing is quiet."

"I doubled up on the mufflers. I basically welded an extra one on after a one-hundred-and-eighty-degree bend in the pipe at the end, re-routing the exhaust back through the second muffler before dumping it out in the center of the car. It's not ideal. It robs the car of a little more power than the single muffler, not to mention the fact that the exit location would make it too easy to gas myself if I sat in it too long with the engine running and not moving, but hey, it's got its purpose and it serves that purpose well."

"You'll hear no complaints from me," Jessie said, admiring the little car. "I only managed to get twelve gallons of gas in all. I'm amazed so many of the cars had already been siphoned dry, but then again, the gang at the bridge had probably been feeding off them since they arrived."

"How far outside of Cortez is your friend's place?"

"A few miles to the east of town. He's on a ten-acre parcel of land."

"I've got maybe eight or nine gallons left in the car here. Once we get to your friend's home and decide whether or not the airplane is a viable option, we can drain the gas from the car as well, if need be. It's not like we'll be needing it anymore from there," suggested Spence.

Strapping the last of the fuel tanks on top of the car's rear deck-lid cargo rack, Jessie walked over to the passenger-side door, began to open it, and said, "Let's stop by the treatment plant. I've got a few things I want to look for that those fithly scumbags took from me."

"Sounds fine to me," Spence replied.

As they closed both doors, Spence started the little car and began to adjust his rear-view mirror, only to realize that the fuel tanks strapped to the rack were blocking his view. "Oh, what does it matter, anyway?" he said with a chuckle as the two began driving down the street.

"Are you sad to see it go?" Jessie asked.

"What?"

"Dolores. Are you sad to be driving out of Dolores for the last time?"

Looking over at him with a serious expression, Spence replied, "Dolores is nothing but a graveyard to me now. Everywhere I look, I see the homes that have become the tombs of my former friends and neighbors. I don't care if I ever see that place again. It's just full of ghosts for me."

Knowing exactly how Spence felt, with similar feelings having driven him from his beloved mountain homestead, Jessie simply nodded to show his mutual understanding.

As Spence pulled into the upper parking lot of the water treatment plant, Jessie said, "Keep the car running. Just because it's safe here now doesn't mean it will be in ten minutes. You never know what's going to come down that road next."

"Roger that," Spence replied.

"I'll be quick," Jessie said as he stepped out of the car, only taking with him, his trusty old single-action Colt.

As he entered the administrative office, the memories of his encounter with Wolf and his men came flooding back into his mind. Walking across the office floor to the far side of the room, just past the doorway leading down the stairs, Jessie opened a door to find a supply room full of office paper, pencils, pens, and other miscellaneous clerical supplies. Closing that door and then moving on to the next, Jessie opened it to find what he assumed was previously used as the manager's office.

Lying on top of the desk in the office were several weapons, including Jessie's beloved Winchester Model 70 that had been taken from him on the bridge. Picking it up, he continued to sift through what appeared to be the spoils of war for the men, who had taken weapons, and other valuable personal belongings from the people they robbed and killed. Numerous watches and other pieces of jewelry were strewn about the desk, as well as several wallets and ladies' purses. *What the heck did these guys think paper money and credit cards would do for them these days? I guess they were stealing for the sake of stealing,* he thought.

Pushing a few watches out of the way, Jessie's heart pounded in his chest as he saw his own wedding ring. Sliding it onto his finger, his pent-up sadness and rage flooded back into his mind, blackening his soul.

Picking up his Winchester, Jessie started to turn and walk out of the room, when out of the corner of his eye he caught a glimpse of his journal lying on the floor, as if it had simply been kicked out of the way. Picking it up and stuffing it into his pocket, Jessie stormed out of the office. Walking with a brisk pace, struggling to hold back his emotions, Jessie returned to the parking lot and got in the car, laying the Winchester rifle alongside the two M-1A's between the seats. Looking at Spence, Jessie abruptly said, "Let's get the hell out of here."

Without saying a word, Spence slipped the car into gear, eased out on the clutch, and off they went across the bridge, heading south on Colorado 154.

~~~~

Arriving just outside of Cortez twenty minutes later, Spence stopped the car and looked over at Jessie, still lost in a rage-filled trance. "Hey. Jessie. Are you okay?"

Turning to look at him, Jessie said, "Yeah, I'll be fine."

"So, where to from here?" Spence asked.

"Stay on 154 until you reach 160. Turn left on 160. It's only a couple miles from there," Jessie said as he rolled down his window.

"Are you getting hot?" Spence asked.

"No. This is a shooting port," Jessie replied. "There will be a lot of buildings of to our right as we travel south. I just want to be ready to engage any potential threats."

"Good thinking," replied Spence as he focused on the road ahead.

With Jessie's M-1A now resting awkwardly on the door of the car, with the barrel protruding outside, they made their way through the outskirts of Cortez uneventfully. Aside from a few signs of smoke from homes off in the distance, the city of Cortez, like Dolores, seemed to be mostly abandoned. The only signs of life were written warnings placed outside of barricaded neighborhood entrances that evoked threats of violence to any outsider who might try to enter.

~~~~

Turning on to Highway 160 as Jessie had instructed, the two men traveled west, leaving the city of Cortez behind. With desolate, wide open spaces in front of them, the scenery turned from the overgrown lawns of the homes and parks in Cortez to dry, brown, lifeless desert-like terrain. Both Jessie and Spence welcomed the emptiness. Deep down inside, they felt a reassurance that the emptiness and desolation of what lay ahead of them would also make it more likely to be devoid of people.

Passing the Montezuma County Fairgrounds off to their right, Jessie broke the silence by saying, "The turn-off to Joe's place is just another mile or so ahead on the right. It's a small dirt road, so it's easy to miss."

Nodding in understanding, Spence asked, "Did Joe have a family? Anyone that we might need to be concerned with that could have also gone to his place to seek refuge?"

"No one close," Jessie replied. "He was originally from California. His father died of a heart attack several years before it all began. His mother passed away when he was younger. He had a sister, but I believe she was killed in a traffic accident some time ago. I think he may have had cousins, but none in the area. It's sad really."

"What's sad?" Spence asked.

"That Joe probably had to go through all of this alone, facing the collapse of the modern society that was keeping him alive during his battle with cancer. Once the attacks started and the infrastructure fell, I just don't see how he could have continued receiving treatment. It would be a rough way to go, being all alone while your body slowly killed itself."

After a moment of silence as the men drove, Jessie raised his hand, pointing up ahead, and said, "There it is. The little dirt road off to the right."

"That's his driveway?" Spence asked, noting that it looked more like a random trail than a road.

"That's the way he liked it. No one was going to accidentally turn down his street," Jessie said, acknowledging the brilliance of his old friend.

"Was Joe a like-minded individual?" Spence asked.

"What do you mean?"

"Was he prepared for the collapse, like us?"

"I wouldn't say I was prepared," replied Jessie. "No, Joe was just a loner for most of his life. I guess, in a way, having a general mistrust of society put him in that category by default.

But no, Joe wasn't a survivalist or prepper. He was just a man who preferred being alone."

As Spence turned down the old worn and rutted dirt road, the low-riding Pontiac Fiero dragged the ground on occasion, barely maintaining its forward momentum as they navigated the road to Joe's home. As they came up to a slight rise in the terrain, Jessie said, "Stop right here."

"Do you see something?" asked Spence.

"No, but we can't just go driving up to this place. Let's shut the car off and observe for a while. No one could have a line of sight on us here from the house, so let's take advantage of that and ensure we aren't driving right up to a dangerous situation."

"Roger that," Spence replied.

Removing his Winchester rifle from the car, Jessie crept to the top of the hill, and lying in the prone shooting position, he began to survey the area down below through his rifle's scope.

Crawling up to Jessie, Spence asked, "Do you see anything?"

"No, not yet. I'm not gonna make the same mistake twice, though, and just go strolling into an ambush. You watch our six while I keep an eye on the place. There's no need to rush this. It's not like we have to be back to work on Monday."

With a chuckle, Spence replied, "Smart man."

Chapter Thirty-One

As the eagle soared high in the sky, gliding on the thermals of air rising from the warm ground below, it spotted the signs of a prairie dog town with numerous burrows following along the natural lay of the terrain that was carved by a small stream.

Hungry for its next meal, the eagle tucked in its wings and dove toward the bustling network of prairie dog-filled tunnels below. Swooping in from a steep angle and at a high rate of speed, the eagle's attack had gone unnoticed by its unsuspecting prey below.

As the eagle began to spread its wings and extend its talons to take its meal, a thunderous crack echoed through the valley, shattering the silence that was, until then, only filled with the sounds of nature. Feeling an impact on its left wing, the great bird looked to see a human appear from behind a constructed blind, who then fired another shot, with a flash of light followed by another thunderous crack..."

"Hey, Jessie. Wake up," he heard as he felt something nudging his shoulder.

Flinching and grasping his rifle, Jessie heard, "Relax, it's just me," coming from Spence's familiar voice. "Everything is okay. You just looked like you were having a bad dream or something. The sun is also starting to come up over the horizon. I thought you might want to enjoy it. Even though we're surrounded by dark things, every morning God reminds us that light will prevail. I for one like to take a moment and enjoy the beautiful reminder."

Rubbing his eyes, Jessie said, "I was just having another dream. My dreams seem more real to me as time goes on. It's almost like they are telling me something, too."

"That could be the Ute in you," Spence said with a smile.

"Yeah," Jessie replied. "That's what my wife used to tell me. So how long was I out?"

"Just an hour or two. It was so quiet out here that I figured I'd just let you sleep. You're still not a hundred-percent with that shoulder injury there. You need to get more rest than you probably want to. Besides, you can't see through your scope in the dark anyway."

"Have you seen or heard anything?"

"Not a peep or movement other than the birds flying overhead."

Jessie replied only with a chuckle.

"What?"

"Oh, nothing."

For the next few minutes, the two men observed the beauty of the morning's sunrise over the eastern horizon. As the sun came up, its rays painted the sky red as it illuminated the high clouds while casting a shadow over the terrain in the distance, creating a striking contrast between the ground and the sky.

"How does it go? *Red sails at night, sailors' delight, red sails in the morning, sailors take warning?* Or something like that," Jessie said, noting the beauty of the bright orange and red colors in the sky.

"I always heard it told as *red skies*, but yeah, something like that," Spence replied. "So, what's the plan?"

"Let's wait here just a little longer. We need to see if there's any morning activity at the house. People generally have a morning routine of some sort and we may be able to spot a sign of it if anyone's around. Let's just give it a little while longer."

"Sounds good to me," Spence replied.

~~~~

As the sun approached the position of high noon, Jessie looked over to Spence, who was clearly becoming restless, and said, "I think we're good. You fire the car up and climb in. Drive slow and I'll walk along beside you. The terrain is too open to try to sneak up on the place. If something happens, I'll be able to use the car for cover while I engage the threat. If we're both in the car, we won't have enough freedom of movement in its tight confines to adequately defend ourselves. If I go down, you get out of here as fast as you can."

"If that's the best plan you've got, then okay," Spence reluctantly replied.

As the two men crept toward the house, Spence driving the Fiero while Jessie walked alongside with his M-1A at the ready, both men kept a keen eye on the home, looking for signs of movement. Just fifty feet from the house, Jessie signaled for Spence to bring the car to a stop.

"What is it?" asked Spence. "Do you see something?"

"No, but I need you to cover me while I approach the house. Leave the car running and get out and kneel behind the door and cover the house with your rifle."

"You do realize these doors are basically plastic, right?" Spence said, referring to the lack of ballistic protection they would afford him. "I've got a better idea," he said as he put the car back in gear and pulled forward, turning sharply to the left. Leaving the car running, but in neutral, he then climbed out of the car and knelt down behind the rear wheel, propping his rifle on the supplies strapped to the rear deck lid.

Shaking his head from side to side in jest, Jessie smiled at Spence and proceeded toward the front door of the older brick one-story ranch-style home.

Reaching the door, Jessie stepped off to the side with his back against the wall, out of view of the home's windows, and looked to Spence. Giving him a thumbs up to proceed, Jessie reached to his left and placed his hand on the doorknob, only to find it to be locked.

Waving for Spence to join him, Jessie watched as Spence shut off the ignition, removed the keys, and slipped up to the house where Jessie awaited.

"Are you afraid someone's gonna steal your pride and joy there?" Jessie said with a sly grin.

"You can never be too careful," he replied. "I sure would hate to hear our gear drive away while we're checking out the house."

With a nod, Jessie said, "Okay, I don't want to just start breaking windows and kicking doors in, just in case someone is around. Judging from the dirt and debris around the front of the house, it doesn't appear anyone's been accessing it from the front anytime in recent days. They could be laying low and using the back door, though. There are no windows on that side of the house because of the garage," Jessie said, pointing. "Let's go around that way and check out around back. We'll look for signs of recent entry first. If nothing presents itself, we'll try the door, or even a window if we must."

Nodding in agreement, Spence followed Jessie around the side of the house, clearing around each corner as they went. Pausing before exposing himself to the back side of the house, Jessie looked around, seeing no signs of recent activity, and said, "Okay, I'm gonna slip underneath those windows. You cover me from here and keep an eye out behind you as well. I'll signal if it's clear."

"Roger that," Spence replied as Jessie worked his way to the back door.

Seeing damage to the door jamb from what appeared to be a forced entry, Jessie thought to himself, *this looks like it was done a while ago. The broken wood looks weathered. Nothing fresh.* Nudging the door open with his left hand, with his rifle slung over his shoulder, Jessie drew his Colt .45, cocked the hammer back with his thumb, and slipped into the house.

Entering through the back door, Jessie found himself in the kitchen. With just enough light shining through the opening between the window curtains to light his way, he could see that the house had been ransacked. Every cabinet door had been left wide open, with the unwanted contents scattered around on the floor.

The house seemed entirely devoid of food products, and on the kitchen countertop, Jessie noticed that the butcher block-style knife holder was completely empty. *I guess knives could come in handy for a lot of things these days,* he thought.

Hearing a bump in one of the other rooms, Jessie spun around with his Colt at the high ready position. Assuming the noise came from one of the bedrooms, Jessie silently lowered the hammer on his revolver and re-holstered it, bringing his rifle to bear. The M-1A, being a full-sized main-battle rifle, could be unwieldy in a close quarters situation, but Jessie felt the extra firepower of the .308 cartridge might come in handy with only flimsy hollow interior doors and sheetrock walls to shield any possible threat from his wrath.

Slipping quietly from the kitchen of the dark and musty house, Jessie saw the silhouette of a man sitting in Joe's recliner in the middle of the room, facing an old television set. Turning quickly and aiming his rifle at the man, Jessie quickly realized the man had long since expired, his body fully decomposed, resembling a mummified skeleton, as nothing remained but dry skin and bones, held in place only by the man's clothing.

Hearing another thud coming from one of the bedrooms, Jessie's feeling of dread that he may have found his old friend Joe was pushed aside while he turned his attentions back to the task at hand. Proceeding toward the bedroom, his rifle pulled tightly against his shoulder, prepared to fire. Jessie noticed a gap of around two inches where the door was partially open. Shoving the door violently open with his foot, Jessie had just begun to shout an order to freeze as something came at him at a high rate of speed, startling him, causing him to fire.

Hearing the shot from inside the house, Spence ran across the backyard and entered the kitchen with his rifle in hand, shouting "Jessie! Jessie, I'm in the kitchen!"

"It's okay. It's okay, false alarm," shouted Jessie from the bedroom. Walking into the kitchen, Jessie said, "I heard activity in one of the bedrooms. It turns out it was a bird trying to find a way out. Air pressure in the house must have pulled the door to a position where the bird could no longer get out of the bedroom, and it started to panic. It flew right at me when I opened the door. Man, my ears are still ringing from shooting inside that small room."

With a chuckle, Spence asked, "Where did it go? Did you get it? That's dinner!"

"No, I missed. It was a reflex shot, and a poorly aimed one at that. The bird flew through the doorway leading into the garage over there," he said, pointing. "There must be a way in and out for them via the attic."

Turning his attentions back to the living room, Jessie said, "I think I found Joe, though," as he walked toward the dead man in the recliner. Looking the remains over, he noticed that no readily visible signs of trauma were present. Seeing a pill bottle on the floor, just out of reach of the dead man's hand, Jessie leaned over to pick it up. Holding it up so he could see the label clearly, he said, "I guess that's how he chose to go. On his own terms. He simply fell asleep and never woke up. Ah, Joe. I'm so sorry this happened to you, man."

"What do you think happened to the house?" Spence asked. "Looters?"

"Yeah, I'd say so. At least Joe didn't have to face them. Going out on his own terms was the only thing he had left to control in this world. Going out at the hands of a thug just wouldn't have been Joe's style."

Chapter Thirty-Two

Standing outside of Joe's barn, Jessie looked at Spence and said, "Well, I guess now we find out if this was a wasted trip or not."

With a nod in reply, Spence said, "The only wasted trip is a trip not taken."

As the two men swung the two large barn doors open, exposing the inside of the barn to the sun's rays, Jessie was pleased to see Joe's old Cessna C-185 parked with its tail to the corner, partially draped in the canvas covering that Joe had used to keep it from being overtaken by dust. Jessie looked around and said, "Someone took his tractor and ATV, and I don't see his pickup truck parked anywhere, but I guess they didn't have much use for an airplane."

"What're the odds the average looter is a pilot?" Spence asked.

Walking over to the plane, banging on the underside of each wing, Jessie said, "Someone drained the tanks. Joe wouldn't have left it that way. He would have had them topped off, with fuel stabilizer added to the gas. He knew the tanks would corrode by the moisture in the air if they weren't stored full."

Standing there scratching his chin while staring at the dust-covered plane, Jessie turned to Spence, and said, "Well, let's get to work. She's not gonna get herself ready to fly with us just standing here."

"What do you want me to do?"

"Go get your car and drive it around here to the barn. We'll use it as a tug to pull her out in the sun so that we can start getting her cleaned off."

"Sure thing!" Spence said with a spring in his step, anxious to get started on the journey.

~~~~

Over the next two days, Jessie and Spence worked feverishly during the daylight hours to get the old, neglected Cessna ready to fly. Sleeping in the barn in shifts at night to watch over their newly acquired mode of transportation, they wasted very little time on anything outside of the task at hand.

In addition to flushing the fuel system of contaminates, they charged the battery slowly over time by use of Spence's solar-charging system fitted to his car. They aired the tires via a bicycle-style hand pump, cleaned several birds' nests from the engine-cowl area, and inspected all control cables and pulleys to be certain they were free of foreign objects left behind by critters looking to use the aircraft fuselage for shelter.

Standing back and admiring the old bird in its now clean and respectable state, Jessie looked to Spence and said, "In regards to fuel for the aircraft, considering its ability to run autogas in addition to avgas, of which we have none thanks to the people that looted this place, the twelve gallons of gas scavenged from the remaining cars in Dolores, as well as the five or so gallons of gas remaining in the Fiero, we've only got seventeen gallons."

"How far will that get us?" asked Spence.

"At fifteen gallons per hour at long-range cruise power settings, we would only get as far as Farmington before we'd have to put her down somewhere and look for fuel."

"That's not very far," Spence replied with a look of concern on his face.

"No. No, it's not," Jessie replied. "We need more, but the way I see it, we have two options: we can take the Fiero back into Cortez in an attempt to scavenge for fuel, or we can go with what we've got, knowing that we'll have to put it down fairly soon and set out on foot looking for fuel."

"Well, since we've got the car, we might as well look for fuel before we leave."

"That's what I was—"

Before Jessie could finish his statement, a man's voice shouted from the direction of the house, "Move one muscle and I'll blow your heads off you damn looters! Now, lay your sidearms on the ground and place your hands on your heads... slowly."

Complying with the man's demands and with their rifles out of reach, Jessie slowly placed his Colt on the ground and began raising his hands to his head as he replied, "We're not looters, we're—"

"Shut the hell up!" the man, appearing to be in his mid-twenties with a thin build and long brown hair, shouted as he began walking closer. "If you're not looters, then what the hell are you doing here and what are you doing with my uncle's airplane?"

Caught off guard by the man's statement, Jessie turned his head and said, "Your uncle? Do you mean—" before finishing his sentence, the man struck Jessie in the face with the butt of his rifle, knocking Jessie to the ground. As the man raised the rifle once again to strike Jessie, who now lay on the ground and nearly unconscious, Spence dove for the man, grabbing him by the waist in a football-style tackle, taking him to the ground.

With the young man now flat on his back, Spence wrestled with him for the rifle, an old Soviet-era Mosin-Nagant bolt-action rifle with the bayonet affixed to the barrel. Unable to pry the weapon from the man's hands, Spence used his body weight to work it up to his neck and began to apply pressure, cutting off his airway.

Just as their attacker began to slip out of consciousness, Jessie came to his senses and pulled Spence off of him, shouting, "No! Stop. Don't kill him!"

As Jessie pulled on Spence's shoulders from behind, the nearly unconscious man released his grip on the rifle, causing Jessie and Spence to fall backward onto the ground. With the rifle now firmly in Spence's hands, he pulled away from Jessie and placed the spike-style bayonet against the man's throat.

"Why shouldn't we kill him?" Spence shouted in a fit of rage. "He attacked us. He could have killed you, and might have before it was all said and done."

"Let's hear him out!" Jessie shouted.

Confused, but trusting Jessie's gut instinct, Spence continued to stand guard over the man but held off on his retaliation.

As the man came to, Spence held the bayonet against his neck and said, "Now, you do what we say, mister. And you had better answer any questions my friend here has, because he is the only reason you are alive right now."

Looking at the man lying flat on his back, clearly fearful of Spence, Jessie knelt down and said, "What's that you said about your uncle?"

Coughing from his inflamed throat caused by Spence's violent attack, the man said, "Joseph Threadgill. He is my uncle. This is his house. That is his place. That is his airplane," he said, pointing to the Cessna.

"How are you related to Joe?" Jessie inquired.

"He was my mother's brother."

"Who is your mother?" Jessie asked.

"Marcie Threadgill. She's no longer with us. She passed away when I was younger. Uncle Joe is the only relative I have left."

Beginning to believe the young man's story, Jessie asked, "Forgive me for asking, but how did your mother die?"

With a confused look on his face, puzzled by Jessie's line of questioning, the young man replied, "She died in a car wreck, but what business is it of yours?"

"It isn't any of my business. I just needed to verify your story. My name is Jessie. I was a good friend of your uncle Joe. I came here to check on him myself, and, well, I'm sorry to be the bearer of bad news, but he's no longer with us."

After a momentary pause, the young man said, "That's what I was afraid I would find. I knew he wasn't doing well before it all started, so, well, it was easy to do the math. I had to know, though. I had to see for myself."

Reaching out with his hand to help him up, Jessie said, "He's good, Spence. Let him up."

As Spence pulled the bayonet away from his throat, Jessie helped the young man to his feet and said, "Forgive us, but what's your name?"

"I'm Mike. Mike Threadgill."

"You took your mother's name?" Jessie asked.

"My father wasn't worth a damn, so yeah, I took her name."

Changing the subject, Jessie said, "Joe's remains are inside the house. Would you like to see him?"

"Yes. Yes, I would," Mike replied. "But before we go in, how did he die?"

"From the looks of things, he overdosed on pain medication. He probably just couldn't take it anymore without medical assistance and went to sleep one day with no intention of ever waking up. He's in his recliner. He looks like he died in peace. Looters have cleaned out the house since then, but he appears not to have been disturbed."

Looking down at the ground, taking it all in, Mike said, "At least he's not suffering anymore. And like I said, I didn't expect him to have made it, but I had to make the trip—just because. I couldn't have lived with myself if I didn't at least try to get to my only living relative. The only one I knew, anyway."

"Where are you coming from?" Jessie asked.

"California originally, just outside of Sacramento in a town called Placerville."

"I know Placerville," replied Jessie. "When I was younger, my father had an old flat-fender Jeep that he had modified pretty heavily for off-road use. He took us on a family trip there once to do the Rubicon trail. It was an incredible experience."

"Yep, that's the place," Mike replied.

"Just before it all started to fall apart, I decided to get myself back into school and learn a skill that could be useful no matter what turn the economy took, so I moved to Ogden and enrolled in the Ogden-Weber Technical College there to learn HVAC. A good friend of mine had gone there and recommended it. Plus, I figured they couldn't outsource that line of work."

"Smart move," Jessie replied.

"A day late and a dollar short, though. By the time classes started, that's when the financial crisis began, followed shortly thereafter by the attacks. By the time I had gotten started, it was all over. I figured being in Ogden, I was half-way between California and Colorado, so I might as well try and find my uncle."

"You've come a long way," Spence said, entering the conversation with a new tone.

"It's been my mission in life since it all went down. What else did I have to do other than just hide out somewhere and wait to die or join one of the camps?"

"Camps?" Jessie asked.

"The government camps," Mike replied. "They lure you in with the promise of food, shelter, and protection. You're nothing but fenced-in cattle in those places, though. That's no life. With the available supplies beginning to dry up, some of the camps are starting break down on the inside. They're just not a good place to be. At least not for me, anyway."

"Me, either," replied Jessie.

Holding up Mike's rifle, Spence said, "Did you make it all the way here with nothing but this old relic?"

"I started with an AR-15. I got into a tight situation just outside a little town called Price, just northwest of Moab. I had a steel-cased Russian-made .223 cartridge jam in the chamber. I hadn't cleaned it for quite some time and I guess that non-forgiving steel case was just a little oversized and got all jammed up in the crud-filled chamber. Slamming it on the ground butt first while pulling as hard as I could on the charging handle wouldn't budge it and I didn't have a cleaning rod handy to knock it loose from the bore side, so I just tossed it and made a run for it. I picked the Mosin-Nagant up a few days later when yet another scumbag tried to rob me. It didn't work out so well for him."

Handing the rifle back to Mike, Spence said, "No hard feelings?"

Taking the rifle with his left hand, Mike pushed his long brown hair back with his right hand, and said, "No, man. We're good."

With a look of interest on his face, Jessie asked, "Oh, yeah, how did you make it out here? I know you didn't walk all this way."

"Different modes of travel along the way. I've got an old S-10 Blazer parked out in front of the house by that little car of yours."

"How much fuel do you have?" asked Jessie, scratching his chin with thoughts swirling around in his head. "I've got a proposition for you..."

~~~~

Early the next morning, as the three men stood around the grave they had prepared for Joe, and after Jessie and Mike both said their final farewells, Mike looked at Jessie and Spence and said, "I thought about the offer you guys made me last night. I've decided to take you up on it. I want to go with you guys. Consider the fuel in my tank and in my jerry cans to be community property for the trip."

"Like I said last night, It's a fool's journey," Jessie replied, "but, it's your uncle's airplane. If you want to go, I'm sure he would have been more than happy to see his only nephew getting some use out of it."

"Great," Mike said, cracking a smile for the first time since they had met. "I've really got no place else to go, anyway. This was as far as my plans took me."

"There's a lot of that going around these days," Jessie replied.

Chapter Thirty-Three

With thirty-three gallons of fuel in the tanks, and after a successful test run-up of the aircraft's engine and one final test of the flight controls, Jessie looked over to Mike sitting in the co-pilot seat, and then back to Spence in the back seat, and said, "Well, guys. If you're gonna change your minds, it's now or never."

With the three of them looking at each other with uncertain grins, Spence said in his best, albeit poor, Scottish accent, "Give'r all she's got, Cap'n."

"All right then, here we go!" Jessie said as he released the brakes and brought the big Continental IO-520 engine above idle, initiating their taxi.

"Are you sure we've got enough room to get this thing off the ground with us and our gear in this small little level area?"

"Probably," Jessie replied. "The 185 is a hell of a bird. It's been used all over Alaska for decades for this very reason—taking off from unimproved strips, that is. We can probably start our takeoff run backed up against the fence behind the barn and head straight for the house. The trees on each side of the house are the highest obstacles, so aiming for the house gives us the best obstacle avoidance."

"Why aim for the house at all?" Spence asked, skeptical of Jessie's plan.

"With such a short takeoff roll, we need a headwind. The winds are blowing out of the west pretty hard. Trying to take off the other way might look clearer, but that tailwind will cause us to eat up too much real estate before we get airborne. It's not about how fast you're actually going, it's about how fast the air is moving over the wings."

"Hmmm," Spence replied. "Okay, then."

Taxiing toward the fence, getting as close to it as he could while still allowing room to swing the tail all the way around,

Jessie locked up the left main wheel brake, and with full tail-wheel-steering deflection, gunned the engine to initiate looping the tail around to put their backs to the fence. Once they were lined up and facing the house, Jessie asked, "Are you boys ready?"

"Nope, but go for it," Spence replied.

"Yeah, let's get it over with," added Mike.

"Alright, then," replied Jessie as he held both brakes firmly while slowly pushing the throttle all the way to the stops. With three hundred horses swinging the propeller at 2800 RPM, the tail began to lift off the ground as the engine fought against the brakes of the forward-mounted main wheels of the old tail-dragger. Releasing the brakes all at once, the aircraft lunged forward, accelerating as he headed straight for the one-story brick home.

Focusing on the house ahead, as soon as he felt the old bird wanting to fly, Jessie snapped the yoke back and pitched up for a maximum-angle climb as both Mike and Spence clutched their seats firmly, bracing for impact as the Cessna barely cleared the house below.

"Wooooo hooo!" shouted Spence. "Hot damn, that was close! How the heck did Joe get this thing back there?"

"I believe he pulled the wings off and had it trucked in."

"Why the heck didn't you tell us that before we pulled that hair-brained move?" Spence asked.

"Then you might have said no," Jessie replied with a sly grin.

"That's just like a shepherd," Spence joked.

"What is?" Jessie asked, curious as to what he meant.

"Earning his sheep's trust before he leads them off to slaughter," Spence replied, chuckling under his breath.

With a simple smile, Jessie turned his attention back to the task at hand and continued their climb out toward the southwest to avoid the terrain that lay just ahead of them. As the aircraft continued its climb, the men sat there in silence, enjoying the beauty of the Colorado mountain west down below. For a moment, the cities and towns didn't look like pits of sorrow and despair. For a moment, everything in the world seemed to be at peace.

~~~~

With Black Mountain to their west at over ten thousand, eight hundred feet tall, and the vast expanse of the southwestern Rocky Mountains to the east, Jessie looked at the others and said, "Okay, guys. We had thirty-three gallons of fuel at takeoff. Let's call it twenty-five now to be safe. At a fuel-burn of fourteen to fifteen gallons per hour once we get her leaned out at a cruise altitude of around ten-thousand feet, we've only got an hour and a half of fuel at best before we need to put her down. At one hundred and forty knots, not taking winds aloft into consideration, that gives us around two hundred miles of reach for this leg. That will put us just past Albuquerque, New Mexico."

Looking out the window, trying to figure out Jessie's rationale, Mike asked, "Why not just go straight over the mountains? Wouldn't that be a lot shorter?"

"Technically speaking, yes," Jessie replied. "However, the Rockies would put us near the altitudes where we would need supplemental oxygen to keep from going loopy, which is something we don't have onboard. Aside from that, I don't want to make that long of a stretch over mountainous terrain using autogas. I'm no engineer so I'm not all that well-versed on the technical details, I only know the basics, but I do know we don't have alcohol-free fuel. As a matter of fact, we've got old, stale fuel. I'd rather not risk having to put her down on the side of a mountain if we lose power due to a fuel-delivery problem. It's cold at the higher altitudes and that damp mountain air could cause us some fuel system icing problems. If we go south and work our way around the terrain toward Albuquerque, we should always be in a position to put her down safely if we lose power."

With a nod, Mike replied, "Makes sense to me. I'd rather not be trapped in the mountains and have to eat you guys like that soccer team, anyway."

Piping up from the back, Spence added, "Yeah, we'd all rather avoid that scenario. At least Jessie and I now know to keep an eye on you if we do go down."

Sharing a laugh, the men settled in, with Jessie focused on managing the aircraft while the other two gazed at the passing terrain below.

As they reached their cruising altitude, Jessie eased back on the throttle and rotated the vernier-style mixture control to lean the engine back to an efficient cruise speed. Looking over to Mike, he said, "Your uncle sure took great care of this old bird. I know he really loved it. He couldn't bear to part with it after he lost his medical, and here we are now. Like it was meant to be."

With a simple smile and a nod in reply, Mike looked back out the window at the passing scenery below.

~~~~

Other than the occasional mountainous-terrain-induced turbulence, the ride had been uneventful and quiet, with each of the men pondering what their futures may bring, lulled into a trance-like state by the droning of the big Continental engine.

Diligently studying the sectional chart for the area, Jessie broke the silence by saying, "It sure was easier when the ground-based navigational aids were still working."

"Not to mention GPS!" Spence exclaimed. "Everyone got so addicted to GPS that no one even had maps on hand when their electronic systems began to fail."

"At least we've got very distinct terrain features in this area. If we make it as far as the plains states, I'll be totally lost except for basic heading. It all looks the same for a thousand miles in all directions."

"What's that?" asked Mike.

"What's ground-based navigational aids?" Jessie asked to clarify Mike's question.

"No! That! Down there," Mike said as he pointed toward the small town below.

Being unable to see exactly what Mike was referring to from his vantage point, Jessie asked, "What do you see?"

"It's a light. Like a signal light. Coming from that cluster of houses."

"I see it, too," said Spence, having shifted in the back seat to Mike's side of the plane. "Well, I'll be damned," he said with bewilderment.

"What?"

"That's Morse code for S.O.S."

Looking back at Spence, Jessie asked, "Seriously?"

"Yep, I'm positive. I've had a lot of time on my hands to study up on this stuff, living all alone. It was that or just stare at the corner and go nuts, so I chose to study."

Turning back in the direction of the light, positioning the airplane so that he could get a look, Jessie looked at his chart and cross-referenced it with an old highway atlas. With his finger on the atlas, he said, "That appears to be a place called Counselor, New Mexico. We're just northwest of Albuquerque now."

Circling high overhead, Jessie looked at the others and said, "That's definitely a distress call of some sort."

"What do you want to do?" asked Spence.

After a moment of silence, Jessie replied, "Let's descend and take a closer look." Looking at the fuel gauges, he then added, "But we can't loiter down here for long. We don't have enough fuel to mess around. We also have to consider what we'll end up burning just to climb back up to altitude as well."

"I agree," replied Spence.

Beginning his descent, Jessie adjusted his fuel mixture and eased back on the power, pointing the nose down below the horizon while holding a right-wing-low spiraling descent so that both Mike and Spence could keep their eyes on the light.

"The light just stopped," said Mike.

"Yep," confirmed Spence.

Unable to see for himself, being on the left side of the airplane, Jessie asked, "Can you see anything else? Anyone who may have been sending the signal?"

"Nope. Not a thing," Spence replied.

"Wait," Mike shouted abruptly. "Go! Go! Go!" he shouted, seeing several muzzle flashes from several of the buildings on the ground. By the time his words of warning reached Jessie, bullets had begun pinging into the thin sheet-metal skin of the aircraft.

As Jessie shoved both the throttle and the mixture fully forward, and initiated a sharp turn to the left away from the threat, a bullet penetrated the bottom of the plane, entering Mike's lower jaw and exiting through the top of his head, splattering blood and brain matter all over the cream-colored interior of the aircraft.

Drenched in Mike's blood, Spence was at a loss for words, frozen in place in his seat.

As bullets continued to strike the airplane, black smoke began to billow out of the cowling, almost entirely blocking Jessie's forward visibility. "There goes the oil pressure," he shouted. "We're going down. I'll put us on that road. Get our gear ready to make a run for it after we touch down."

Hearing no reply, Jessie looked back to Spence, seeing him covered in Mike's blood, and shouted, "Spence! Get our gear ready to run!"

Snapping back into the moment, Spence muttered, "Yeah... Yeah, of course," as he began reaching into the cargo compartment behind the back seat, pulling their packs and rifles onto the seat alongside him.

"Seatbelts and brace!" shouted Jessie as they neared the road, still barely able to see in front of him from the thick, billowing cloud of oil smoke and oil droplets spewing from the damaged engine, completely covering the windshield.

Using the visibility from his side window, Jessie attempted to steer them toward the small paved road. He controlled the rate of descent by pitching the nose for the aircraft's best glide speed, the propeller now completely stopped as the engine finally succumbed to its damage and seized.

As he neared touchdown, Jessie flared slightly to arrest the decent rate, attempting a three-point touchdown in the old tail-dragger. Misjudging slightly, the tailwheel struck first, initiating a slight bounce that brought the mainwheels down hard. Unbeknownst to Jessie, the right front mainwheel tire had been struck and blown to pieces by the barrage of bullets that had killed Mike, causing the aircraft to swerve violently to the right. Unable to control the yawing motion with rudder alone, the Cessna ground-looped, striking the left wingtip on the ground. As the aircraft continued its deadly spin, the tail spun completely around and the old Cessna flipped over on its top and slid violently to a stop.

With smoke billowing out from the engine compartment, Jessie frantically grabbed the cockpit-mounted fire extinguisher and began discharging the bottle through the now broken windshield in a desperate attempt to stop the hot splattered engine oil from catching fire.

"Get out! Get out!" he shouted to Spence as a vehicle came to a screeching halt approximately twenty yards away.

Among the unintelligible shouts, Jessie clearly heard the phrase, "Allah be praised," in Arabic, along with other celebratory chants.

Being only able to see the boots of the men as they approached, still hanging from his seatbelt and pinned down in the wreckage, Jessie reached for his Colt, flipped the leather retaining strap off of the hammer, and cocked it. *Only six shots, but I'll make'em count,* Jessie thought as he feared the worst.

As the men neared the wreckage, Jessie whispered to Spence, "Don't let them take you."

"Same to you, Jessie. Good luck," Spence softly replied.

As Jessie heard the familiar sound of an AK-style rifle chambering a round, gunshots began to ring out all around them.

Expecting a barrage of bullets to start ripping through the thin aluminum aircraft fuselage, Jessie heard only a few direct hits. Confused about what was going on outside of the plane, the man standing closest to Jessie fell to the ground, and now lay dead, blood draining from his bullet-riddled corpse. The man, appearing to be in his mid-thirties of undeterminable ethnic origin, with a long beard and loose-fitting clothing similar to middle-eastern attire, lay with his back to the pavement, his eyes wide open and seemingly devoid of life, staring directly at Jessie.

Within moments, the gunfire subsided as Jessie and Spence both heard the coordinated movements and commands of several men outside.

Hearing one of the men shout, "Clear!" followed by several more, Jessie noticed a pair of tan desert boots jogging over to the fuselage.

"Are you okay in there?" a voice in English with a standard American accent asked.

Jessie responded, "Two survivors. One dead."

Seeing a man drop to his knees and look through Jessie's side window, the two made eye contact as the brown-haired, blued-eyed man in his early thirties said, "Hang on. We'll get you out. We've got to move quick."

Almost instantly, Jessie's door was aggressively pulled open, exposing the aircraft's interior to the daylight. "Come on," the man said as he reached out to take Jessie's hand.

Putting one hand above his head against the crumpled ceiling to arrest his fall, Jessie released his seatbelt buckle and rotated sideways, exiting the aircraft. Looking back toward Spence, he saw two of the men pulling Spence through the side cargo-door opening.

"The other one is dead?" one of the men stated, looking for clarification.

With a nod in the affirmative, Jessie acknowledged the sad fact as the man then said, "Okay, we've got to move before they send backup."

As a desert-tan Humvee pulled alongside the crash site, the men led Jessie and Spence to the cargo area in the rear, as it was set up in the M998 cargo/troop transport configuration. As soon as they were all aboard, the Humvee, along with a second one directly behind them, sped away from the smoldering scene of the crash.

Chapter Thirty-Four

Running down the road at what appeared from the back to be the Humvee's maximum speed, one of the men, with a medium build, sandy brown hair and brown eyes, looking to be in his late twenties to early thirties, said to both Jessie and Spence, "My name is Denny. Are either of you hurt?"

"We can't leave him there, Denny," Jessie insisted.

"What?" the man said over the roar of the engines and the noise generated by the off-road tread tires of the Humvees.

"We can't leave him there," Jessie said, this time shouting.

"Sir, there was nothing we could do. We barely had time to get you out of there, much less extract the body. Our spotters have already indicated that backup arrived on scene just after we left."

"Who? Who are they? Whose backup?"

"We'll explain more when we get to where we're going. For now, you two just take it easy and try to relax."

"We just freakin' got shot down," Spence shouted. "That doesn't just happen every day. We've got a lot of questions."

"Like I said, we'll be able to explain more when we get to where we're going. For now, sit tight," the man said as he turned his attention back to the men in the front of the Humvee.

"Are they Army or Guard?" asked Spence, looking to Jessie with concern.

"These are Guard Humvees, but these aren't guardsmen. Well, they aren't at the moment, at least," Jessie replied as he looked around trying to get a mental grasp of what had just happened.

Noticing that the men wore a mix of civilian and military attire, and carried what appeared to be MIL-SPEC select-fire M4's, as well as each of the men wearing a load-bearing vest supporting numerous STANMAG 5.56 NATO magazines, Jessie knew there must have been a government connection at one point.

As Jessie watched the men in the front of the Humvee, one of the men talking on the vehicle-mounted radio tugged on Denny's shoulder, seemingly notifying him of some sort of incoming news. Quickly looking behind them at the Humvee in trail, Denny scurried back to Jessie and Spence in the rear and said, "They're on us. There are two vehicles chasing from behind. They're gaining on the other truck. We're gonna split up so that we can take them on our terms. With luck, they'll split up and follow us both. Hold on."

As Denny took a seat and held on tight, the Humvee veered hard left, nearly sliding Jessie across the back of the cargo area and into Spence's lap. Becoming slightly airborne over a rise in the terrain off to the side of the road, Jessie watched as the other Humvee split off to the right and led both pursuing vehicles to the other side of the road. Both Humvees now having departed pavement and heading in opposite directions, Jessie, Spence, and Denny watched as gunfire erupted between the three other vehicles. To their horror, a shoulder-fired, rocket-propelled grenade was launched from the bed of one of the pursuing pickup trucks, striking the Humvee. The impact knocked the severely damaged Humvee off course, sending the vehicle, now engulfed in flames, rolling and flipping violently end over end until it came to rest on its top.

A look of sheer horror came over Denny's face as they drove away, out of sight and over the next hill, with the knowledge that their friends in the other vehicle had been killed before their eyes.

Silence consumed the men as the Humvee maintained its course off-road, speeding and bouncing along, until reaching a ravine with a dry rainwater wash at the bottom. The Humvee drove into the ravine and handrailed the wash, struggling over the harsh terrain until reaching a point where they could cross, climbing the hill on the other side and up onto an old dirt road.

Following the dirt road to the north for another half an hour, they finally reached a small camp hidden from plain view by large rocky outcrops in the terrain. Without saying a word, Denny jumped out of the Humvee and ran toward camp as several other men ran out to greet him. "Jörgen!" he shouted to one of the men.

"Where's the other truck?" Jörgen asked with an obvious Swedish accent.

"We lost them."

"Did they follow you here?"

"We're not sure. Their trucks were stock four-wheel-drive pickups. They could outrun us on the road, but they'd have a hard time coming the way we did." Pausing and looking back to the direction from where they came, he then said, "They could follow on foot or with some other vehicles in the very near future, though. We've got to go."

"Right," said Jörgen as he turned and shouted the order to break down camp to several others in the camp.

With practiced precision, the group immediately began breaking down and packing up their tents. Most of their gear, already being in large portable containers, was thrown onto an old International flatbed truck.

"How can we help?" asked Jessie.

"Watch our backs while we pack," Denny said, tossing Jessie an M4. "Do you know how to use that?"

"Absolutely," replied Jessie.

"Great," Denny replied as he opened one of the containers, removed another rifle and tossed it to Spence. "You guys get on that hill over there and keep an eye out. When we're all packed up, we'll call you in and you can bug out with us. Got it?"

"Got it!" Jessie replied.

As Jessie and Spence watched for any sign of activity off in the distance, the others frantically packed their gear onto the flatbed truck, into the remaining Humvee, and into an old Jeep Wrangler. Both the flatbed and the Wrangler appeared to have been painted desert-camouflage in a very rudimentary fashion.

Once the gear was all loaded, Jessie heard a whistle and turned to see Denny waving them down. "Come on, guys. Let's go!"

Running down the hill, Jessie and Spence climbed into the back of the Humvee with several others, as the vehicles sped away.

~~~~

As the sun began to set, the silence between the men and the only woman in the Humvee was overshadowed by the engine and road noise created by the speeding vehicle. They had all lost friends that day, and each person was beginning to cope in their own way.

Breaking the silence after several miles, Jörgen spoke up and said, "Denny and his group were out making observations when they saw your aircraft overhead. They said they saw you descend closer to the old Navajo boarding school and begin to circle when you started taking fire. Who are you, and what were you doing over the boarding school?"

Jessie and Spence both began to explain their situation, and how their individual journeys had brought them together with Mike. Jessie then continued, saying, "So anyway, we were on our way toward Albuquerque where we were going to have to stop and scavenge for fuel. Mike, the poor kid with us in the plane who didn't make it, saw a signal light. Spence here verified that they were signaling S.O.S. so we went in for a closer look. That's when they took us down and your guys showed up. And look, we're sorry about what happened to the other half of your crew.

We'd have rather died on that road at the hands of whoever the hell that was than to have put your guys at risk."

"They died doing what they felt they had to do," Jörgen explained. "This world we've all inherited—this catastrophically broken world—only has one chance to make it back to any recognizable form of civilization. That is, if the good people stand together and fight, even in the face of death, against a seemingly superior force. In the recent past, too many people just rolled over and capitulated when faced with injustice and corruption. As you can tell from my speech, I am not originally from the U.S. I am originally from Sweden. I have always had a soft spot in my heart for the freedoms you Americans had. You have no idea how many books I have read and how many old John Wayne movies I have watched. As my country was being taken over from the inside by complicit politicians, and wave after wave of migrants from the Middle East and other places, who did not want to assimilate as Swedes, but rather sought to convert my beloved country into an image they wanted, I took a job in Albuquerque on a H-1B visa to get away from it all and start over. You see, my government, just like yours, was just letting it happen. Some of which was intentional, and some of which was simply the inept being pawns in the greater game. It happened to us sooner because of our geographical location as well as the economic fragility of the Eurozone caused by the European debt crisis.

"Political correctness, and the fear of standing up for who you are and what you believe because you might be ridiculed, led to my nation being paralyzed. I felt like I was having a bad dream from which I could not awake. Even before the bombings started and the waves of crime and violence spread like wildfires, I just could no longer recognize my beloved Sweden. Working in emergency services back home, I heard it all first hand. It was obvious to me that it was not going to get better, either. The politicians and government leaders did not have the will, and the general population did not have a way.

"Due to our very stringent gun laws, the citizens of Sweden did not have access to firearms like here in the United States. That meant mounting a serious opposition without any sort of outside help simply was not as feasible.

"Sadly," he continued. "Moving to the U.S. did not allow me to escape what was happening back home. When the global financial collapse began, followed by the attacks and the infighting on U.S. soil, I felt like I was living it all over again.

"Shortly before the final stages of the collapse, myself and a few other like-minded individuals started a mutual-assistance group in the event we felt things started to reach the point of no return.

"When it was clear that the end-game was upon us and was not going to be stopped, we bugged out together as a group and eventually joined up with Denny. He and several other former National Guardsmen who joined our group, several of whom lost their lives today, were able to help us out in regards to supplies. They had managed to get their hands on a few helpful items on their way out the door.

"Since then, we have been trying to do whatever we could, to help whomever we could. What purpose is there in living if you are not making a difference?"

"I agree with you completely," Jessie replied.

"Amen to that!" added Spence. "I've made it through all this by hiding out, but no more."

Looking back to Jörgen, Jessie asked, "So, what were you observing? Who was that back there?"

"So you know how the NWO leaders used terrorist cells to do some of their dirty work?"

"Yes, we do."

"After the organized fighting stopped, the Jihadist movement didn't. Just prior to the collapse, there were numerous terrorist training camps located along the southern side of the U.S./Mexican border, poised and ready to strike. When it all started going down, the cells activated and moved easily into the U.S. through the mostly undefended and porous border. Many were killed in the fighting that ensued—killed by citizens standing their ground as well as the NWO-elite-controlled forces that set out to stop the jihadists once they had begun to abandon their alliances and turn on them. The ones who remained were left with a chaotic situation in which they could thrive."

"Just as ISIS had no trouble recruiting before, in the days leading up to the collapse, the groups that are now here in the U.S. are not having trouble, either. Some of those who join are die-hard radicals who truly believe in the cause; others are self-radicalized individuals who relish in the opportunity to rape, murder, and be a part of something that exerts power and superiority over others. Either way, the end result is the same."

Coughing from the dust being kicked up by the trucks, Jörgen cleared his throat and continued, "The area you were circling is a point of interest for us because a jihadist group has taken over the previously abandoned Navajo boarding school located in Counselor, New Mexico. They have kidnapped at least fourteen young girls that we know of, to use as both sex slaves and as young brides for the jihadists themselves. The girls that resist are often raped, tortured, stoned, and killed, becoming an example to the others if they do not conform to the new way of life being forced upon them. It is the same old song and dance that we have seen in the Middle East for ages, only now, it is here."

"Are these guys in particular hardcore radical jihadists, or are they self-radicalized individuals?" Jessie asked.

"A mixture of both, from what we can tell," replied Jörgen. "We believe their leader to be Imad al-Din Hashemi. He is the real deal from what we know. Probably a survivor from the wave that came across the southern border during the onset of the attacks. Many of his followers, however, are homegrown."

After a moment of silence to take it all in, Jessie and Spence shared a look of mutual understanding as Jessie turned to Jörgen and said, "We'd be glad to help out in any way we can. Your guys died saving us. It's the least we can do. Not to mention the fact that there is no way either of us could just walk away knowing what's happening to those girls."

With a look of appreciation, Jörgen said, "Considering our losses today, we can use all the help we can get. What you have seen is all that is left. Marissa here is a registered nurse by trade and was a nurse in the Guard as well. She has been acting as our field medic and camp doc."

"Pleased to meet you," Marissa said with a nod.

"Likewise, ma'am," Jessie and Spence both replied.

"Denny and Curtis are former active-duty Army turned National Guard infantrymen," Jörgen continued. "They have been the trainers for the rest of us. Frank, the gentlemen driving the flatbed, was an over-the-road trucker with lots of firearms experience as a hunter and outdoor enthusiast. Tommy is the younger fellow driving the Jeep out in front of the flatbed. He is young at only nineteen years old, but he has got a lot of fight in him. He and others like him are the future of this country and this world, if you ask me. The man riding shotgun for him is Leland. Leland was a retail store manager turned preparedness minded survivalist. He, like myself, did not have any sort of fighting experience before this all happened, but we have all gotten our hands dirty several times over at this point. What about you two? What are your backgrounds?"

"Spence here, is a doctor," Jessie said, nudging Spence in the side.

"A Doctor of Veterinary Medicine," Spence clarified.

Looking at Spence, Jessie said, "You yourself said that's the best kind of doctor. Remember? You can perform your procedures in a barn without all of that fancy stuff."

Blushing slightly, Spence looked to Jörgen and Marissa and said, "I would be happy to assist Marissa in any way I can."

"And you?" Jörgen asked, looking at Jessie.

"Most recently, I was a simple shepherd and homesteader. I was in law enforcement prior to all that, though."

"That is a good skillset to have," Jörgen said. "Your law enforcement experience will come in handy now, and your animal husbandry skills will surely come in handy when the world starts to recover."

Changing the subject, Jörgen said, "We will be at our next campsite soon. We will practice light discipline tonight and forgo the bulk of the setup until morning. Other than those on watch, everyone will just sleep in, around, or under one of the vehicles. When we get a chance to settle in, I will talk to Denny and the others and we will get you both on board with our plans, if you are willing. For tonight, though, just get some sleep and we will work on the details tomorrow."

"Are you in charge of the group?" Spence asked Jörgen.

"No. No one is in charge. We all have a role to fill and we each understand that role. I was an emergency services manager, so I am good at staying on top of all the details amidst chaos and disorder, of which there is no shortage here."

"Roger that," replied Spence. He then turned to Marissa and said, "It's your show, ma'am, I'm at your assistance."

"Like Jörgen said, it's no one's show, sir," she replied. "We're all in it together here."

"Of course," he replied with a smile.

Chapter Thirty-Five

Early the next morning as the first rays of the day's sunlight began to warm the camp, Jessie awoke to the feeling of something crawling on his forehead. Smacking at it, still half asleep, Jessie looked at his hand to realize it was oil dripping down onto his head from the undercarriage of the flatbed truck, under which he had been sleeping.

Great, he thought as he attempted to wipe it off with his sleeve. Crawling out from underneath the truck, Jessie saw Denny sitting atop a nearby hill, glassing the area off in the distance with a pair of binoculars. Walking up the hill to Denny, Jessie said, "Good morning."

Without deviating from his scan of the terrain below and in the distance, Denny replied, "Any day you wake up starts out as a good day. It's up to you to screw it up from there."

With a chuckle, Jessie replied, "Yes, sir. That's a fact. I can relieve you, if you want to catch a nap."

"Don't sweat it. I'm all right," Denny replied as he lowered the binoculars, hanging them from the lanyard around his neck. "You've got a busy day ahead of you, anyway."

"I do?" queried Jessie.

"Yeah, well, if you're gonna join us at the boarding school that is."

"Of course, but what's the plan?"

"First off, we've got to get you two trained up. I'm sure you can handle a weapon just fine, especially with your background. We just want to make sure everyone is on the same page here. Being half prior-service and half civilian-trained, we've sort of developed our own style over time. We've got some rather unique hand signals and whatnot that you'll need to be well versed on before making any sort of a move on the boarding school, which they've turned into quite the compound, by the way."

"When do we start?" Jessie asked.

"Leland is our mess crank of the day. We rotate that duty to everyone. If you want to see if he needs any help, give him a hand and get yourself something to eat. After breakfast, we'll all get together and go over everything." Turning to look at Jessie with a facial expression that indicated his seriousness, Denny said, "We're gonna have to hit them soon, whether we're ready or not. From what we've seen, we can't leave those girls down there any longer. If we wait until we're ready, it might be too late for many of them. That's just not acceptable."

"What do you know of the girls? Do any of them have a family?"

"Not that we know of. We'll have to debrief them once they've had time to decompress, to try to find out if there is somewhere we can try to take them. I can't imagine the families that lost the girls fared very well during the struggle, though."

"So what's your plan, then?" Jessie asked. "You know, afterward."

"Don't have one," Denny bluntly stated. "Hell, we may all be killed and there won't be an afterward. We've learned to take things one step at a time. Planning is critical, but around here, planning too far into the future just sets a benchmark for failure. We've come to learn to just roll with the punches and accept the gifts when they're given."

Nodding as if he understood, while not fully agreeing, Jessie said, "Well, I'll leave you to your work. I'll go see if Leland needs my help."

~~~~

After breakfast, the group gathered together and caught Jessie and Spence up to speed on their group's standard operating procedures, as well as taking the time to get to know one another. Once they were on the same page, Jörgen spoke up and said, "I was speaking with Denny and Curtis earlier, and given the sudden change in our manpower, we feel the time to make a move on the compound is now. We lost some good friends yesterday. That is something that seems to happen all too often.We cannot afford to take any more hits. If we lose anyone else, we may not have adequate resources to get the job done. The weaker we are as a group, the more dangerous the situation will become for the girls if we do make a move. With Jessie and Spence onboard, we have to assume that we are at our peak for the foreseeable future."

Jörgen looked around the group, seeing that everyone was nodding in agreement and said, "Spence, we want you and Leland to stay back and be our support team."

Caught off guard by Jörgen's statement, Spence held his protest to hear him out.

"We have to assume there will be casualties or injuries. Marissa will be going along as our field medic. In the event we..." pausing to find the right words, Jörgen continued, saying, "In the event we do not have the luxury of her services after the fact, we will be well served having you ready to receive any of the wounded, as well as to provide any medical assistance to any of the girls that we may be lucky enough to free. You and Leland will stay with the flatbed several miles away from the boarding school, ready to assist with extraction or medical care as needed."

"Jessie, we need you to go along with the rest of us. It is going to take every person we have. Denny and Curtis are finalizing the plan, which we will go over prior to making our move. That gives us you, Frank, Tommy, Denny, Curtis, Marissa, and myself. By our estimates, they have the advantage in numbers at nearly two to one, but why let math get in the way, right?"

Sharing an uneasy smile, understanding the full weight of the situation they were about to face, the group dispersed and spent the rest of the afternoon preparing their gear, each person taking the time to focus on the gravity of the situation they were about to face in their own way.

As Spence and Marissa got to know one another and went through the group's medical supplies, Jessie found shade under the rear of the flatbed, reached into his pocket, and removed his journal. Silently staring at the cover for a moment, Jessie flipped it open and began to write.

It seems like both yesterday, and an eternity ago, that I was living a happy life on my family's homestead. I had everything I wanted, yet it was all taken from me. In that darkest of hours, I had nearly lost all hope for humanity and for myself. Setting out to shed myself of the emotional pain and suffering I would have surely endured if I would have stayed, I have encountered the best and the worst humanity has to offer.

The hope and spirit I've seen in people like Ash, Spence, and now Jörgen and his crew, and their steadfast determination to retain their dignity and humanity in the face of the ultimate tests of strength, has rekindled my hope for the world and for myself.

I'm not sure where I am supposed to end up in life. Not a day goes by that I don't long to be in heaven with my wife and children. Not a day goes by that I don't want to break down into tears from the pain in my heart that I hope never goes away. I never want them to slip out of reach of my memory and that pain, no matter how emotionally debilitating, keeps them close to me inside.

Still unsure why I have been spared, I no longer feel as if I am making my own way through the world. I feel as if I am being led through it, as if there is a destination that I am meant to find, although I know not what it is.

Pausing to look up into the sky, Jessie saw a great eagle circling overhead. Momentarily losing his thoughts to the grace and majesty of the bird, Jessie smiled and then returned to his thoughts.

If my journey is to end tonight, so be it. If it does, I just pray God reunites me with my wife and children in heaven. If it does not, if my journey is meant to take me to another place for some reason as yet unbeknownst to me, I will dutifully follow. I have countless debts to repay for the blessings that have been bestowed on me and intend on settling those debts no matter what the cost.

Tucking his journal back into his jacket pocket, Jessie laid his head back on his pack and watched the eagle as it flew higher and higher, disappearing from his view into the rays of the sun.

Chapter Thirty-Six

As the moon replaced the sun in the sky, and as the cool desert breeze flowed through camp, everyone readied their gear and made their final equipment checks. With an M4 carbine and his trusty Colt on his side, Jessie slipped the last of his six thirty-round 5.56 magazines into his load-bearing vest and ensured that everything was snug and secure. With the body armor they had given him underneath, he felt overloaded and cumbersome, but he knew it was better to be over prepared than under prepared.

"Are you all set?" Denny asked, walking up to Jessie.

"As ready as ever," Jessie replied.

Looking around to the entire camp, Denny shouted, "Okay, folks, listen up. Everyone gather around. Curtis is about to go over the final plan."

Stepping up onto a portable storage container, Curtis said, "Here's the plan: Jessie, you're gonna go with Marissa in the Jeep. To our knowledge, they've never seen our Jeep, or Marissa for that matter. You two are going to create the initial diversion. You two will drive up Highway 550 toward the boarding school. We don't imagine they'll let your presence go unanswered. As soon as you see activity, and they get a good look at the two of you, get the heck out of there. Head west until you reach the abandoned post office.

"Upon reaching the post office, exit 550 onto the dirt road just behind the post office and follow it back to what used to be the local government building. Jörgen will be lying in wait on one of the rooftops, or a similarly advantageous position, and will begin to pick off your pursuers. Engage them there once Jörgen begins firing on them and keep them occupied. If you can take them out of the fight and join up with us, great. If not, hold them off there as long as you can to give us time to hit the remaining threats at the compound and attempt to extract the girls.

"Denny, Frank, Tommy, and I will take advantage of the diversion to make our move. Denny, Tommy, and I will be lying in wait in the darkness. Frank will be positioned on one of the roofs at the old stockyard across the road from the boarding school compound. He'll have the fifty cal—"

"You've got a fifty?" interrupted Spence.

"Yeah, we've got a fifty," Curtis replied, seemingly annoyed by the interruption.

"So, like I was saying," he continued. "Frank will be on top of one of the buildings at the stockyard, putting a world of hurt on any of the jihadis who show themselves at the compound."

"Will Frank have any sort of night vision?" asked Jessie.

"No, he won't. The fifty-cal has a damn fine scope on it, though."

"Will he be able to acquire his targets in the dark with a conventional scope at that distance? How is the lighting at the compound?" asked Jessie.

"It will be fine," insisted Curtis. "Frank knows what he's doing. To get back on track here, Frank will provide cover for us to move in on the camp while you've got a handful or more of them tied up behind the post office down the road.

"From what we know, the girls are being kept mostly in the main T-shaped building. That's where they seem to always be led in and out of when we've caught a glimpse of them through our optics while out on our observations. We'll take out anyone we encounter as we go, until we find them."

Looking at Marissa, Curtis said, "Once you and Jessie take care of the jihadis who follow you to the post office, join up with Jörgen and make your way back to the compound to provide cover-fire while we extract the girls."

Seeing the look of concern on Jessie's face, Curtis said, "Do you have a problem with something?"

With tension now clearly in the air, Jessie replied, "Look, I'm not trying to be confrontational. I'm just trying to make sure we've covered all the bases here. If I poke holes in your boat and it still floats, it's a good boat. If it sinks, we need another boat, that's all."

"So what's the problem?" Curtis asked again.

"The plan, as you presented it, makes a pretty big assumption that a group will peel away from the compound to follow Marissa and me. What if that doesn't happen? Without a reduction in force at the compound, as you've clearly tried to address with the vehicle diversion, you'll be three on the ground facing their full strength."

"They'll follow," Curtis insisted.

"He's got a point, though," Spence interjected. "What if they don't?"

"Who saved who?" Curtis replied in a very pointed manner. "If I recall, you got yourself into a bind and we had to bail you out. At the expense of some of our finest people, I might add."

Stepping forward in an attempt to calm the tensions between Jessie and Curtis, Jörgen said, "He has got some valid questions, Curtis. Let us just work through them so that everyone is clear. There is no reason to get upset."

In a defiant tone, Curtis said, "If you want the new guy to lead this, then I'm out. We risked our lives to save him and his friend over there and now you're letting them disrupt our way of doing things."

"You have done a fine job for us, Curtis," Jörgen replied. "We will never forget that, however, past success does not prevent future failures. Just hear him out. He was in law enforcement before all this."

"He was a shepherd," Curtis responded sharply.

With his hands pulled back and open, Jessie said, "I think you're misunderstanding me, here, Curtis. I'm not trying to start anything. I'm thankful and grateful of what you guys did for us, but I'm thinking of those girls. Not me, not you, but them. Sure, we've got a lot to lose here if we bungle it up, but unless we are successful, those girls have a much rougher road ahead than any of us. Dying by bullet tonight will be an easy way out compared to the fates that await them. Now, let's just work this out and get on with it the best we can."

Stepping up to Jessie with his chest forward and his arms back, Curtis said, "Look, I worked with special forces in the Army. I don't need any lip from some failure of a cop who ran off to raise goats in the mountains while the rest of us were still knee-deep in it."

"Sheep," Jessie snapped.

"What?"

"They were sheep. And besides, if you'll explain your experience and expertise to me, in regards to you working *with* the special forces, maybe I'll better understand. Were you *in* the special forces, or did you work *with* them, and who exactly?"

As Curtis began to tense up and pull his right arm back, Denny stepped in and snapped, "Curt! That's enough."

Turning to Jessie, Denny explained, "We're all just a little tense tonight. There's a lot at stake and that's enough to stress anyone out. Just trust us that we've handled a lot of bad situations in the past and we'll handle this one just fine as well."

"As long as no one's pride is being put before the safety of those girls, I'll follow your lead," Jessie replied, looking at Curtis out of the corner of his eye.

Assuming control of the situation, Denny shouted, "Okay, let's all just go get some rest. As soon as the sun goes down, those of us that are assigned forward positions need to get on the move. Leland, you and Spence have everything you need ready to go for any casualties, and have the stake-sides on the flatbed for evac of the girls. When we call you in, bring the flatbed ASAP. Marissa, unless you hear from us otherwise, roll on up the road toward the compound at zero-three-hundred hours. By that point, we should have each had time to get into position and the compound should be bedded down for the night, ensuring that most of the girls will be in the main building like we discussed."

~~~~

Later that evening, Denny, Curtis, Tommy, Frank, and Jörgen set out in the remaining Humvee to a pre-planned location where they would each hike to their respective positions under the cover of darkness. As Marissa and Jessie readied the Jeep, Marissa looked at Jessie and said, "I'm sorry about Curtis. He can be a hothead at times, but he and Denny have really gotten us through a lot."

"What did he do on active duty and in the Guard?" Jessie asked.

"You're still on that?" she asked.

"This plan is far from solid. Have you guys ever made an assault like this before?"

Pausing for a moment, she replied, "Well, no, we've mostly done hit-and-runs or ambushes, but Curtis and Denny did in the Army—at least I assume they have. This is Curt's first time leading, though. Jeremy—he was one of the men killed in the other Humvee—was usually in charge of this sort of thing."

Knowing it was too late to push the issue, Jessie simply nodded in reply and went back to the business at hand. Marissa could sense Jessie's doubt about the plan, but like Jessie, she knew the ball was already rolling and they needed to see it through.

Breaking the silence as they finalized their preparations, Jessie said, "If we keep our M4s between the seats, they'll be hidden until we need them, yet still be easily accessible. I think we should lose the top and doors, too."

"Why?"

"The most this fabric top will do for us is to provide us with a small margin of visual cover. However, when and if you're trying to return fire, it could be a big hindrance. Not to mention the fact that once we get to the ambush site behind the post office—if we make it that far—we'll need to egress in a hurry and get in a position to fight. You won't want anything slowing you down."

"Makes sense," she replied.

As Jessie and Marissa began removing the top and doors, Leland and Spence approached. Leland said, "Anything we can help you two with? We've got the flatbed ready to roll, and all of the first-aid and trauma gear is staged and ready as well."

"No, I think we've got it," Jessie replied. "But thanks."

"No problem," Leland replied. "You've got the tough job. I feel like I should be doing more."

"Don't look at it that way, Leland. Just think, if you were a soldier in a bind, would there be anyone more important than your extraction team?"

With a chuckle, Leland said, "Yeah, I guess. When you look at it that way, I suppose I feel a little better."

"If you get called in the middle of a firefight, you two make sure you keep your heads on straight yourselves. No one is safe until they're back at camp. Don't forget that."

"Jess," Spence said, getting Jessie's attention.

"Yeah?"

"I just wanted you to know you've saved my life several times over, and I appreciate it."

"What are you talking about, Spence? You patched my busted butt back together after I looted your house," Jessie replied, rubbing his still achy shoulder wound.

"Something I never told you... Well, you see, when I came back to my home in Dolores, I subconsciously expected it to be for the last time. I think I wanted it to hurry and end. Now, I wasn't planning anything in particular. I just kind of felt it coming. Having you there, well, it gave me a reason to be me again. Why do you think I was so quick to sign on to your cross-country suicide mission? Meeting you, having a true friend in this world when I had been alone for so long, brought me back out of a dark place that perhaps I didn't even realize I was in. I've been more alive since I met you than for as long as I can remember. Take care of Marissa here and take care of yourself. This world, as screwed up as it may be, still needs men like Sheriff Townsend around."

"Thanks, buddy," Jessie said as he reached out to shake Spence's hand, only to be embraced in a big bear hug by the burly old fellow.

Chapter Thirty-Seven

As the wind buffeted throughout the cab, the now topless Jeep drove through the night toward the boarding school. Jessie turned to Marissa, who was in the passenger seat, and asked, "How are we doing on time?"

"It's two-fifty-five. We'll be right on time."

"I just hope everyone else is," he replied.

Seeing the lights of the compound off in the distance, both Jessie and Marissa felt their tension rise as they were entering the point of no return. With their headlights on bright, they knew they had undoubtedly been spotted by now, even if the camp did not have forward lookouts.

"Here we go," she said.

"Yep," Jessie replied.

Sharing a glancing smile, the two looked ahead at the daunting task that awaited.

~~~~

From atop the main building in the stockyard, Frank could see the headlights of the Jeep approaching in the distance. His pulse raced as he knew it was all about to hit the fan directly in front of him. *I sure hope everyone else is ready,* he thought, knowing he would be an easy target, alone on the roof, if the occupants of the compound were not held at bay by the impending attacks.

Looking through the scope of the big Barrett M107, Frank struggled to find any potential targets at the compound with the low level of available light. *Oh, well, I'm sure the place will be lit up well before long.*

~~~~

Jogging through the desert brush toward the buildings behind the post office, Jörgen looked at his watch and thought, *They should have given me more time! I had the furthest to go on foot!*

Increasing his pace, Jörgen reached the cluster of buildings and frantically looked for a suitable place for the ambush. Seeing a large steel dumpster with a sliding metal door on the front, just to the right of the local government building, he ran up to it and gave it a good whack with his knuckles. *That will do,* he thought, noting the thickness of the metal.

Sliding the door on the front of the dumpster partially open, Jörgen climbed inside on top of the trash and refuse. He then pushed the door half closed. This would give him a shooting port, as well as the benefit of having double the thickness of the metal where the door and the dumpster wall overlapped.

Looking again at his watch, *Three o'clock. Here we go,* he thought as he double-checked his rifle as well as his H&K USP .40 sidearm. Settling into the trash as best he could in order to reduce his chance of making unintentional noises, Jörgen watched carefully out of his shooting port, hoping to see a sign of the Jeep at any moment.

~~~~

Giving Tommy and Denny the hand signal to spread out to their pre-planned positions and wait for the Jeep, Curtis began his long, low crawl toward the compound, from the rear, opposite the road. With the Jeep driving past the road on the other side of the boarding school, the jihadist's attention should be diverted toward the road, allowing them to make their move on the compound as planned.

Looking at his watch by the glow of the moonlight, Curtis's heart rate intensified and he could feel beads of cold sweat on his forehead as the moment had arrived. Looking off in the distance to the east, he could see the faint lights of the distant but approaching Jeep. *C'mon, C'mon, work… this has got to work,* he thought as he watched Jessie and Marissa get closer and closer to the dangers that awaited them.

Seeing movement around the compound, with someone yelling orders in what appeared to him to be Arabic, his heart sank in his chest as he heard the compound's diesel generator spool down, causing the lights that they had depended on for Frank's overwatch to extinguish, leaving them in complete darkness. *Oh, no… God, no…*

~~~~

"Jessie!" Marissa said as she saw all of the compound's lights go dark.

"Yeah, I know," he replied. "There are two quotes I've always held to be the absolute truth," he said as he scanned intensely through the bug-splattered windshield for signs of anything up ahead.

"What's that?" she asked.

"The first one is from Colin Powell. He said, 'No battle plan survives contact with the enemy.'"

"What's the other?" she asked.

As he began to answer, they passed the wreckage of Joe's Cessna 185, still resting on its top. Jessie couldn't help but wonder if poor Mike was still inside. Looking at Marissa, he said, "If I'm still alive after tonight, I'm coming back to give him a proper burial."

Approaching the now-darkened compound, she asked again, "So, what's your second favorite quote?"

Before he could answer, he said, "What the heck is—" Slamming on the brakes, Jessie swerved as a large-diameter steel cable was being reeled across the road, snapping tight directly in front of them, several feet above the ground. Barely recovering from the swerve without rolling the little Jeep, Jessie pressed the accelerator to the floor as he pointed the Jeep directly off the road.

He shouted, "It's from Sun Tzu, who wrote 'In the midst of chaos, there is also opportunity!' Now hang on!" as the Jeep launched over the earth berm along the side of the road, becoming airborne momentarily before bouncing violently from the impact. Regaining control just in time to avoid a small tree, Jessie steered the Jeep directly for the compound, yelling to Marissa, "Grab the flares!"

Swerving erratically, Jessie slid the Jeep sideways around a small outbuilding on the eastern side of the compound. "Stay down the best you can!" he shouted, as he drove the Jeep at a high rate of speed between the buildings of the compound, with several of the jihadists diving out of the way as Jessie barreled through the compound like a mad man. He knew staying in close while keeping his speed up and driving erratically was his best chance to avoid gunfire from the compound itself, following the same tactic as an attacking helicopter would, staying in close and tight, approaching at rooftop level to avoid being shot at from a distance.

With bullets pinging through the thin sheet-metal side of the little Jeep, several shattering the windshield, he shouted, "There! The tank! Pop the flares and throw them at the tank!" as he drove wildly toward a large LP gas tank that supplied fuel to the compound's generator and heat.

Marissa got two of the flares ignited and tossed successfully in the vicinity of the tank as Jessie slid the Jeep around it, the tires spinning wildly, kicking up dust and debris that clouded the area, adding to the confusion of his attack. With the flares in place, Jessie pointed toward Highway 550 and the stockyard where Frank was supposed to be positioned.

With the two left tires on the Jeep being penetrated by gunfire, and nearly shredding themselves completely off the rim, Jessie began to lose control. Suddenly, he felt a heavy thud directly in the center of his back. Being unable to breathe or speak, Jessie signaled to Marissa to use the radio and he mouthed the word, *Frank.*

Immediately understanding Jessie's plan, Marissa got on the radio and yelled, "Frank! Hit the flares! Hit the tank by the flares!" as the Jeep once again hit the berm separating the compound from the main road.

The Jeep, now nearly out of control, hit the berm at an angle, causing it to careen to the right as it became airborne, impacting the pavement on its left-hand side, initiating a violent tumble as both Jessie and Marissa were tossed from the crashing vehicle.

~~~~

Patiently waiting in the dumpster for the ambush that was now overdue, Jörgen began hearing small arms fire off in the distance. *Crap! Here they come!* he thought.

Readying himself for the pursuit he expected to see come barreling around the corner of the post office at any moment, Jörgen heard the pounding blasts of the fifty-cal from Frank's position as Frank began hitting the compound upon Marissa's order. After four shots of the big fifty, Jörgen heard a massive explosion and saw the sky light up from a distance.

Something is not right! he thought as he climbed out of the dumpster, slung the rifle over his back and began running toward the explosion.

~~~~

As Curtis and the others watched Jessie's headlights swerve erratically through the camp and begin to take on fire, Curtis ordered Denny and Tommy to engage. "Cover that crazy bastard!" he shouted as he saw Jessie and Marissa taking on gunfire. "I don't know what he's doing, but cover them!"

With all of the attention in the compound focused on the Jeep, Curtis, Denny, and Tommy left their positions of cover and advanced on the boarding school. As they advanced, Denny saw a muzzle flash out of the corner of his eye as a man dressed in all black began firing on them with an AK-style rifle. Feeling a searing pain in his left leg and side, he focused on the man and returned fire with his M4, taking him out of the fight with three well-placed hits.

Seeing that Denny was no longer moving forward at an aggressive pace, Curtis dropped back to his position to see that he was bleeding profusely. Pulling his own trauma pack from his gear, saving Denny time, Curtis tossed it to him and said, "Get a tourniquet on your leg and stay put. I'll be back."

"No!" Denny shouted. "I'm good."

"Like hell you are!" Curtis said as he watched Tommy round the corner of one of the buildings, disappearing from his sight.

Dropping to his knees and taking cover behind a small pumphouse, Denny said, "Go! Keep an eye on him! I'll be fine. I'll cover you from here if you have to fall back."

Patting Denny on the shoulder, Curtis said, "Take care, brother. I'll be back," as he turned and took off running, following Tommy around the building.

As Denny watched his friend rejoin the fight, a huge fireball erupted on the far side of the compound. The massive LP gas tank exploded as the leaking gas from Frank's direct hits reached the smoldering flares left behind by Jessie and Marissa's last minute change of plans.

~~~~

Knocked nearly unconscious from the violence of the crash, Jessie regained his senses, coughing several times, feeling intense pain when he inhaled. *Thank God for this vest,* he thought as Frank began sending a barrage of lead into the compound after receiving Marissa's orders.

Looking across the road, Jessie saw several armed men dressed in all black advancing on his position, when a massive explosion erupted from the compound, coming from the location of the LP tank.

"Let there be light," he said as the compound was lit up like Times Square on New Year's Eve.

Hearing gunfire from his immediate left, he looked over to see Marissa firing on the men with her M4 carbine, dropping both of them in quick succession. Realizing his M4 was still in the Jeep, having nothing but his Colt at his side, Jessie crawled over to Marissa, who was clearly in a lot of pain.

"My leg and my hip," she said. "I can't get up."

Placing his arms underneath hers from behind, Jessie started to drag her clear of the Jeep and toward the buildings in the stockyard when she screamed in agony.

"No! No! Oh, God, something's wrong," she said with pain in her voice.

"I'm sorry. It's gonna hurt, but we can't stay here," he said as gunfire again erupted from the compound.

Desperately looking around, Jessie said, "I've got to get you into one of those buildings until this is all over. They'll find you out here. They'll come to the Jeep if they get past the other guys."

Nodding that she understood, Jessie started to once again attempt to lift Marissa and drag her clear as he heard Jörgen's exhausted voice yell, "Jessie! Jessie!"

Steven C. Bird

Turning to see Jörgen, drenched in sweat and out of breath from his run, Jessie said, "Help me get her in that shed. She's hurt."

Nodding in the affirmative, nearly unable to speak from exhaustion, Jörgen helped Jessie move Marissa into the relative safety of a corrugated metal shed in the stockyard.

Hearing the powerful shots of Frank and the big Barrett from the rooftop of the central building as he relentlessly pounded the compound, Jörgen asked, "What about the others?"

"I'm not sure," Jessie replied. "It sounds like there's been a gunfire exchange going on out back."

"Are you ready to move?" Jörgen asked.

Doing a quick function check to determine the extent of his injuries, Jessie said, "Yep. I'm hurting, but I'll be fine. I took a hit to the back earlier, but the vest stopped it. I almost got my lights knocked out from the wreck, too, but as long as my heart is beating, I'm still in the fight."

Looking at the Jeep, now destroyed and on its side, Jörgen asked, "What the heck happened?"

"I'll explain later. Let's get moving," Jessie replied, patting Jörgen on the shoulder.

~~~~

Catching up to Tommy, Curtis gave him the signal to hold his position while he caught up. As he reached Tommy and began to speak, Tommy shoved him to the side and simultaneously opened fire with his M4, downing an attacker that Curtis hadn't even seen coming.

Once Tommy had determined that the man was down hard, he looked back to Curtis and asked, "Which building? Where are the girls?"

Looking around to get his bearings, Curtis pointed and said, "That one... I think. Remember, we're guessing here. We're not the CIA."

As the gunfire started to subside, Tommy and Curtis worked their way through the compound, one aiming high, and one aiming low, advancing together as a team, just as they had trained for so long. With Tommy in the lead, as they worked their way around the corner of one of the buildings, Tommy caught a glimpse of movement coming from the darkness just ahead. Almost immediately on the target, he started to squeeze the trigger as Curtis violently pulled his rifle down, discharging the weapon into the ground just feet in front of them as Jörgen and Jessie appeared in the light of the now dissipating fire.

"Holy crap, that was close!" Tommy shouted.

"Tell me about it!" Jörgen exclaimed. "I thought I was smoked when I saw your muzzle flash."

"Where is Marissa?" asked Curtis. "I can still hear Frank pounding away so I assume he's all right."

"She's hurt, but she'll be okay. We've got her in a safe place below Frank. Where is Denny?"

"Same," Curtis responded bluntly. Looking at Jessie, he said, "And just what the heck was that all about? What were you thinking?"

"This isn't the time," Jessie replied sharply, shutting down any discussion of the matter. "While working our way over here, we saw four or five armed men enter the long rectangle building on the east side of the school. Are you sure the girls are in there?" Jessie asked, pointing at the T-shaped building.

"We've not seen them tonight, but there's only one way to find out," Curtis said. "Who's got point?"

"We do!" answered Jörgen, nodding at Jessie, who immediately followed his lead with Curtis and Tommy bringing up the rear.

Working their way to the side entrance of the T-shaped building, Jörgen gave the men the sign to rally on him. Once they were formed up, Jörgen said, "Curt, you and Tommy go to the far side of the building and watch that door. Jessie and I will make our entry on this end. If we bump them out that way, we need you there. If we all go in the same way, they could usher the girls out the other side and we would never even know it."

"Listen," Jessie said, whispering.

Together, the men came to the realization that the gunfire had ended. The only sounds that remained were the crackling of the fire, along with the moans of an injured fighter somewhere off in the darkness.

"Go! We may be running out of time," Jörgen said as he and Jessie made a move for the south-facing door.

~~~~

As Frank frantically tried to get the bolt of the big Barrett to cycle forward to chamber the next round, he saw two armed men off in the distance, working their way toward the downed Jeep.

"C'mon, baby. C'mon. What's the hold-up here?" he said to himself as he repeatedly tried to shove the bolt forward and fully into battery. Looking back down at the Jeep again, he saw the two men dressed in all black disappear into the darkness on his side of the street, just beneath him. *Ah, hell,* he thought.

Giving up on the M107, Frank picked up his M4 and began to work his way across the rooftop of the old livestock building toward the ventilation cupola located in the center. Removing one of the vented louvers, Frank squeezed himself inside, disappearing into the roof itself.

~~~~

Lying flat on her back in the old tin shed, Marissa heard footsteps as well as what appeared to be the sound of someone's clothing rubbing up against the outer wall of the sheet metal structure, only feet from where she lay. Hearing hushed voices, her heart raced as she realized it was men from the compound. *They must be after Frank. Why has he stopped shooting? Why is it so quiet out there?* she asked herself as thoughts raced through her mind, secluded in total darkness, unaware if her friends were still alive or dead.

Listening for a moment more, she heard the men start to move across the wall from her right to her left. *I can't let them get to Frank,* she thought. *If they got the others, I'm dead anyway,* she thought as she blindly aimed her rifle in the direction of the sounds, opening fire, emptying the remainder of her thirty-round magazine into the thin sheet metal wall. The flashes of light from her muzzle and the deafening sound of the high-velocity 5.56mm rounds echoing inside the small metal building disoriented her.

By the time she had fired her last shot, she was unsure if she was even still pointing her gun in the right direction. With her ears ringing and seeing nothing but spots from the blinding flashes of light in the darkness, Marissa quietly slipped a fresh magazine out of her vest and reloaded by feel alone. Listening... waiting for the next move to make, in total darkness... all alone.

~~~~

As Jessie turned the knob and pushed the door open, Jörgen rushed into the room and flipped on his weapon-mounted tactical light, quickly scanning the room for any possible threats.

Entering behind him, Jessie scanned high while Jörgen scanned low. Reaching behind and pulling the door closed, Jessie whispered, "We don't want anyone coming in behind us without us knowing."

Nodding in agreement, Jörgen motioned for Jessie to follow as they pressed on through the building. Entering the next room in the same manner, Jörgen saw movement in the far corner, followed by a flash of light and the shockwave of a round blasting into the sheetrock wall directly next to his head. Diving out of the way while returning fire, Jörgen hit the man directly in the throat with the high speed 5.56mm projectile, severing the man's jugular vein, causing blood to stream out of the man's body as he fell to the floor, a pool of blood flowing outward from his now lifeless body.

Clearing the rest of the room, Jörgen heard crying through the next door. Turning to Jessie, he whispered, "Careful in here. Don't risk any blind shots."

Nodding in agreement, Jessie cautiously followed Jörgen to the door, where they each took a knee on opposite sides. Reaching out and turning the knob, Jessie pushed the door open as Jörgen shined his light into the room, only to hear the muffled cries of scared little girls. As Jörgen entered the room, he held his hands out to show that he wasn't a threat and put his finger to his lips to signal to the girls to be quiet as he looked around the room.

His heart broke to see a group of young girls, battered and bruised, tied together like animals. Turning to signal to Jessie, a blinding flash of light, followed by the thud of an impact and the crack of a supersonic round as he fell backward to the floor. Lying on his back, Jörgen looked up to see Jessie fire two quick shots at his attacker.

Jessie knelt and looked into his eyes and said, "Jörgen! Jörgen, are you okay?"

Unable to talk and finding it hard to breathe, Jörgen patted his hand on his chest and mouthed the word, *vest,* with a smile.

As Jörgen struggled to his feet, coughing, trying to catch his breath, Curtis and Tommy entered the room from the far side with their rifles at the ready. Signaling for them to take it easy, Jessie said, "Careful. Let's get these girls out of here."

Chapter Thirty-Eight

Once they had freed the girls from their bondage and Jörgen went around to each one of them, reassuring them that everything would be okay, Jessie looked at Tommy and Curtis and said, "Okay, guys. The game has changed. We are no longer in fight mode. Now we are in flight mode. Avoid contact if at all possible. Let us work our way back to the south side of the compound. I do not think the road is safe at this point. The sun will be up in a few hours. Let us bug out into the brush and hunker down until first light. We need to get some distance between ourselves and this place before we call in the flatbed. We do not know how many of these guys scattered, but the road may not be safe."

"Agreed," Curtis said, nodding in the affirmative.

"Jörgen, radio Frank and see if you can reach him on the radio. See if he can get to Marissa from where he is. We're not leaving her there, but we can't bring the girls into that area."

With a nod, Jörgen picked up his radio and transmitted the message, "Frank. Report."

~~~~

Alone and in severe pain from her injuries, Marissa was starting to doubt if she was going to make it out of her current situation. The jihadis from the compound seemed to have silenced Frank above, and several had already made their way across the road from her position. Gripping her rifle tightly, she debated in her mind if she was capable of taking her own life if her capture became unavoidable. She did not want to die by her own hand, but she knew that the horrors that awaited her in the hands of the enemy was a far greater fear.

With the sounds of footsteps outside the building once again, her morbid thoughts were interrupted as she was snapped back into the here and now. Blindly aiming her rifle toward the sound, she listened for any sign that it may be either friend or foe.

Feeling her rifle in the dark, double checking its readiness, she gently placed her finger on the trigger, ready to shoot, as she heard the staticky crack of a hand-held radio receiving the message, "Frank. Report!" followed by Frank's muffled voice in reply.

"Oh, thank God! Frank, it's you!" she cried as tears rolled down her face, lowering her rifle. "In here. In here," she said softly.

~~~~

"Eleven, I'm counting eleven," Jessie said as he and Curtis took a headcount of the girls, who were still in shock and afraid to utter even their names. They had clearly been through a true living hell in the hands of their captors, and Jessie knew it would be some time before they could expect to earn the girls' trust.

"He's got her," Jörgen said with an excited tone.

"What?" Curtis asked.

"Frank's got Marissa. He said he'll get her somewhere safe for the night and will find a way to hook up with us after sunrise. He agrees it is too dangerous out there in the dark right now with no idea how many more of these guys are out there."

"She's gonna need medical attention right away," Jessie replied.

With a nod of understanding, Curtis said, "We'll get her to Spence as soon as it is safe. For now, though, we need to all make it through the night. We can't have Spence and Leland blindly roll up in that big ol' flatbed if there are guys in black pajamas still running around out there with rifles, and in the dark, we have no way of knowing."

"Yeah. Yeah, you're right," Jessie replied, though the guilt of his role in her injuries was eating at him inside. He desperately wanted to get her help right away, but he knew she would want him to ensure the safety of the girls first.

Taking control of the situation, Jörgen looked at Curtis and said, "Where is Denny?"

"He's behind a small pumphouse on the south side of the compound. He said he would cover for us on our way out."

"Okay, then, we will work our way back to him. We can pick him up on the way out. Curtis, you know the way. You take point. Tommy, you take up the rear. Jessie and I will stay in the middle with the girls."

Answering with a nod, both Curtis and Tommy took their positions as the group of four men and eleven young girls began working their way out of the building in which they had been held captive, and into the darkness of the night.

Once outside of the building, darkness had reclaimed the night as the fire had subsided to a mere smoldering flicker. The night was still and silent; the familiar gentle breeze was the only movement throughout the compound that was, until a few moments ago, the scene of a violent struggle for life and death.

Nearing Denny's location, Curtis motioned to the group that he was just ahead. Reaching Denny, Curtis dropped to his knees in horror, finding his friend dead. He had been beheaded and stripped of his weapons and gear. The soil beneath his body was drenched in his blood, which was now soaking into Curtis's pants as he knelt by his dead friend's side in a state of shock.

Feeling a hand tug at his shoulder, Curtis heard Jörgen's voice say, "Come on. We have got to go. We have got to get the girls out of here."

Reluctantly struggling back to his feet, his knees trembling, Curtis got his head back in the game, knowing the girls would not be safe until they had gotten far away from this cursed place.

As they quietly worked their way away from the compound, one of the girls turned to Jörgen as if she had just remembered something and said, "Emma! He's still got Emma!"

Kneeling in front of her, Jörgen asked, "Who? Who do they have, and where is she?"

Mustering the strength to speak, the girl said, "The man... the man who says he speaks for Allah, took her to his bedroom tonight. He said we are all gifts from Allah to him and his men. He wants to make her his bride. He forces her to stay in his room almost every night."

"I'll go," Jessie said. Looking at the terrified young girl, Jessie asked, "Where? Which building?"

"The one across from where we stayed," she said, struggling to speak through the tears.

"I'll go, too," Curtis insisted. "I've got a score to settle."

"No," Jessie said firmly, "these girls need you more than your anger needs to be quenched. Jörgen and Tommy might not be able to handle what lies ahead alone. You go with them. You've lost enough. Now go. I'll catch up with you all somewhere, sometime. Go and don't slow down until you see the sun come up. Just keep going."

And with that, Jessie slipped off into the darkness as Jörgen said, "You heard the man, let's get moving."

~~~~

Slipping silently back into the compound, Jessie worked his way back to the building that the young girl had described. Pausing momentarily, closing his eyes and listening intently to his surroundings, Jessie focused as the night's breeze blew across his face, carrying the smell of burning embers—a silent reminder of the violence that had just transpired.

Crouched down in the darkness at the side entrance to the building, Jessie turned the knob ever so slowly, ensuring that it did not make a sound. His heart raced as he slowly opened the door. As he released the knob to bring his rifle to the ready position with both hands, a gentle gust of wind pushed the door open, causing it to bounce against its door stop, making a thudding noise that startled even Jessie.

Damn it, Jessie! he thought, unable to believe he had made such a rookie mistake. Continuing inside, he left the door open, knowing that if anyone else inside the building had heard the same thump, a rapid egress might be a priority in his near future.

Flicking on his weapon-mounted light momentarily to scan the room, and then quickly off again, Jessie worked his way through the building repeating those same steps until he reached a room that made his heart skip a beat at just the sight of the door. He didn't know why, but his heart felt heavy and chills ran down his spine. He knew this was the room. This was the room where the greatest of the evils these girls suffered had transpired.

Checking the knob, Jessie found it to be unlocked. Quickly pushing the door open and then stepping back out of the way, Jessie popped back into the room, flicked on is light, and began to scan the area.

A large four-poster-king sized bed, adorned with rich fabrics and silk pillow cases resided along the wall on the far side of the room. Off to the left of the bed was a large, ornate tub of water with several red silk towels with gold trim folded neatly in a stack to its left. At the foot of the bed was an elegant rug, with scenes depicting a great battle of days gone past. As Jessie continued to scan the room, on the other side of the bed, in the furthest corner, he heard a whimper.

He worked his way silently around the bed, his rifle leading the way. Once he rounded the corner, he saw a young girl of no more than twelve years of age with long brown hair wearing a silky gown, appearing to be wearing nothing underneath.

"Shhhh," he said, holding his finger to his lips. "It's gonna be okay."

With fear in her eyes, she shook her head and mouthed the words, *No, it won't.*

Feeling the hair stand up on the back of his neck Jessie quickly turned around just in time to stop a large curved blade with his rifle. A tall man, seeming to be nearly a foot taller than Jessie, with a long dark beard, began swinging the blade wildly, striking Jessie's rifle over and over again. The constant attack prevented Jessie from bringing the rifle to bear on his attacker, forcing him into a frantic defensive position.

As he fought off the relentless assault, the blade repeatedly clanging against his rifle with great force, Jessie fell backward onto the floor as the man kicked the gun out of his hands. His sling having been severed by the repeated strikes, the rifle slid unimpeded across the freshly waxed floor, out of Jessie's reach.

Before Jessie could reach for his Colt, the man was upon him, thrusting the blade downward toward his chest, clutching it tightly with both hands. Reaching up and grabbing the man by his wrists, slowing the attack, Jessie supported the man's entire weight with his bare hands as the blade inched its way closer and closer to his heart.

Jessie's strength beginning to wane, the knife made contact with his flesh, just above his ballistic vest, piercing into his skin. Jessie's heart raced as he felt the sting of the blade entering his body. His vision becoming cloudy, he felt that he was hallucinating as he looked into the man's eyes and saw the devil himself. Never had he seen such pure evil in human form. As the knife began to slide up his sternum and toward his throat, splitting his chest as it went, Jessie could feel the blade pushing its way through the bone as his arms trembled, pushing forth with every ounce of energy he could muster.

For a moment, Jessie lay there in silence. He felt the struggle no more as he heard his wife Stephanie's voice. "Jessie," she said. "You have to stay there. You have to stay."

Looking back at his attacker, he now saw fear in his eyes instead of the pure evil of the moment before. He felt the man grow weak as he fell to the side, releasing his grip on the blade and exhaling his final breath as his head rested on the floor beside him.

Jessie turned his head to look for his wife, only to see the terrified young girl standing over him with a long slender dagger in her blood-covered hands. The young girl had killed the beast that had kept her captive all this time, saving Jessie from death's cold, icy grip.

~~~~

With the sun now up and lighting his way, Jessie's legs quaked as he pressed on, utilizing the last of his remaining strength to get the tormented young girl to safety as she clung to his back, her arms around his neck and her legs around his waist. Knowing he could not make it all the way back to the camp on foot, Jessie scanned far into the distance, hoping to see a sign of the others.

His legs finally failing him, Jessie dropped to his knees, awakening young Emma, who had fallen asleep while he carried her. "It's okay," he said calmly. "I just need to rest for a moment."

"What's that?" she said, pointing off in the distance.

Looking up, Jessie said, "What?"

"I see... something. Over there."

As a trail of dust became visible in the distance, Jessie soon recognized the silhouette of a Humvee as it raced across the dry and arid terrain toward them.

As Emma turned to run away, Jessie said, "No! Wait. It's them. They're back."

Stopping just shy of Jessie and Emma, Leland climbed out of the driver's seat and ran to Jessie's aid, helping him to his feet. Out of the passenger side appeared Frank, with a smile on his face from ear to ear.

"You look like you had a heck of a night," pointing at Jessie's blood-stained shirt.

"The others?" Jessie asked with a trembling voice. "Where are the others? Marissa, did you find Marissa?"

"Yes," Frank said reassuringly. "I managed to get Marissa far enough away to have Leland and Spence come and get us. Marissa's with Spence now. He's taking good care of her. Jörgen and the others contacted us first thing this morning and we met up with them, traded them the flatbed for the Humvee, and headed this way to search for you. They're probably back at the camp already. We can go over the specifics later. Let's get you and this young girl out of here."

Chapter Thirty-Nine

Three months later...

As Jessie sat on a hill, watching the girls who had remained with his new group as they tended to the animals below, he looked down at his journal with his pen in hand, at a loss for words. After a few moments, he began to write:

So many things I want to say. So many feelings I have trapped inside of me that I want to get out. Yet I am at a loss. I feel as if the whirlwind of change that has blown through my life in recent times has been merely a dream. A dream like the many I continue to have that are either there to haunt me, or to guide me; of which, I am not sure.

All I know is there are places I seem to have been led, like to Ash, who was as lost in this world as me, with nothing to live for except revenge. I can only hope and pray that she and the young girl escaped and are headed toward a better life, wherever they are. I see great plans in her future. Her strength, her passion to do what must be done for the betterment of those around her, all of her attributes are what this world is in desperate need of. I only hope I live long enough to someday see her once again. God willing, of course.

I know I can't undo the past. I can't bring people back. I can't change the course the world took that led to the demise of our once polite society. The one thing I can do is to continue on my quest to find my sister and lend a helping hand to humanity, whenever it is needed along the way.

As it currently stands, I plan to...

"Jessie!" Spence shouted as he walked up the hill.

Snapping back into reality, Jessie tucked his journal into his pocket and said, "Hello there, Spence."

Sitting down beside him, Spence said, "Can you believe how fast this place is coming together. I mean, just a few months ago we were just setting out for this place with Jörgen and his group, and here we are. The first cabin has been built, the garden is planted, and we've even managed to barter for a few goats to get us well on our way to stable meat production. If nothing else, those silly goats sure give the girls something to entertain themselves with for now. I know they're goats and not sheep, but you've made quite a few little shepherds out of those girls," he said with a smile.

"Yes, a lot of things are hard to imagine, Spence. It wasn't long before that when you found me in your home, injured and headed for death."

"As was I, my friend. As was I," Spence replied, staring off into the distance.

"How's Marissa coming along on her new crutches you made for her?"

"She's a trooper. She's got a long row to hoe, but in the long run, she'll be just fine."

"I've been meaning to have a talk with Jörgen and the others, but I wanted to speak to you first," Jessie said as he watched the birds soar high overhead in their search for food.

"About what?"

Pausing for a moment, Jessie replied, "Nothing. It's nothing."

"We're your family now, too, Jessie. We always will be. You know that, right?"

"Yes," Jessie said with a smile. "Yes, you are," he said, turning to look at Spence. "You belong here. This is what you needed, and they need you. Marissa wouldn't have made it this far without you, and you're just the kind of man these girls need to have around to help watch over them while they grow and learn to cope with all that has happened, not just to them, but to the world. Me, on the other hand…"

Placing his hand on Jessie's shoulder, Spence said, "I know, Jessie. I know."

~~~~

A few days later, slipping out under the cover of darkness, Jessie began hiking east on the next unknown leg of his journey to find his sister. He was beginning to feel that all too familiar feeling of comfort with Spence, Jörgen, and his group, now including the orphaned young girls in their care. No, Jessie knew deep down inside he must keep the fire inside him burning in order to stay focused and find his sister. Comfort was an unwelcome guest to Jessie. He knew it would lead him astray, so press on he must.

Watching as the sun illuminated the eastern horizon, its rays seeming to set the morning's clouds on fire with brilliant displays of red and orange, Jessie looked up at the sky to see an eagle circling overhead. The eagle, in search of its morning meal before the small creatures of the night scurried away, served as a reminder to Jessie that the circle of life continues, no matter how bleak the situation might seem.

~~~~ The End ~~~~

A Note from the Author

First off, let me thank each and every one of you for reading The Shepherd: Society Lost, the first book in The Shepherd Series. I thank you from the bottom of my heart and I will always be grateful for your readership and support.

All of us are likely to face tragedy at one point or another in our lives. We are likely to face times when we just want to give up when faced with what seems to be overwhelming odds. Jessie Townsend is no different, and that's something that I tried to portray throughout the book. When confronted with insurmountable odds, or pain that seems too great to overcome, we have two choices we can make: we can give in, or we can use the hardship as a forge that tempers us into someone who is even stronger than before.

As Winston Churchill once said, "Never give in. Never give in. Never, never, never, never—in nothing, great or small, large or petty—never give in, except to convictions of honor and good sense. Never yield to force. Never yield to the apparently overwhelming might of the enemy."

The enemy or struggle you face may not always be clear, but when dealing with life's hardships, no matter what form they take, keep those simple words in mind, and never give in.

I invite you to visit my website/blog at stevencbird.com and sign up for my newsletter as well as to join me on social media at facebook.com/stvbird, facebook.com/homefrontbooks, and Twitter @stevencbird.

Respectfully,

Steven C. Bird

Made in the USA
Columbia, SC
06 August 2018